SCARLET

SCARLET

A. C. GAUGHEN

Walker & Company ✹ New York

First published in the United States of America in February 2012
by Walker Publishing Company, Inc., a division of Bloomsbury Publishing, Inc.
www.bloomsburyteens.com

For information about permission to reproduce selections from this book, write to
Permissions, Walker BFYR, 175 Fifth Avenue, New York, New York 10010

Library of Congress Cataloging-in-Publication Data
Gaughen, A. C.
Scarlet / by A. C. Gaughen. — 1st U.S. ed.
p.   cm.
Summary: Will Scarlet shadows Robin Hood, with an unerring eye for finding treasures
to steal and throwing daggers with deadly accuracy, but when Gisbourne, a ruthless
bounty hunter, is hired by the sheriff to capture Robin and his band of thieves, Robin
must become Will's protector risking his own life in the process.
ISBN 978-0-8027-2346-8 (hardcover)
[1. Robin Hood (Legendary character)—Juvenile Fiction.   2. Friendship—Juvenile
Fiction.   3. Folklore—England.]   I. Title.
PZ7.G23176 Sca 2012   [E]—dc22   2011006395

Book design by Donna Mark
Typeset by Westchester Book Composition
Printed in the U.S.A. by Quad/Graphics, Fairfield, Pennsylvania
2 4 6 8 10 9 7 5 3

This book is dedicated to my mum.
You taught me what it means to be strong—
and how to make up my own vocabulary.
I love you.

SCARLET

CHAPTER

ONE

No one really knows 'bout me. I'm Rob's secret, I'm his informant, I'm his shadow in dark places. No one ever takes me for more than a knockabout lad, a whip of a boy. They never really see. And I don't mind that they don't see. Like, when you walk through a room full of big men drunk off their skulls, it ain't so bad to be ignored.

I opened the door to Friar Tuck's and the air fair slapped me 'cross the face. It were too hot and stank of beer and men, and I smiled. It were rough, but none here would turn me out for being a thief and a liar. I slipped in the door and moved quiet past Tuck, the innkeep, and went into the barroom. It were heaving with bodies, laughs, and mugs slinging 'bout. The lasses pushed through the lot, using a smile or slap as needed to get their own way.

I went through the big room to the small room Tuck keeps

for Rob. It's got a few secret passages and Malcolm, the big Scot that keeps bar, lets us know if anything's amok. Which comes in handy seeing as, though I'm the least moral minded of the bunch, I ain't alone in doing things contrary to the law.

One door went out the side of the big room, and then the door to our little room were down the hall a bit, so we could still look out a touch and see who were coming. John were sitting there, at the end of the bench, watching like he always is.

Rob looked at me, and as were fair usual, I felt my heart jump. He has a way of looking at me in particular that I'm none too pleased 'bout. I like slipping around and not being noticed. But Rob sees me. He even saw me before I knew he were looking.

"Scarlet, finally." That were Rob's version of a greeting.

"Rob. John. Much," I muttered. I sat down next to the last of the three, part because it meant I could skulk in the corner and part because Much didn't look to anyone but Rob. Much had some bad luck as a lad and he were the sweet sort, so most people just gave him their pity like scraps to a dog. He were the youngest of us, too, bare sixteen, which didn't help none, but Rob knew what Much were capable of in true. It meant Rob were his hero, above and beyond, and I could understand. If I were the sort that had heroes, I'd have pegged Rob for it straight. Twenty-and-one and the oldest of us, Rob were the natural one to lead us, but more than that, Rob tended to see the bit of bright in all of us.

John passed me a tankard, and I took a deep swig of the ale.

"What word?" Rob asked. He kept his hood up, most

because the sheriff were hiring new mercenaries all the time and just a bit because the people loved it. They called him the Hood—the least he could do were wear it.

"Two words. First, Freddy Cooper were arrested," I said, looking round. It weren't good news.

"Fred?" Much repeated. "He's just a boy."

"Old enough to poach for his family," Rob reminded.

John crossed his arms. "He's the oldest son. We should have made it clear that he could have come to us, Rob."

Rob looked at him. "First sons think they can provide best for their family, John. They don't ask for help. You know that better than most."

"Well," I cut, "it weren't quite for poaching."

They all looked at me. "What for, then?" Rob asked.

"Mistress Cooper went to the sheriff today. Asked for more time to pay her taxes, and he said no. Then he took Freddy and said if she can't pay, he'll swing."

The lads stared, and I scraped my nail into the wood table 'stead of looking back.

"The sheriff is taking collateral now?"

"Collateral?" Much asked.

"He's holding people ransom for debts," Rob said, lowering his hood and rubbing his hands into his hair. His eyes looked up under his hand and he nabbed me looking.

His eyebrow drew up, but I looked at the table again, hoping it were dark enough to hide cheeks that went red without my say-so.

"If he gets it into his head that this is a good idea, we could have a lot of children strung up from Nottinghamshire," John said.

"He shouldn't. Unless, of course, more people let him think they can't pay," Rob said.

"Which they can't," Much said.

"The sheriff doesn't know that. And scooping children up without cause would incite a riot, which isn't his intention. Fear is much more effective. It does mean, however, if anyone can't pay come tax day, the people of Nottinghamshire will feel the burden in horrific ways."

The lads settled quiet as we all considered that. Things were fair rough already; we'd be fixed if they got worse.

"I'll get him out," I told them. "I found a new way to sneak into the prison today."

"What?"

"What?"

"What?" All came at me at once.

I blinked. Honestly, they all heard me. I'm not in the habit of repeating myself.

"This your idea, Rob? Send her into the *prison*?" John growled.

So I'm a girl. Most people miss that 'bout me. The boys'll call me Will Scarlet if other people are 'bout; a few people know it's just Scarlet, but most think I'm a Will.

"The first thing I'm concerned with is Scar's safety, John," Rob said, his voice low enough that it made me look to him.

A muscle in John's jaw bunched, but he didn't say nothing.

"Scarlet, what on earth were you doing inside Nottingham Castle, much less inside the prison?" Rob asked.

I took out one of my daggers. It were a little rough, but I had filed the blade down sharp. It made me feel a little bit easier, having all these eyes on me, if I had a knife in my hand. "I were bored. I went for a lookabout."

"Scar, you can't just—" Rob started.

"Neither you, *Your Grace*, nor you, John Little, can tell me where to go or not go." Much leaned forward and I glared at him. "Don't even think it, Much."

John's mouth tightened. "You're not going back to the prison without me."

"You can't quite squeeze into my entrances, John."

"And you can't quite take a punch, Scarlet."

"No one's been able to catch me to try it."

"You caught the rough end of something one time," he reminded, pushing his thumb over the thin scar that ran the length of my left cheekbone.

Fury pounded behind my eyes and I grabbed his wrist, twisting it and pressing my dagger to his vein.

He pulled his hand away slow, his mouth twisted in a bit of a smile. "I'll go with her to get Freddy, Rob."

Rob were scowling. "Fine. Just get him out of there, and look after Scar."

"Honestly," I spat. I could look after myself, after all.

"And Scar, you look out for John. We look out for each other," he reminded me. "That's what a band does."

I frowned. "You blackmailed me into this, *remember?* I'm in no one's band," I told him. Every time I said that, he looked like I kicked his kitten.

"Thought no one made you do anything against your will," Rob said, crossing his arms.

"They don't. I can choose whatever I wish. I just chose to help you instead of being sent to prison."

"And you've been choosing that for the past two years."

I crossed my arms. "Yes. It ain't like I can't leave anytime I want."

His blue eyes caught some of the candle flame and flickered it back like his eyes were wicks. His head bent forward and the blue of his eyes felt more like a riptide. A rakish smile slipped over his mouth. I sucked in a breath, trying not to notice.

"Then it's not blackmail, is it, Scar?"

My mouth tightened.

"We look after each other," he repeated. He looked to the others. "Much, get over to Freddy's mother, make sure she's calm. I'll get them enough food for a while." Rob looked out the door, toward the tavern. "It won't answer the larger problem, though. First, we'll have to hide the other Cooper children too."

"Whole family," I said.

Rob nodded. "And we have to make sure that every other family can pay. We have less than a month before tax day, and how much do we have stockpiled?"

Much sighed. "To cover the villagers' taxes for them? Not near enough. And what we do have is needed already—the people barely have enough food and money to survive, much less be taxed on."

"It's stupid to do this every time," I said. They looked at me like I were Satan. "It is! We scramble to keep everyone floating and then the sheriff just sinks us harder."

John rolled his eyes. "Sorry you have to work so hard, you lazy thief?"

"It ain't getting us nowhere," I snapped, glaring at him.

"She's right," Rob said. "We've seen already it takes more to stop the sheriff than just to protect the people."

"Don't see why you don't just go blazing in there," I said. "You're the rightful earl. You grew up as such. All the people still think you're their lord."

"I was," Rob reminded. "But now I lack the right and the army to take it back, Scar."

I shrugged. "I could kill him."

"You wish you could kill him," John said with a snort.

I kicked his shin and he gave a low grunt.

"Killing him wouldn't restore my right. Not after Prince John named my father a traitor—after he was already dead and while I was away and unable to defend his name," he said, pausing as his fists went tight like bowstrings. He shook his head. "Prince John stripped that right and *gave* it to the sheriff, so unless the prince has a change of heart, killing this sheriff will just allow a new one to rise. Regardless," Rob said, "we need to grant the people some kind of reprieve. They cannot endure this oppression."

"Sheriff stands on money, guards, and meanness," I said.

"Money he taxes back," Much reminded.

"Guards he pays with the money," John said.

"A perfect problem," Rob said. He sighed. "And one we can't be concerned with right now. We need to focus on getting the people enough money to survive tax day—and enough meat to survive the night." Rob nodded and stood, and I raised my eyebrows.

"Not so fast. It ain't the only information I have. There's more. And it ain't good."

"What is it?"

"Nottingham's bringing in a thief taker. From London. I didn't catch the name, but I'll get it."

John looked round. "Why should we worry about some mercenary who catches thieves?"

Much turned to him. "John, we all could very easily be tried and hung as thieves. We steal things."

"Do you know of any thief takers?" Rob asked.

I nodded. A thief in London learned quick who to avoid. "You're right as rain, unless it's Wild. Or one or two others." Like Gisbourne. Though really, it's me that will be in serious trouble if it's Gisbourne.

"How much will he get in our way?" Rob asked.

"Enough. And while we're thinking after other things, like protecting people and getting coin, he won't. He'll be looking to make his bounty and go, which means your head—or all of ours—on a pike."

John grinned, leaning back. "We can't be caught."

I hit him. "Don't be a fool," I snapped.

His eyes narrowed at me and I gave a yelp when he pinched me.

"Enough," Rob said, cutting in with sharp eyes for John. "Scar, keep your ears open." He tried to stand again and looked at me. "Do I have your leave now, milady?"

"Don't call me that."

"Even a thief deserves some respect." He gave me one of the warm, heroic smiles that made my cheeks flush, and I ducked my face under my worn felt hat. "John, make sure she eats something. I have to get hunting." He walked out of the room, and with a glance to John and me, Much followed him.

"I'm not hungry!" I told Rob's back. "Or some whelp that needs looking after, for that matter."

John slid closer to me with a smile that meant he'd listen to Rob over me.

"When shall we break into the jail, then?" John asked.

"Midnight. The guard changes then, and you'll fair certain look less conspicuous in that crowd."

"So you think I look like a guard? I'll take that nicely." He took a drink of his beer, his eyes shining at me over the brim.

I flicked my eyes over him. "Brutish and stupid? Yes, you look quite like a guard."

The shininess cooled. "Never nothing kind to say, Scarlet."

"Only 'cause you think I can't go in alone. You have no idea what I can do. I'm quicker'n lightning."

"I know you can handle yourself. Other people are the tough part."

"I ain't made of glass, John. Someone hits me and I don't shatter."

"Listen good, Scarlet. Long as I'm around, if someone wants to hurt you and I can stop it, I will."

I flicked my eyes over to him, and he were staring at me in that way that I hate, like if he looked long enough he'd see everything I were. "I'm going to throw some knives around."

"No, no, no," Tuck called, pushing through the door frame and blocking my exit. He had a platter of food. "Robin says you eat."

"Bugger off," I snapped.

He scowled. "Scarlet, you wouldn't refuse my food, would you? Drive an old man to drink?"

"You're already a drunk and a terrible cook."

"Now that's just mean. Sit. Eat," he told me. "And I'll have a drink while I watch you." He smiled, and his cheeks caught the light and filled with good-natured redness. He herded me back to the table, and John pushed closer so that they caged me in. Tuck put a bowl of venison stew in front of me.

I knew the more I ate the less they'd stare at me, so I choked down a few bites before they started chatting with each other. I chose that moment to duck under the table and slide out the back way before they could catch me.

It's not like I don't eat. I eat. I just don't like charity and I don't like them thinking they can put their noses into my life. Rob wants us all to be like a family, but I don't. I want them kept far away from me.

Besides, I had errands to run. I managed to get a few loaves of bread from the sheriff's baker and some clothes off the line from the keep's laundress, and it weren't like I had any use for that. Friar Tuck's Inn were in Edwinstowe, the small town that were closest to our camp in the forest, and we knew the people there the best, so I knew who needed what. The thatched houses were so close together, like huddled-up children, and it always made them seem weak, vulnerable. Like they could be crushed. I left little packages in front of the doors; the people looked for them in the morning, and I knew, in some bit of a way, it bucked them up.

I did as much as I could, but it weren't like I could get everyone something every night. That seemed like the cruelest part. I tried not to think 'bout the people that woke up and rushed to the door and didn't find nothing; it made my chest hurt.

CHAPTER

TWO

―o―

I went back to the inn to meet John a while before midnight; Edwinstowe were to the north of Nottingham and we had ground to cover to get to Castle Rock. John weren't there yet, and I didn't go in, just leaned against the tree and blended in.

John came out of the inn with Bess, one of the prettier, bustier wenches at Tuck's. He were grinning and let her push him against the wall, pressing her mouth to his. Despite all the noise of the forest, I could hear every sloppy motion of the deep, open kiss. She dug her fingers in his hair, and he chuckled.

He pulled away with a wide smile. "I have to go now, m'love. Why don't I sneak into your window later on?"

"I'll leave the usual sign."

He pushed her back to the inn. "Off with you, then."

As she closed the door with a giggle, I came out from the

SCARLET

trees. I didn't say anything, and he just nodded with a grin and pushed away from the wall.

"No remarks?" he asked when the inn were out of sight. The road were rough beneath my shoes, and without a lamp, the clouded-over moon were the only light, shining silver and soft on the way. It were like the road we walked near every day were gone, and we were walking to a fey and foreign place instead of the sheriff's keep. I could just bare see John.

"I suppose you want me to say what a tart she is. Or you are? But really, every time you climb in her window, you make her think that's all she's good for. Bess is a nice girl."

"You must have known all sorts in London."

I didn't say. I don't yap 'bout London. And besides, he didn't answer me 'bout Bess.

"You ran out pretty quick from Tuck's."

"I do that when I'm being bossed 'bout," I said, cutting a glare to him.

"So how are we getting into the castle?"

I looked up. "Good night for a climb."

"Aw, Scar," he moaned. "I hate climbing, and you know that. And it's not a good night. You did that on purpose."

I didn't say that neither. I walked faster.

—◦—

They call Nottingham Castle the Castle Rock for good reason; it's built on a big pile of rocks. One side is sheer rocks and the other side is a series of heavy fortified baileys. Most would think that's the way to go, but I see rocks and I can't help but climb 'em. The rocks are the fortifications, not the walls on top. An army can't scale rocks, can it? And castles are built to keep armies out, not thieves.

Rob used to live there, before the Crusades—and before the sheriff, with Prince John's approval, took over the keep. They called Rob's father a traitor after he died and said his lands were forfeit to the English Crown. It weren't that he were a traitor in truth, but there were lands and there were no Rob here to defend them, so the Crown took what it could—and yet they call *me* a thief. When Rob heard his father died, he came back and found there weren't nothing here but pain and suffering all around. While he were off defending his country, they were taking his birthright.

Rob used to be an earl, if you can believe it. It's why he feels so particular 'bout his people, and why they feel so particular about him. Most still call him Your Grace. He'll be an earl again when King Richard comes back for sure. Rob's the one who taught us most of the ins and outs of the castle, but some I've found on my own, from listening and watching and general poking round.

"Scar?" I heard in the distance. I looked down. John weren't far up at all. "Don't go so fast."

I smiled. "I'll wait for you at the top." 'Course, I weren't honestly going to the top. Three quarters up there were a secret entrance. But he didn't need to know that; I could get in and out with Freddy before he would even be up there.

Climbing up were quick and steady by the bright light of the moon, making the handholds gleam like the moon were pointing them out to me. There were a big rock overhanging the tunnel entrance, hiding it from sight, and I scrambled under. From there it would all be dark and lightless, but that were well enough—I had no need to see the crawlers hiding in the rock.

The tunnel were small and bits were caving in, but it were still intact, and I kept low and ran the length of it. It went right to the apartments in the main bailey up on the top of the rock, and from there it were an easy, shadowy walk down to the prison on the middle bailey. The castle were set up like a giant twisting staircase, and each bailey were the flat of the stair, a walled, defensible castle unto itself. The top bailey were the best protected and held the people and the storerooms; the lowest were guards, and the middle bailey held just about every-thing else.

Now, the prison had one entrance in the front, and that were all. Under the ground in the middle bailey, the prison didn't have any windows. It did, however, have an air vent that were almost my size exact.

I slid down headfirst, holding inside the vent to see if any-one were in the hallway. It were clear, and I dropped onto my hands and tucked down, staying quiet and sticking to the walls. There were rats all over the place, and the squeaks and claws covered my noises.

"*The Hood!*" I heard someone whisper. I wheeled my head

around. A prisoner stood, plastered to the bars. "Are you looking for the boy?"

I nodded, keeping my head down. He pointed me to the end of the row. I could see the guard straight ahead, turned away from me, and Freddy's cell were off to the left. It were perfect. I slid my pick from the inside of my belt as I snuck closer. Freddy were curled on his filthy bedroll. He looked even younger there, and a big bruise showed on his face.

The locks weren't difficult to pick, but it still took a few moments, and it weren't even the hard part. Going painful slow, I yawned the door open, drawing out the squeak till it were quiet.

With a breath, I snuck into the cell and pulled Freddy up, shushing him as he woke and pulling him onto my shoulders. He didn't question me, holding on tight as I walked him out and shut the door slow behind, waiting for the heavy *click* of the lock.

I ran him back to the air vent and pushed him up, then scrambled up the wall myself. He wriggled up without being told, but at the top of the vent he turned back. "Where do I go?"

"Stay against the wall."

He cleared the top, and I heard Freddy give a yelp in the dark beyond. With the fear of God in me, I scrambled up to the top in time to see John lean forward and grab my arm. His grip were bruising. "I will kill you later, Scar."

I rolled my eyes. "Follow me."

We came up the gauntlet to the upper bailey, ducking into the alley that stood between the thick wall and the artisan shops. At the end of the shops, there were a gap to cross over to the apartments. I edged along the wall, waving them back until I got a clear lookabout.

The daub wall were rough against my back. Sneaking slow, I went to the wooden post at the corner and peered around it.

I whipped my head back, the breath rushing from my chest. I froze.

"I expect this will garner results, Gisbourne."

The name burned through me like a falling star. My throat felt like a hand were closing hard around it, pressing my pipes in, strapping my lungs closed.

I hadn't seen him in four years, and now here he were, less than an arm's length 'way from me. I'd run from him and kept running, and now it seemed fate'd run straight back around to slam our lives together.

"If by 'results' you mean a gang of thieves to string up while the adoring people watch, I assure you it will," came the smooth, dark voice.

I screwed my eyes shut; his voice ate through me like acid. I felt sweat jump out of my skin, and my chest burned from not breathing. My fist found its way tight round a knife, and I sucked in a tiny breath.

"But when, Gisbourne?"

He laughed. "Very soon."

"Make sure of it. The Hood and his men are the scourge of the forest. Prince John himself has written me that these thieves must be put down like dogs. The people protect them, and I can't *find* them."

"I can. Thieves are prey like any other, Sheriff. I hunt them, I track them, and I kill them."

My heart dropped out from my chest, and my hands set to shaking.

"Good. I'll see you to your apartments, then."

The two of them crossed the bailey with a flank of guards and I crouched low, part because I didn't want them to turn and see me none and part because my knees had gone fair wobbling. I waited until they were inside the apartments and then signaled to John. He and Freddy slid up beside me, and I jumped when Freddy touched my arm.

"The tunnel is behind the residences," I whispered. I glanced back to watch a guard stay out front, pacing, and I sucked down a breath. "When he paces in the other direction, we can go one at a time."

John sighed heavy. "Christ, Scar. I'm good for something." He kicked a bit of a cracked cobblestone loose and picked it up. He heaved it back the way we came, and the guard went on alert. A moment later he jogged toward the noise.

"Go!" John ordered.

I scowled but began to run. John picked Freddy up under one arm and kept pace with me, flying 'cross the open courtyard to round back of the residences, tucked safe in shadow. That were the only rub about the tunnel; it were far from everything in the castle.

We made it to the tunnel, and I felt relief shake through me. John closed the trapdoor behind us, and once in the dark I heaved a sigh.

"It's dark," Freddy pointed out.

"I'll go first, Freddy," I told him. "You follow behind me."

"Fred," he corrected.

"Fred. Make sure not to lose John?"

"I will."

We went quick through the tunnel, and at the mouth, in the dark, Fred pressed close to my side. "I'm not good with climbing."

I crouched down. "I'm good with climbing. Hop on."

"Don't be silly," John muttered, picking Fred up and slinging him onto his back. "As much as I'd like to see Will fall down Castle Rock, I'd like better for you, Fred."

"Everyone knows Will Scarlet can do anything," Fred told him.

John rolled his eyes.

I decided I'd steal Fred something extra this week for that.

—⁓—

Fred were quiet most of the way back, and John and I walked with him in between us, staying pretty close to each other. I felt like Fred needed people standing close to him right then, and I got an inkling John might've had the same notion.

Every step with the castle at my back meant I could breathe a touch easier, but even away from Castle Rock, and farther from Gisbourne, I didn't feel no safer.

Edwinstowe were due north on the main road from Nottingham. It weren't big like Worksop, and Lord Thoresby, the nobleman responsible for the town, didn't have the sorts of coffers for his own private guard. So more often than not Edwinstowe bore the sheriff's anger like a little one bears a bully. Besides, past Edwinstowe the road snaked through the forest before it went to Worksop, and that were where we made most of our money, watching over the road in the shelter of the forest, if you will. It meant that the sheriff came down much harder on towns what were close to him than he did on those through the forest.

When we walked through the town, the Coopers' home were the only one with a candle burning inside, and I saw John hesitate as we went close. He stopped at the gate, and I stopped with him. "Go on now, Fred," I told him. "We'll wait."

Fred went forward slow, and in the low light he looked pretty white. Didn't blame him. Mothers could be tough.

His mother opened the door when he knocked and burst out sobbing, hauling him inside without a glance to us.

"Where are we taking him?" John asked.

I examined a scrape on my hand. "Much's father will take in the family in Worksop until we can find them something elsewhere." Licking my thumb, I rubbed out the dirt on my hand.

"You lied to me tonight," John said.

I shrugged. "I lie to you a lot. Reckon you might want to be more specific."

"You said you'd wait at the top. You said we'd go together."

"Well, yes, that was a lie."

He turned his head. "I don't give a damn if you lie to me, but if you do it when the life of a boy is on the line again, I swear I'll knock your block off."

My ears were burning, most because John were the type that wouldn't even joke about smacking a girl, but I just shrugged. "I got him out, didn't I?"

"How do you know Gisbourne?" he asked.

I froze. Most people, when they're frightened or something, they shriek and run away and general make it fair obvious. I've learned you should be very careful about what you show, so I just kind of freeze up and try to think quick. "Don't."

"Yes, you do. I've never seen you look one inch of scared, and tonight you had a little touch of it, which I reckon means you were terrified. Did he collar you in London?"

"I don't know Gisbourne. I know his name. That's all."

He shrugged. "You don't have to tell me. But I will tell Rob, and he'll get it out of you."

"Nothing to get."

Fred opened the door then with a small bundle of clothes, and his mother and sisters stood behind him. The candle in the window had been put out. "Ready to go, Fred?" I asked.

He nodded. John put his arm on Fred's shoulder, always the older brother.

—⁂—

We walked him to Worksop, and dawn were breaking as we got there. We went to Much's father, a miller whose shop were set away from the market center. He always needed apprentices, so it weren't too unusual to see a young boy there. He gave us some eggs and bread for breakfast and John and me went on about our way.

"Sorry you didn't get back to Bess," I said.

"Should have figured." He tugged a loose strand of dark brown hair that had escaped from my cap. "You're coming undone."

I pushed it under the cap and pulled the cap down tighter. I felt heat on my face and hated that the sun would show me blushing.

"I don't know why you don't chop it off. No one would ever know you're a girl, and isn't that the point?"

"Why, so then you could knock my block off without feeling guilty?"

His face flattened a bit. That were fine. Getting him angry meant I didn't have to fess to the fact that I liked my hair. I liked even more that no one saw it but me. And it reminded me of someone who I liked to remember—just me. "I wouldn't really ever hit you, Scarlet," he grunted. "You better know that."

"Then don't talk about it. If you just said what you mean, you wouldn't have to yap so much." I shot him a glare. "Besides, you did once."

"I didn't hit you that time, I tackled you. Which was a hell of a way to find out you were a girl, by the way. Never would have done it if I'd known, and then Rob starts in on me with a holy fury, telling me not to hit a girl, because *he* knew." He scowled. "Why do you tell Rob everything first?"

"Didn't. He figured it out on the way up from London."

"How?"

"I wouldn't never bathe with him or pass water when he were near. He got suspicious quick. Seems real boys are awfully eager to parade their bits around."

He snorted. "You know, that one tackle was too long ago for you to still be complaining about it. Boys settle things by fighting each other."

I nodded. "That were right when I got to Sherwood. Before Much were one of us. Before there were even really an us." I kicked the leaves at my feet. It were strange how short and long that seemed in the same breath. Forever, and a blink.

John spat. "Before Nottingham cut off Much's hand, you mean."

I shrugged up. I didn't like to think on it, much less to say it aloud.

We hit the main road from Worksop to Edwinstowe, and there were a brewer with barrels of grain for his beer on a wagon. It might've even been Tuck, but I didn't catch the front end. I ran up to it and hopped on the back, and John followed me. I gave him my hand to pull him in.

We hid behind a barrel of grain—not from the brewer, mind, because few tradesmen around here would refuse us anything, but sometimes the sheriff's men patrolled these parts.

"Wonder how Rob fared," John said.

"I saw some deer meat at the Coopers'. Edwinstowe will eat today."

"I saw some bread on the step at the Woods' house."

I didn't say a word.

"Take it that was you, then."

"You think I bake?"

"No, I think you steal. Despite saying that you're in this because Rob blackmailed you into it."

"I ain't Rob's servant, you know. Honestly, you people think I'm chained to the man."

"Aren't you?"

"No."

"Well, how did that all work out, then? You're blackmailed or you're not."

I sniffed. I didn't want to admit none that Rob caught me stealing from him. Less than that did I want to remember the awful days leading up to that. "Rob gave me a devil's choice. Told me I had to help him or he'd send me to the prison—not the gallows, with a nice quick drop and a sudden stop, but the bloody prison, where you die slow with your inner bits rotting out. But Rob ain't the sort to really throw me in prison, is he? Didn't know that then. But I could leave now. Fact, I might not stay much longer."

His eyebrows pushed together. "What?"

Honestly. Why all the questions? He's not deaf.

"Why?" He leaned forward. "Why would you leave after, what, two years of us being a band? Two and a bit. Now, when things are worse than ever? Why just change your mind?"

"I'm not from here, John." Lie. "It's not like these are *my* people." Lie. "I don't owe them anything and I'm getting fair bored of you and Rob always acting like you're my fathers,"

I said with a sneer that I couldn't hold back. That were a lie and a truth. Kind of.

He shook his head. "First off, it's daft to say I'm your father. We're both eighteen. It's not even possible."

"Then quit actin' it."

"You know, I always thought you just liked us to think that you're a rat. But you really are a yellow-bellied coward of the first order. How can you save Freddy and then think you have nothing to do with this? 'Will Scarlet can do anything,'" he mocked. "''Cept be a good person. I used to wonder how a girl like you could be a thief, but I guess it figures perfectly."

He spat on the wagon bed by my feet, and to my horror I flinched a little. He didn't notice, though. He were too busy scooting to the back of the wagon and jumping off.

I pulled my knees up away from the spit and stayed on the wagon as it justled deep into the forest. So I lied to him and poked him a little. Still, that kind of hurt. I weren't a rat. Not by my own making, at least. Besides, the only thing that made me blurt that out in the first place were Gisbourne. He were the one person in the world I should be keeping far away from, and I couldn't ever tell the boys why.

Last I'd seen Gisbourne's foul mug, I had been thirteen, bare days before my birthday, but I ain't forgot a bit of his face. Now Gisbourne were in Nottingham, and he were coming for Robin and the lads. And me.

If there were ever a good time to leave everything and run as far and fast as I could, it were now.

I jumped from the wagon when I were close as I could be to our spot in the forest and made it back to the camp before John. I ignored Rob, climbing up the Major Oak. It were a broad, tall old tree, but I were the only one who could climb to the top, and I had built a little hammock up there. It were rare for birds to make perch that high. Instead of looking at great green forest and brown earth, all I could see were trouble-gray sky and spiny treetops, a whole world of Sherwood no one else could know. Rob's band couldn't follow me up there, and it were the only place I felt like I could sleep.

CHAPTER

THREE

—o—

I woke to the sound of Rob banging a pot in my direction. I leaned over the edge of my bed.

"Luncheon, Scar," he called.

Sighing, I rolled back into the hammock. John would have talked to him by now. And John were probably down there as well.

My hat were half off my head, so I twisted my hair back and pulled the hat down low over my eyes. I began hopping through the branches—I liked that part. The branches were a little rough underhand, and I gripped one, then the next, dropping through the tree and wending a path through the branches. I fancied going where lugs like John couldn't.

With a final jump, my feet hit the ground and I crouched over them. Robin were standing right in front of me. "We need to talk, Scar."

Much were over by the fire, stirring a pot, and John were sitting in the crook of one of the lower branches, but he didn't look over to me.

I crossed my arms. "Talk."

"Walk," Rob said, pointing to the trail. I scowled.

We began walking away from the others, and I kept a fair distance from Rob. I always have. He's just . . . he's the type you get attached to pretty easy, and I don't want that. I always figured staying away from him is best. He weren't a lug like John by any stretch, but he had broad shoulders that took up most of the path, and I shrunk into some shrubbery to keep away.

"Gisbourne is the thief taker?"

I nodded.

"How bad is that for me?"

"Bad."

"And how bad is that for you?"

"Worse." It popped out of my mouth before I could stop it. Rob had that effect on me.

He fell silent for a while, and the dry leaves were pretty loud underfoot. I counted out paces in my head.

"Will you ever tell me how you got that scar?" he asked.

I covered it with my hand. Why did he think of that? "Not if I can help it," I told him. "But it's old. From a whole different life."

He raised an eyebrow and I swallowed, knowing that were the first time I'd let on that I weren't exactly born into thievery, or London for that matter. There were another existence before this one. I liked this one better.

He stopped, and I leaned against a tree, fixing my hands behind me so they were pinned there. I tried not to look back. He were handsome, God knows that. All soft wet-wheat hair, eyes that were gray blue like the English Channel, and a jaw that were strong enough to take a few punches. "Are you thinking of leaving because of Gisbourne?" he asked, his voice soft. He came close to me. His hand rested on the tree by my head, and he were close enough that his body were warmer than the rest of the forest.

I nodded. My pipes felt thick, like I couldn't swallow proper.

"When you're ready, Scarlet, you can trust me. I'm not going to force it out of you. And as far as leaving goes, you know I won't keep you here, especially if you're in danger. But if you stay, I'll keep you safe as best I can."

Our eyes met. I didn't like to do that real often because I have funny eyes, and people both tend to remember them and tend not to be too comfortable with them. Especially during the day. See, when Rob says stuff like that, it sounds like he's just worried about me. But I watched him swallow and I weren't so sure. I've been with Rob a long time, and he's lost people like I've lost people. He's alone like I'm alone. And I may be stupid, but I think me leaving would hurt him too.

"I'm not going. Just thought about it," I told him. "'Sides, we keep each other safe." I said it for Robin, but I weren't so sure. I weren't sure if anything could keep me much safe from Gisbourne.

He sucked in a breath, holding my eyes, and his face came a little closer to mine. He were looking at my scar when he said, "Yeah, we do." He let the breath go, rocking his body back and away. "Don't go to the prison alone anymore, all right?"

A frown rolled over my face. "Don't make me promise that."

"Scar, please. Doesn't matter who you take, just take someone with you. It's not much to ask."

'Course it were. I weren't the sort to have people to go with, people looking after, and I were fair sure I didn't want to change that none.

We turned around to go back, and his shoulder brushed against mine. He pulled away quick. I scowled.

That's how it were between me and Rob—he'd say such things that made my chest feel like porridge instead of a heart, and just when I thought it might mean something more than me being a fool girl, he'd pull away sharp. It were just Rob's way—he were the hero with everyone, and like Much couldn't help but be enthralled, sometimes his hero's ways sucked me under like a current.

But it weren't nothing. He were the leader and I were the bandmate, and any words I heard come soft from his mouth were just my mind tricking me. Again.

When we turned the corner to the camp, I felt John's eyes burning into us from 'cross the camp. I moved away from Rob, going to sit by Much.

"We need to talk about Gisbourne," Rob said, sitting on the log closest to me and Much. John hopped down from the tree, coming over to the fire.

Much passed me food first, some kind of slop with barley and carrots in it and a hunk of stale bread. I pushed the bread into the bowl while he passed food around to the others.

"Rabbit stew," Much told me. "It's good. Mrs. Cooper told me the recipe."

My fingers curled round the bowl. It were hot, and it smelled fair good, but the thought of Mrs. Cooper and her little ones made my stomach fill with ash 'stead of hunger.

"Scarlet, you're the only one who's heard of him. What do you know?" Rob asked.

I shrugged. "He's ruthless. Cruel." Rob's mouth got a little thinner, and for a breath he looked so much older than his twenty-one years. "He's got a fair sterling name as a thief taker. He's the oldest son—doesn't need the money. He does it for sport. Hasn't got a family. He were set to marry a while ago, but the girl died."

"Did he have anything to do with it?"

I looked down. "She hanged herself, so I'd reckon so."

I felt their eyes on me.

"And he never married?"

"No." 'Course, there were much more to the story than that, but it didn't matter. They didn't need to know the rest of it. "Most of the thief takers in London, they get some of the action. They're crooks themselves, right, and say they're thieves.

Well, they get a crew together, make a few big thefts, and then the thief taker turns one of his own men in to the lords what hired him. Thief taker usually cuts his man free from the hangman's noose, too, but he ain't always so lucky and sometimes a thief has to die. Don't matter none. The takers collect a bounty for the thief and keep collecting from their thefts. Fair heartless work. They still make a big profit, but the law don't look too hard as long as they keep turning people in."

"Cunning," said John.

"Yeah, 'cept Gisbourne never did. He only turned them in when he had to; he prefers to send them for a sleep in the Thames with a grinning throat."

"What does that mean?" Much asked.

"He'd slice their throat before putting them in the river," Rob said.

Much shuddered. "I don't know if we're lucky or not that there's no river. The Trent would be a bit of a walk."

"Not," the rest of us chorused.

Much looked into his food.

"He's prideful to a fault. I could listen outside his window and he'd never suspect a thing because the palace is fortified. But we can't pull the same gag twice—he'll learn right quick."

"And for reasons Scarlet won't let on, I think if Gisbourne finds her, he'll kill her," Rob told them.

"He won't know me," I promised. 'Cept the eyes.

"Regardless, we all keep him away from Scar, all right?" Rob asked.

Much nodded, and I were surprised that even John nodded without hesitation.

"He won't know me," I said again.

"Yeah, but you're the only one who's an honest-to-God thief by trade, Scar. Know him or not, I reckon we should keep you away from the thief taker," Much told me.

"You lot steal just as much as I do."

Rob smiled. "You taught us how."

My eyes went to Much's arm, where it were missing a hand. I didn't teach Much soon enough, and the sheriff had cut off his hand when he'd tried to steal food for his family. That were before I met him, but it still didn't sit easy.

"Freddy got to m'dad's okay, right?" Much asked through a mouthful of food. I looked down at my bowl. I ought to at least eat a bite. I took a piece of the broth-soaked bread.

"Just fine. He's a brave kid," John replied, slurping up some of his stew.

"Scarlet, I want you to keep an eye on the family. John, you too. I'm trying to get them a place to stay and positions outside of Nottinghamshire, but they'll have to stay until we can arrange it. We'll get them to Worksop first thing in the morning, but the sheriff will be looking for blood, so we need to have someone keeping watch."

"I locked the cell," I told them. "After he were out, I locked it again."

Rob grinned. "Ha! They'll probably think he was small enough to slip out."

"They hit him, you know. Whipped him, too, reckon, but I didn't see." I hadn't really wanted to know.

"I don't think they did," John said, and his voice were softer, like he were trying to make me feel better. I didn't like it. "I grabbed his back and he didn't react."

I nodded but didn't look up at him.

"Boys, why don't we patrol the roads today, see what we can stir up. And Scar, I want you to keep an ear out for information."

"You get more loot when I'm with you," I reminded. I were good at spotting who had money and where they kept it.

"But we need information more than money until we know what Gisbourne's about."

I touched the brim of my hat in his direction.

"And I would like you to eat more of your food."

"Stop pushing food down my throat, Rob. I eat when I'm hungry."

He cocked one eyebrow, and I glared at him. I don't back down. Rob worries. There were times when we first met up that I were awful sick on account of how long I didn't eat, and he never forgets it. 'Course, I don't forget it neither, but thinking of it makes things worse. I remember that I've gone weeks without eating much, days without eating nothing, and I can survive. I reckon the little Cooper kids couldn't.

And Rob should understand. He takes the guilt and

responsibility that others can't. John takes the punches. I just take the hunger, and most times it feels like awful little.

"Well, if you're not hungry, I am," John said, coming and taking the food away from me. He were doing it to be mean, but I really weren't hungry, so I let him.

He sat down next to me and ate it noisy. He sat right up against me and pressed his elbow into my side. I hit his arm and he spilled the spoonful down his tunic. "Perfectly good food, Scar."

"Maybe you shouldn't sit so close to me."

He pushed closer, which only made me push against Much. "Didn't think you'd mind."

I stood up and slapped his bowl up, spilling it over him. "Didn't think you liked sitting with rats," I snapped, stalking off.

"Scarlet!" he roared.

I smirked but kept ambling on. Served him right.

—◦◦◦—

I made a pass through Edwinstowe, keeping my head down but eyes open. The houses were all set off from the central water well, little thatched roof bits with rickety fencing for their chickens, if they were lucky enough to have one or two. There were one or two farmers in Edwinstowe and they kept their livestock in a corral by the well.

I didn't see any castle guards or any of the sheriff's men. They were the only ones around here who wore armor, so it made them easy to spot. Lady Thoresby walked the small town as well; she were the wife of Lord Thoresby, who protected the town from the sheriff. He weren't very good at it, but he did his best.

Lady Thoresby were pretty as far as those things went. So pale and blond, she kind of looked like the sun in the day and the moon after night fell. She were taking her pretty skirts to the Coopers' house; I wondered if she were fixing to tell Mistress Cooper that her son had escaped the prison. She were kind like that—even if she couldn't do much, it were a help to warn the family that the sheriff might be coming down on them. It made our job easier too.

She had a guard with her, but he were no threat to the townspeople, so I began to walk toward Nottingham. It weren't really the right time of day for wagon fare, so I climbed a tree and began to run through the overlapping branches. The trees were old and the branches were decent thick; as long as I ran fast, they bare had time to bend. It were the best way to get around during the day. It didn't make too much of a clatter neither.

Nottingham were a market town, but the market weren't as good as Worksop, most because the sheriff just scooped up anyone who were any good and stationed them in the keep. As sheriff, he set the taxes in Nottinghamshire, and it were how his big castle ran itself; they taxed the grain from the farmers, the weapons from the smiths, the cloths from the weavers and dyers, and so on. Sheriff never had nothing what he made himself. He also had a tendency to take the best grain and food as a tax. Showing at Nottingham meant you'd often lose your wares, but some still did it.

I nicked an apple as I went past, leaving a coin in its place. The coin were worth far more than the apple, but that didn't matter much. I didn't steal from people who couldn't afford it, but I also didn't like to barter neither.

A little girl and her brother were curled on the ground beside their father's shop, and the whole set looked threadbare and thin. My stomach growled—I were a little hungry for once, not having eaten the yesternight—and I sighed. Without looking at her, I pushed the apple into her hands, sinking back into the crowd before she really saw me.

The gates were open, so I walked right in past the heavy guard. I'm fair good at not being looked at.

I walked round the lower bailey, listening. The laundress and baker were down in the lower one, and they were women with other women working for them, so they tended to cluck up a storm while they worked.

I had sewn my vest special; it had a pocket against the small of my back that I could fill up with whatever I needed, and despite making me look a fair bit thicker, you couldn't tell what were in it. I began sliding rolls into it and nicked a fine pair of black woolen hose. Then I just leaned into a shadowy corner and listened. I considered eating one of the rolls, but too many faces from the village popped into my head. Tuck would give me food later on.

One of the girls laughed, and I heard a snap as she whipped out the wet cloth. "These that fancy man's things?" she asked.

"Aye," said the laundress.

"They're not much more than threads!" she said.

"He's been wearing them, but they're not his," another girl said. "Jameson told me that his things are being sent up from London." She made a noise. "Don't like him. Eyes look like God took the light from 'em."

The laundress laughed. "Jameson? Like him well enough to be running off with him every chance I give you."

"Oh, no, I like Jameson very well. That Sir Guy. He's terrible."

"Least he keeps his hands to hisself," another said.

"God's truth."

"I heard he was in the Crusades."

"I heard he's killed a hundred thieves. God's own work, that man is after."

I heard a splash. "That's not on, Margery. He's been called to string up Robin Hood. Not God's work at all."

"Careful with that tongue, little one. You may be new here, but there are things we can't talk about."

"Well, the Hood may help us with the washing, leastways," said the one who carried on with Jameson. "I heard they're awful afraid that Hood's men will nick Gisbourne's things. They were sending it up the river, but Jameson's been sent to bring it through Sherwood, disguised somehow."

The laundress laughed. "Robin Hood won't be fooled by a disguise! Best tell Jameson he's off on a fool's errand."

"I tried, but he's gone already. Hopefully they'll be back with it tomorrow."

The women started whistling, though I couldn't much tell

why. "Remember, lass, there's the milk and there's the cow, and the cow part should come first."

The women hooted at this, and the girl were giggling too.

I left Nottingham fair quick; it were a walled city, and they closed their gates at dark. For the hour after the end of the market, in the late afternoon, the city emptied of people, and I could hide easy in the tide.

I went to Edwinstowe and got there just before dark. Men were out corralling their livestock, and women were taking in the laundry. I went through the town and passed out the rolls where I could, and I gave the hose to Mistress Clarke. She had three growing sons and her husband's harvest hadn't done well.

I tried to leave the things in such a way that I wouldn't have to face their thanks. I didn't like being thanked for my sticky fingers. It ain't me going to Heaven, so no need to fuss about it.

I were due at Tuck's, which were by the road, a little farther away from the villagers and the manor, and I were on my way there when I heard someone bawling. And then a crack, like someone got hit.

I crouched down to the ground, listening. I heard it again, and I whipped around the corner to see two of the sheriff's men holding Amy Cooper by the dress front. She's bare nine, a little slip of a girl. She were carrying on and had a big cut under her hair, like the brute hit her with his armored hand.

I slipped a knife from inside my vest and aimed at the brute's open hand, the one not shaking Amy, with the unprotected palm toward me. I whipped it at him and yelled, "Amy!"

He dropped her with a roar of pain, and she shrieked and ran to me. I crouched down and caught her. "Run to your mam's; don't open the door for them," I whispered to her.

She continued to cry but she obeyed me, running like the Devil himself were on her heels.

The man pulled out the knife as his counterpart unsheathed his sword. Swords are terrible. They are naught but big, heavy knives that most don't know how to use right. I drew two more knives as they came at me.

"You'll regret that, lad," the one said. His hand were dripping red, though, so I were fair sure I wouldn't regret that.

"Make me," I challenged.

They ran at me and I turned and bolted, hearing them chuckle as they chased me against the tanner's fence. 'Course, this were my plan.

I didn't hesitate, leaping up and using the fence to flip over their heads. I dropped behind the uninjured one and sliced my knife along the back of his knee, and he screamed. I didn't like to kill people, but that kind of slice meant he couldn't do much chasing from here on.

The injured one hammered his sword down, aiming to hack my head, but I slid back and he caught just my knife, snapping the blade.

"Son of a whore," I snarled. His blade stuck in the soft ground, and I slammed a punch to his crotch. He let go of the sword with a growl, but he cuffed me with his bloody hand.

I twisted away with stars in my eyes, but the instant thought of John Little saying I couldn't take a punch gave me iron in my blood. I turned back to the guard and threw a fist as fierce as I could muster to his face, the little of it not covered by chain mail. He fell and hit the ground, and I took off running into the forest.

I didn't go far, 'course. I wheeled back through the woods and came up on Mistress Cooper's house. Seeing a light go out, I looked in the window and started swearing.

Mistress Cooper were there with Amy. The others weren't; they must have gone on to Worksop already. They had a bundle on the ground, and I reckoned they must have been packing up a few more things. I climbed the thatch, hanging on the ridge of the roof to watch over the door. I still had three knives on me; if they came to bother Amy or any other Cooper, they'd have me to deal with.

My heart beat like the drum of a Scot, hard and even. I had that animal's blood on my face, and I tried to wipe it off. The hand that I punched him with were bleeding and hurt—I never punch people. I just cut them. Bastard broke my knife.

It were pitch-black and more than an hour before I moved, and then only when I saw John walking through town, his eyes casting over the Cooper home.

I gave three short whistles and he stopped, looking up into the trees. He lowered his gaze a little and squinted at the roof. Even he couldn't see me. I dropped from the roof and went around the side of the house.

"Christ Almighty," he said, grabbing my face and twisting it. "What happened?"

Swiping at the blood again, I pushed his arm off me. "It's not my blood. The sheriff's men went after Amy Cooper."

"Why wasn't she in Worksop? I thought the whole family went over earlier."

"I ain't a mind reader, John," I snarled.

"Is she hurt?"

I nodded. "He smacked her up a bit. She were terrified. She and her mam are here. We can't move them till dark, and even then we best use the forest."

Swears jumped from his mouth. "All they had to do was listen to us and no one would have been the wiser to them in Worksop. And who the hell hurts a little girl?" He shook his head fierce and crossed his arms over his big chest. "Are you hurt?"

"He broke my knife," I told him, showing him the hilt with the jagged remnant.

"I'll fix it for you." As he picked it up, he brushed my knuckles. I hissed.

He grabbed my hand and tried to see it in the dim light. "What did you do, punch him out?"

I pulled my hand away from him. "Yes."

"You busted up your hand pretty good. You might have broken it."

"It ain't broken."

He took my hand again, pocketing the remains of my knife

to push his thumbs over my hand, working each finger in turn and testing the bones. It hurt, but I grit my teeth. "Not broken."

"Told you."

"Get over to Tuck's and have Robin clean you up. I'll keep watch."

I shook my head. "I'll stay."

"Scar, you know I lost my little sister, right?"

I swallowed. I did know that. A little sister and little brother and his parents in a fire. He never told me that, though, so I weren't sure if I should fess to knowing it. "Yeah."

"So, they aren't going to lay a finger on that little girl while I'm standing in front of this house, you understand?"

"If they come back with more?"

His eyes glinted even in the dark. "I'm hoping they will."

"I'll be back soon with Rob."

He nodded.

I jogged over to the inn. My head hurt and, with the anger gone, I were starting to feel a little dizzy. I went in the back door to the side room, checking that Rob and Much were there before edging into the doorway. "Rob," I said soft.

He looked up, and his face changed. "Go downstairs. Much, you stay here."

Much looked up at me and swallowed. "Jesus, you all right, Scar?"

"Fine, Much." I smiled at him, and he smiled back. John and Rob, they were the same sort. They thought it were up to them to save the rest of us, and most people looked at them and agreed. People pushed me and Much aside. They thought I couldn't never do nothing, and they thought Much needed to be coddled on account of his bad arm. "Amy and Mistress are stuck in the Cooper house. Need you to figure a way to get them to Worksop."

Much nodded. "We're sending them on to Dover tonight anyway. My aunt can get them work there. Rob, can I go over there now?" he asked.

I scowled. "It ain't like you need his permission, Much."

Much's mouth tucked under, and I felt bad.

"Downstairs, Scar. We need to take care of whatever is cut under all that blood," Rob said sharp.

I nodded, going down the back stair to the underground storeroom. It were cold down there, and I knew why Rob sent me. Tuck had a big water supply he kept in the cold ground, and I fished the rocks out of it and dried them off. I held one to the side of my head. It felt like ice against the pain.

Rob came down with a candle and I looked at my other hand, the one with the busted knuckles. They were torn open and already swollen. I scowled. My aim would be off.

Rob didn't say anything. He kept trying to swallow like something were stuck in his pipes while he pressed another rock to my hand. I hissed at the contact. He took a cloth and began to clean off the blood in little dabbing motions.

"It's not mine," I told him quick, taking the cloth and wiping the blood off, rubbing at the dried bits even as it scraped at my cuts.

"Some of it is," he said, his voice low. "Can I take off your hat?"

I bit my lip, chewing on it a moment. Swallowing a breath, I looked down and reached up and pushed it off, pulling my long hair to the side.

My fingers felt something thick and clumpy in my hair, and I frowned and scrubbed at the matted blood with the cloth.

He sighed. "Would you give me that? You're making it worse. I know how to tend a cut, Scar."

I glared at him but handed the cloth over. He began dabbing again, but this time at the cut on my cheek, which were fair awful. Even the dabs made my teeth grind.

"Going to tell me what happened?"

"The sheriff's men went after Amy Cooper. She and her mam came back to their house. One hit Amy."

Rob looked up, his eyebrow raised. "Is the sheriff's man still alive?"

"They both are. I cut one behind the knee and the other's hand. He broke my knife," I said, bitter.

"So, you punched him?"

I nodded.

"You're no good for punching, Scar. You could have broken your hand."

"That's what John said."

"I take it he's at the house, or you wouldn't have left them."

I nodded.

He pressed my cheek with the cloth again, and then his

hand touched my cheek, hot after the cold water. "I hate seeing you hurt."

The air whooshed from my chest but I rolled my eyes 'stead of letting on. "No one gets all bent up over John being bruised."

He stepped back, looking into my eyes. I felt like my eyes were unprotected without my hat.

"Scar, you walked in here covered in blood. You don't see how that would upset us?"

"No."

He caught my chin in his fingers. "Like it or not, Scar, we're your friends. We care about you. I care about you."

I pulled away from his hand, pushing my knuckles forward.

He tore up strips of old, worn linen and wrapped my knuckles with them, tying them off in my palm.

"We should get back to Little John. If the soldiers come back, he'll need help."

Rob nodded. His head were low and he weren't looking at me. He wiped the stones and put them back in the cold water. "I'm sorry I got you into this, Scar."

All my rage bubbled up, mixing with the little bit of fear I didn't want to cop to. I pushed him back, shoving my hat on my head though it stung fierce. "Stop it. You ain't sorry you got John and Much mixed up in this. You ain't sorry I'm outta London. It ain't no tragedy that I bleed, so just let it lie."

He looked at me with his funny, lopsided grin, like he knew how tough I were and it weren't half what I wanted it to be. "I'm saying I'm sorry you got hurt, Scar."

"And I'm telling you I make my own decisions. Including who to fight for and when to get hurt. So let's go."

His mouth twitched into a smile. He nodded. We went to the top of the stairs and he gave me a hard look, but without any yap, we went out into the night. It were cold, but we moved pretty fast to the Coopers'. Part of me thought we'd find the house on fire, but John were where I left him, looking out from the side of the house. He were kind of like a big, shadowy gargoyle on a cathedral, keeping the place from demons. It made a shiver run up my spine, but I shook it off. I pretty much think I ended up on the wrong side of God, even if I spent most of my time trying to make up for it.

Much were around the side, and he came over as John came from the shadows and Rob went to the back door. I heard Rob knock and softly speak to the Coopers, and I leaned against the wall.

"Find anything out today, then?" Much asked.

I nodded. "Gisbourne is here but his belongings ain't. They were going to ship them up the Trent and then bring them down to avoid Sherwood, but they decided to disguise the goods instead. They're coming up tomorrow, as early as dawn."

John smiled. "Rob will like that."

My fingers brushed the empty space where my knife usually sat. I wondered if John would actually fix it. He used to be a blacksmith, so I knew he could. Couldn't much trust people to do favors for you, no matter if they were strangers or bandmates. I guess I could steal it back if he didn't fix it.

"Do you know what the disguise is?" Much asked.

"No. I'll spot it, though."

John elbowed me. "'Bout the only thing you can trust a thief to do is spot treasure."

I scowled. "It won't be any great treasure. Some money, but his belongings foremost."

"Well, why do we want it?" John said.

"Because it will make him very angry," Much said. "Which probably isn't such a good idea."

John smiled and gave a dark, throaty chuckle that put gooseflesh on my arms. "Angry is always a good idea."

Much scoffed. "Why do we always start the trouble?" he mumbled to himself.

"We don't," I said, probably a lick harsher than were right. "We finish the trouble they start." Much looked down, and I sighed. I didn't like making Much feel small but I weren't the sort to apologize. "Did you get good loot today?"

John scowled. "No. Pains me to admit, but we need you on the roads with us."

Rob came out from around the building, sliding in the darkness and nodding to us. "The family is safe and calm." He nodded to me. "And grateful, Scar."

I nodded back. It were dark, so they couldn't prove I were blushing.

"Much, why don't you and I take them back over to Worksop? Scar, John—go back to the Oak. We need to be on the roads early tomorrow, and I want your eyes sharp."

"Scar has information that Gisbourne's effects are coming up through the forest. At dawn, disguised," John said.

Rob smiled. "Very interesting. We'll all meet at the archway an hour before dawn. Agreed?"

We nodded, and I took my chance to run off. And I ran. And ran. It took an hour to get to Thoresby Lake, the farthest bounds of Lord Thoresby's property far in the deep of Sherwood Forest, so I were running as hard as I could. I felt filthier than in London. It weren't the blood. He hit me and broke my knife. For one measly second I were scared, and I needed to get that off me before the dawn, before we patrolled the roads, when I couldn't be one inch of scared.

My fists were shaking as I ran, sweat pushing out the filth, desperate for the water. I jumped the big rock and dove in, breaking the surface and crashing into fierce cold.

I hung there, under the water. My eyes were closed and my skin went fair numb. My lumps and slices went to ice. There were no room for nothing in my mind but cold.

When I pulled out of the water, heaving shivery breaths on the shore, I were fearless.

CHAPTER
FOUR
~o~

The air were fair crisp, with the kind of crunch to it like a sweet apple. The leaves hadn't fallen yet, which were good. When the leaves fall the trees get thin, and I have to try harder to hide. When the leaves fall, though, the whole forest is covered in a blanket. Leaves cover the pitfalls and ditches and level off the bumps, but it's all lying in wait for them that don't know what's there. I like to know my forest better than those that might chase me into it.

I were crouched low on the archway. It weren't a proper arch: two trees knitted together over the road years ago, forming a big curve with their branches. I couldn't see John, Rob, or Much, but I knew where they were, and they were waiting for my signal. It were dawn and the road led to the markets, so several wagons had come through. Most of them we knew; some of them were strangers, but they didn't look like they had much in the way of coin. Besides, this morning weren't about money.

The wind were coming through the trees fair hard when I spotted them down the road. It looked like a coffin cart, with two souls in boxes, and two monks were at the reins. It were a good disguise, but the monks were half a belly short of the typical breed, and the chain mail beneath their robes clinked soft with every pitch of the wagon. What mucked it up true, though, were the horses. No religious house would have solid war destriers like that.

I threw a small dagger with a long red ribbon attached to it into the tree by Rob's hiding spot. I never heard so much as a rustle, but I knew they'd be ready.

When the cart rolled close, I dropped to the ground, my thinning wool coat spreading out beneath me. The leaves whooshed away and I smiled, lifting my head slow.

"Whoa," they called to the horses. "Out of the way, ruffian!"

"You ain't no monks," I said. "And those ain't no bodies."

They jumped to their feet at this, pulling swords from their robes. "Let us pass, or our master will make you regret it."

"Don't put much faith in masters, myself," I told them. "So, are you gents going to pay the forest tax?"

"You want a tithe of a body?"

I looked them over. "If you're offering, then I'll take your hand. Maybe a foot. You have lovely feet, sir."

"He meant the corpses, whelp."

"Oh, are we still trying to wink by that you have bodies in those coffins?"

The one on the left jumped down, and I heard the chain mail rattle like rainfall. I stepped back, crossing my arms over my chest to grab two knives under my coat.

"Time to run off now, vermin."

Honestly. Why does everyone think I'm a rat? "So you'll not be paying the tax, then?"

"I'll take a tenth of your neck if you try," he growled.

I shrugged. "S'pose that's fair. I'll be on my way. You might want to make sure those bodies are still safe, though. Don't want a dead'un rolling around."

I grinned, and they both turned to look at the cart that were very much empty. By the time they turned round again, I were hidden in the tree and they were cursing a blue streak.

They hacked around in the underbrush for a little while, but they couldn't find our men. The longer they looked the more they argued with each other, and after a bit they got back in the cart, red faced, and drove on to Nottingham.

As they drove, I hoped they were the sheriff's own men. Then, at least, Gisbourne wouldn't have no authority to kill them where they stood.

I helped John with his coffin while Rob and Much struggled with the other; my arms were right sore by the time we got it back to the cave, and that were even with John hauling most of the weight. I hated that I weren't more strong. Much were sweating and pale, leaning back against the weight with his one good arm. Maybe it weren't the worst fate to be the weakest of the group.

We brought it deep into the cave. We kept this place separate from our camp; we found it last winter and stored any loot we came 'cross here until we could get it to the townspeople. We also had a few crucial supplies that would get us through the winter and such. A calico cat had taken up in here to have her babies, and one of the little kittens seemed to like me. He clawed up on my shoulders like always.

"Hey, Kit," I said, scratching his ear. He were warm at least.

"Let's crack them," John said.

I nodded, kneeling down to the locks and pulling my pick from my vest. I had the lock opened in a second or two. I stood and John stretched out his arms.

"Why couldn't I just break them?"

I crossed my arms. "I reckon if you continue being yourself, we'll need a coffin that's fully intact in short order."

Rob scowled at us. "Lads—and Scar—there's loot to be sorted. Does this not hold your interest?"

I blushed. "Interested."

John kicked the box open. They bent over it, pushing through things, but I stood rooted to the floor. It were sitting there, on top of everything: a lock of dark brown hair wrapped in bright red ribbon. The scarlet ribbon were too close to the ones I tied to my knives; even if the boys didn't know whose lock of hair it were, they'd yap about the ribbon.

I reached in and grabbed the hair, twisting it round my

hand in a trice to hide it from the lads. Rob looked at me quick, but we just kept digging through the things. There were clothes and boots, some money but not a lot. Much got into the jewelry, which we could melt down and sell for the most money.

"What's this?" asked Rob, looking over his shoulder. He picked up a small ladies' ring. "This is the Leaford crest, isn't it?"

"Leaford were his fiancée," I told them. "The one that killed herself."

"He kept her ring? He must have taken her death hard," John guessed.

Honestly. "You've no idea what you're talking about or what a villain he is, John," I told him.

Rob looked at me in that way of his, and I looked down.

"What's that mean?" John asked.

"He just wanted to own her, like he owns her ring. And she killed herself rather than have him."

It felt like a wave of water were coming to crush me with the weight of Rob's stare.

"You knew her."

I couldn't cop to that. That would put me in Leaford's lands, which weren't far from Nottingham. "She had a sister. I knew her sister." Even talking about Joanna made my pipes hurt. I couldn't swallow proper.

I weren't sure if Rob believed me or not. He kept looking at me, like I left a door open and he were trying to crane round the side to peek in.

John looked up at me. "So you must know more about him than you're letting on. What do you know?"

"Nothing useful. Nothing good."

"Tell us, Scar," Much said.

"There's nothing you want to hear. She just said he were awful. Signed the contract before it were even legal to wed and set the date for the first day it were. She said that her sister cried and cried to her parents that she didn't want to be married, and they didn't care. He wanted the land, and her parents wanted his money, and that were all there were to talk about."

"So she killed herself," John said.

"So they say."

"That really doesn't sound all that awful," John muttered. "Not worth dying for."

"You know nothing of it, John. To be silenced when your wishes don't matter, to be sold like property, and to a man like him?" I spat at his feet. "A man would know nothing of it."

"And what would a thief know of it?" John scoffed. "Like you've ever done a damn thing you didn't want to."

I shook my head. "I know what it's like when you can't get no one to listen to you. When what you say don't matter. I half think every girl knows what it's like to be silenced."

"It's a terrible practice," Rob agreed. "Most parents wait longer. Most suitors want them to."

"Let's open the second one," I suggested, kicking it open like John did. My foot rang and jangled with the contact, but it felt good after all the talking.

"Ooh, weapons," Much said.

John pushed him aside. "You don't even know what to do with them, Much."

Much scowled dark, and before I could fuss at John for it, John tossed me a set of knives. I caught them.

They were treasures, the metal darker than most I'd seen. There were a fine grain where the metal had been folded. "This is Saracen metal," I breathed. Both had a small ruby set in the hilt, a finer version of the garnet in my favorite knives.

"Easy, Scar—we should sell those," Rob reminded.

I frowned. "You'll never get a good price for these here, not what they're worth. Besides, I can steal back the value if you give me the say-so."

"Maybe she is a girl after all, hankering after shiny baubles." John laughed.

My fist balled up but I didn't sock him. Me wanting shiny knives and fool girls' sighing over shiny jewels weren't near the same thing.

"Do whatever you think is right, Scar. I can't tell you what to do—isn't that what you always say?" Rob said. He weren't smiling at me, though, and he turned away, as if he didn't want to see me nick them.

My mouth tightened and I tossed them into the pile that we'd sell or give away. I don't have no grand thoughts of myself—I ain't no saint to be sure—but thinking of Amy Cooper and the people who didn't have nothing to eat, it's not like I could keep them fair. Nothing were fair.

We kept digging through Gisbourne's belongings, and the only thought that cheered me up were Gisbourne's mug when he found out.

Much and I set to sorting the clothing into packages that we could give away. We could do that with the clothes since none were too distinct, but the jewelry and metals had to be melted and broken to sell raw. See, if Gisbourne were to find someone with something of his he could recognize, he'd kill the lamb for sure, innocent or not, and we couldn't risk that. John and Rob took to hacking and snapping the other bits.

"Will you show me how to throw a knife, Scar?" Much asked, quiet.

I looked up at him. He weren't looking at me; he were tying off a package of clothing. "Not sure if it's your weapon."

He frowned. "I know I'd have to borrow your knife."

I shook my head, pointing at Rob with one of my knives. He had his long bow strapped 'cross his back. "Bow is Rob's weapon. It suits him. He moves with it; it works like his arms got pulled out and shaped to a bow."

"It's part of him," Much said, tucking his bad arm 'neath his cloak.

I nodded. "I'll teach you, but I ain't sure it's your weapon."

"Of course it's not," he muttered, piling more clothes.

"Hey," I said, enough bite that he looked up. "I ain't saying you don't have a weapon, Much."

His eyebrows got bunched up tight together. "Sure you are. I only have one decent arm. How can I fight worth a damn?"

My mouth twisted, and I pushed him. "Shut it, Much. People think I can't fight worth a damn, even not knowing I'm a girl, and I prove 'em wrong. We prove 'em wrong. And I have an idea, all right?"

He shook his head. "You lot think I'm not good for anything. John says as much every chance he gets."

"Oh, and he would know? All he does is hit things."

He rubbed his chest where I shoved him. "You do a fair lot of hitting yourself, Scar."

"Don't make me do it again. John ain't the be-all of opinions."

He sighed, going back to his pile of clothing.

"Look, I ain't saying it will be fair easy." I pushed up my sleeve and showed him loads of little white scars from nicks and cuts. "I were terrible with my knives when I first started, but they were the only weapons I could hold and hide, so I learned them." I showed him the ribbon on one of them. "And then they learned me."

"I don't understand."

I ran the ribbon through my hands. "I used to tie ribbons on them to grab them quick. They're my hair ribbons. And then when Rob nabbed me in London, I wouldn't tell him my name. So he called me Mr. Scarlet till he found out I were a girl. Then it were just Scarlet."

"It's not your real name?"

My eyes met his, fair serious, fair dark. I shook my head slow. He looked at me for a long time, and I looked down. When his mouth opened, I said, "What's the rock you've been cutting at?"

He looked up. His face changed a little, and for a breath he were looking at me like he looked at Rob. "Want to see?"

"I asked, didn't I?"

He smiled and jumped to his feet. I followed him, going to the fire pit. He took a smaller log from the banked fire and went into the corner of the cave. I could see he'd hollowed out a vein in the big rock, collecting the graveled bits in a bowl. He put the torch on the ground, then stepped far back, pushing me with his bad arm.

He took a pinch of the grayish powder. "Don't scream," he said with a smile.

I scowled. "I don't scream, Much."

"You might."

He flicked the powder toward the flame.

It caught, flaring up in a bright white flash that looked like God himself came into the cave with no burning bush to announce him.

I knocked Much over, covering our heads, slamming to the stone ground in a pile.

He were chuckling as my vision came back slow. White light were still arcing 'cross my eyeballs, but it were beginning to feel more like the Devil's work than God's.

"What in Christ's name was that?" Rob shouted. Smoke were rolling out of the cave, but the burning were done. He and John were waving their arms like it would do any good.

"Not sure," Much called.

I slapped his chest. "Me neither, but good job, Much." I looked to him, and he smiled. "Rob, I think Much might know a way to stall the sheriff a bit."

"I do?"

I sat up, pulling Much with me, and looked at the powder. "Don't you? Seems to me the only thing we didn't reckon is that the sheriff can't go after the people if he's busy with his own bits."

Rob came forward. "You want to set an explosion?" He looked to Much. "Do you have enough of this powder?"

"To tumble Castle Rock? No, but maybe I can find some more in the other caves."

"Do it."

—⟋⟍—

It took us two full days to move what we could, sell some of the metal, then give away the clothes and stockpile the jewels and coin. It also meant two days off the road, and it felt like time were sinking its claws into us.

We met in the inn that night, and I came in unnoticed as usual. My head were beating like a hammer from the cut and bruise surrounding it; since the guard clobbered me it had lumped up and colored dark, and my hat pushed on it tight. Still, I'd rather the pain than strutting 'bout without my hat, so I were fair out of luck. I also had bad news, and that never put me in a good mind.

John nodded to me as I slid in.

"Rob's not here yet?"

"No. Tuck made you a meat pie," he told me. He moved over, meaning I should sit next to him. I looked around. Much were sitting on the edge of the other end of the bench, no room beside him. The bench kind of curled around the table. I sighed and sat next to John. There were a pie, and it had an *S* cut into the top of it. It smelled better'n Heaven. I picked up the spoon and stabbed it, taking a scoop and eating it. My stomach rolled and I stopped, wondering if I had waited too long to eat. I could feel John looking at me, so I tried another bite.

Rob came in then, and his eyes went straight to me and the food. I took another bite and my stomach twisted. "Finish that, Scar. You didn't eat breakfast."

"And you only took a bite of dinner last night," Much reminded.

I glared. "Thanks, Much."

Rob crossed his arms, and I took another bite. Sweat broke on my head; I felt like I were going to retch it all back up.

"Well, the good news—after a fashion—is that I couldn't fence the weapons; they are too distinct. No one around here is selling anything like them. So we all just got new weapons. Scar, you just got your knives back."

I winced out a bit of a smile, and he stayed watching me for a second. I took another bite. I held it in my mouth, trying not to swallow, but he just watched me.

I swallowed, and he looked away.

"Christ," I moaned, jumping up and slamming out the back door. I just made it outside when all the food rushed back up. My knees wobbled and gave out as I retched again, but Rob's arm caught me around my waist, holding me against him.

I retched one more time and tried to get my legs under me. "Easy," said John's voice.

I looked up, trying to pull away. It were John? Why had I thought it would be Rob catching me?

"Easy, easy," he repeated, rubbing my back.

"Stop touching me, please," I muttered. He stopped rubbing, but his arm didn't leave my waist. I pushed him off, crouching down over my knees. I closed my eyes, taking a deep breath. My head were beating out a mean tune.

"You all right?" Rob asked. I turned and saw Rob and Much standing there. Rob's arms were crossed and he looked dark. I hated the way they were all looking at me.

"Fine," I said. I stood, feeling only a little wobbly.

"Scar, you're sick," Rob said, and his voice were rough and a little frightening.

"I ain't sick," I snapped. "I just told you, I eat when I'm hungry."

John were still on one knee. "You're too hungry. That's the problem, isn't it?"

I crossed my arms, and he stood up.

"That's what happens when you don't eat enough—you can't even eat when you want to. That's it, isn't it?"

"I eat, for Christ's sake," I growled. I moved to go back into the tavern, but Rob wouldn't budge.

"Still, after all this time?" Rob asked, soft. "You've been lying to me about eating more?"

"It's not about you, Rob," John said.

Rob's eyes shot to John, but I didn't dare look at neither. "No, it's about her. I promised I'd look out for you, Scar. After you were so hungry in London, I swore to you that I'd get you fed. Why have you lied to me all this time?"

I felt shame rising up in my throat behind the food, and I hit his chest. "Because it weren't what you wanted to hear, Rob!"

"Well, I'm listening now, Scar."

I shook my head. "I'm fine! I eat. But these damn bruises make my face hurt so much my stomach twists up. And sometimes just thinking of all these people that can't even scrape up a crumb, that twists up my belly too. But there ain't much I can do 'bout it." I glared at him. "And it doesn't go away. It ain't something you can fix. I were hungry for a long time, Rob, and much as I'd like, bits of me won't never get over that. No matter what you grump at me 'bout."

He grabbed my arms, bringing me close to his face, and his eyes looked like the ocean, deep and dark and full of things I knew nothing 'bout. "We don't lie to each other, Scar. Especially not about things that mean I might lose you."

My breath froze in my chest. Did he just say that?

He let me go. "Because losing one member would put the whole band at risk. Do you understand?"

Just like that, I felt all the heat leave my bones, and I shivered. I nodded, and John put his arm around me. Christ, he were warm all of the sudden. "Let's get inside." To me, quieter, he said, "Try eating some bread or broth. They'll go down easier than a pie."

I nodded and let him keep his arm around me as we went in. John sat real close to me, warm and protective. He pulled a piece of bread off the plate with the pie and pushed it toward me.

In all the time I'd known John, he'd played the older brother to most everyone at some point, but never with me. And to have him do it then felt fair strange.

I picked the bread up and took a little bite, gnawing on it a bit. "I have some information," I said, hating how feeble my voice sounded.

Rob didn't look at me. "Go ahead."

"Gisbourne's getting us back. He's tripling the forest patrols, day and night. Anyone caught poaching will be strung up the next dawn."

Rob nodded. "Well, he could have done worse. We're prepared for worse. Just tell the townspeople that we'll get them food; they can't risk it themselves."

"I don't think it helps," Much said. "They all know if they get caught, we'll get them out, so they try it anyway."

"Then tell them Gisbourne intends to kill them on sight," Rob said. "Because I'm sure that's what he really has in mind anyway."

I nodded. "He's every kind of awful."

"Which also means for the next few days, we all will be

hunting and patrolling the forest in pairs, then scaring up the roads in the morning." He sighed, and his shoulders bent a little, like someone were shoving down hard. "We can sell the furs, at least."

"And antlers," I added.

He nodded. "If anyone's not up to doubling their time over, say it now."

We all were silent.

"Good. Stay sharp. We can't afford mistakes right now. Scar, since you and I are the hunters, I'll take John and you take Much."

Everyone stopped at this.

"That's foolish. I'll go with Scar," John said. Rob's face turned stormy, but John continued. "Rob, I'm no hunter, but if she runs amok of Gisbourne's men, I'll be more help than Much." Much frowned, and John shrugged. "Sorry, Much."

Much sighed. "He's right. We're the scrawny ones, Scar."

"But we both have our uses," I reminded.

"Fine," Rob said, his teeth gritted. "John, go with Scar."

I waited for John to make some rub about going with me, but he didn't. Who knew it took retching for a lug like him to be friend-like? Not that I expected it to last long, mind.

"Should we go now?" Much asked.

"Would you two wait outside for a moment?" Rob asked, nodding to John and Much. "Can we talk, Scar?"

I didn't nod, but I didn't leave neither. I let John out from the bench and leaned against the wall, crossing my arms and looking down. He leaned against the opposite wall, looking at me. "What should I be doing for you, Scar? Honestly."

"Doing?" I repeated.

"When we left London, you weren't eating, and I tried so hard to get you to eat more. For *years* now I thought it was working. I thought you were eating just fine. But you're not, and I don't know what to do for you." He raked his hand over his hair, and it went every which way in his wake. "You scare me," he said. "Thinking of you hurting scares me. So I have to do something. And you need to tell me what it is, because obviously what I was doing before wasn't right."

"I don't know," I murmured.

"You don't eat."

My mug felt hot. "I don't need much. After London, it were always fair hard to eat much. Having none for so long weren't easy. And now that I do, there are other people that need it more."

"Why didn't you eat in London? You're one of the best thieves I've ever met. You could have stolen your body weight in food."

A scoff jumped out of my throat. "I were barely a thief then. Besides, there were other people that needed it there too."

"Was there a person in London you were stealing food for?"

"We're honest with each other, right, Rob?"

He nodded.

"Then don't make me answer that."

He looked at me for a long time, and I wouldn't clap eyes on him. "So what can I do, then?"

"It's life, Rob. Nothing to be done."

"Make no mistake," he told me. I looked up. "We do what we do—" He halted, then stepped one foot closer. "I do what I do because I will always believe that no matter how awful life gets for however many of these people, there is something I can do about it. There is something I *will* do about it."

I nodded. "That's why you're the hero, Rob, and I'm a thief."

I turned out the back way then; there weren't much more to say.

He caught my wrist before I were full out the door. "Scar," he said, rough, like rocks were running over his tongue. "I have done so many unforgivable things in my life. Don't let failing to save you be another."

I pulled my hand away. "I never asked to be saved!"

That were enough. I went outside, eager for the cold on my hot cheeks.

—∞—

John and I stayed quiet that first night. I weren't much in the mood for chat, and he had to listen for game as best he could anyway. I stayed high in a tree for most of the night; I caught more moonlight up there and I could see farther, so I could aim better when I saw a deer. I were better on the ground with knives, of course, but in the sky I didn't mind using a bow.

I were fair decent with it; none so good as Rob, but I managed. I killed two, and John dressed both. I didn't like that part, seeing all the inner bits come out. I always think how easy it would be for someone to slit my belly and watch all my inner bits slide out.

We took them back to the cave, and John and Much set to skinning them and cutting the meat. I watched, sharpening my knives and unstringing my bow. I never liked hunting. Well, I liked hunting right fair, but I didn't like blood. So much of it had to come from an animal to feed a town, and it felt strange to me.

This, more than stealing baubles, were what made us thieves, and outlaws, and all the names the sheriff called us. Sherwood were the king's forest, a protected land that were meant to be his hunting grounds. But England were a country without a king. King Richard, him they called the Lionheart, had taken his lion paws over to the Holy Land. He were off fighting infidels while his people—while *my* people—starved. There wouldn't be no game left for hunting when Richard returned. 'Stead of deer, England would be full up of wolves, the biggest among them Prince John.

John and Much wrapped packages of meat in the skins, and Rob and I set off quick. Rob headed for Worksop and I went to Edwinstowe, delivering the meat before sunup.

We parceled out the meat as best we could, trying to get to each family a cut that would feed them for the day at least. Some of the families had more luck than others; farmers had crops to feed their families, and some of the summer crops did fair well. Even if they were settled, though, when we got food, we shared it round.

I were through most of Edwinstowe when I heard the soldiers. I slid against one of the house frames, hoping they didn't have a dog with them. I were covered in the smell of raw meat.

"Damn night patrols," one grumbled.

"Gisbourne's a fool. Everyone knows the Hood's just a ghost."

"Yeah, but somebody's poaching, ain't they? And we're meant to catch the poachers."

"And kill them. That ain't on."

"We bring 'em in and the sheriff'll kill 'em. We don't have to do it ourself."

"I don't get the plan. He thinks killing all them we catch together in some big thing will get the Hood to come out. Hood's a ghost!"

"And if there were a Hood, and I were the Hood, I'd get them out the night before. Gisbourne's none too smart."

"No."

"Maybe we can amble by Tuck's. Rosie's had that sparkle in her eye lately."

The other chuckled. "Mind it ain't no apple in her eye, lad."

"Sheriff won't never know. Let's go over."

The other man nodded.

I stayed hidden until they cleared, and then I bolted to Major Oak.

"It's fine," Rob said when I finished telling him all I heard. "We just don't let anyone get caught poaching."

It didn't feel fine. It felt like a big storm, and Gisbourne were in the eye of it.

CHAPTER

FIVE

The next morning were a long one spent on the road. There were a slew of travelers that morning, and I felt fair flush as I sussed them out. Some lords tried to look like the poorest of men, but they still rode huge horses and were hale and fed. Shameful. I liked picking those out the most. One set of knights were hauling a big chest of jewels for a lady, delicate and fine indeed, and when we cracked it open, far to the side of the road, I felt a smile bubble out of me.

"This will cover most of the people in Nottinghamshire," John marveled.

I let a string of diamonds run through my fingers like rainwater. "Feed 'em and clothe 'em too."

Robin winked at us. "That was a good spot, Scarlet."

I grinned, watching the sun bounce off a silver bar. "Oh, I know."

"This is excellent news, lads. Once we fence most of this, we'll have time to spare for tax day." Rob nodded at me. "And we can focus on running Gisbourne out of town."

I nodded back, sucking in a breath that made my chest swell up. He were right, 'course. It would all be fine, and we were safe as houses.

—∞—

It were later that afternoon when I walked through the market in Worksop with Much. The people in the shire towns liked Much best; he were an awful good listener, and they all knew him from a whip of a boy. Only, he didn't always know which were the important bits, so I went with him to listen to what he heard.

It were strange. People looked at him and they gave everything over. They wanted to talk to him, and they wanted to pat his good hand and kiss his cheek and stand next to him. I weren't the same as him. I stood alone, though I weren't fair sure if that were by my own choice or not. Honestly, watching him, I felt like a leper.

I also felt a little noticeable. "Hello, Will," I heard from beside me. Two girls were crowding around a launder basket and beaming at me. I tucked my hat down lower and frowned.

"Everyone's heard what you did for Freddy Cooper," her friend said.

I scowled. "You think yapping about that will be good for anyone?"

They shut their mouths. "We weren't."

"You were. Your mothers should have taught you better."

They both flushed, but one still bit her lip like she were sweet on me. I scowled again. Stupid chit. I shook my head, looking over to Much, and by the time I looked back she were next to me; she took my face in both her hands and kissed me.

I whipped away, sputtering oaths as she went back to her friend and ran off, giggling the two of them.

And they weren't the only ones. Much were bent over in laughter. I pushed him, and he rolled to the floor without my intended insult. "Come off it!" I stamped my foot.

"What's so funny?" John asked, coming over in the middle of eating an apple. He tossed me an apple and I threw it at Much.

He only laughed harder. "K-k-kissed Scar!" he hooted.

"Someone kissed you?" John asked, turning to me. He didn't look like it were too funny. "Who is he?"

This made Much laugh more.

"None of your business, John Little," I told him.

He stepped closer to me with a flat face that, if I could ape it, I'd never be kissed by a stupid girl when I didn't want to be. "Who, Scar?"

"Jenny Percy!" Much roared.

John's face broke open, like a smile could split a black mood. "Wait till Rob hears this."

"You two are nothing but loose lips," I snapped.

John grinned. "Sounds like Jenny just got your lips a little looser."

"It isn't funny."

"Look at Much. Of course it's funny. I'll tell you, though, wouldn't I have loved to see the look on your face."

"What happened to her shining on you? Weren't you fiddling around with her?"

"Her cousin, Emma." He smiled. "Now she had lips that could do quite a bit of loosening on me."

I shook my head, disgusted, and then a shine caught my eye. I grabbed John's shirtfront and dragged him back behind the weaver's shop. Much jumped up, but I shook my head. It were too late; he'd look suspect. John didn't crack wise as I drew my knives, hooking eyes round the corner to watch Gisbourne come through the market.

He stopped in the center of the market square, stepping up on a small fountain. "Perhaps I should introduce myself," he called. People stopped to look at him. He were wrapped in violence as if it were clothes, his cloak like death, his armor like blades. His hair were shaggy as an animal's and it looked like the Devil were trapped in his head.

"I am Guy of Gisbourne, and I have been hired by your sheriff to hunt down the one you call the Hood. I've been informed that rather than outing this criminal amongst you, you protect him." His lip curled, and the points of his teeth shone like a snake's fangs. "Now, I don't know how long it will take," he said, and his voice shook me like a dry leaf. Everyone went dead quiet. "But I'll track the Hood and his men, and I will find them. When I find them, I will kill them. Anyone along the way that I even *suspect* of helping the Hood and his gang will lose everything—starting with his life."

He snapped his fingers, and his guards brought forth two men. I looked to John. "Stay. I need to get to the side."

He nodded, and his hands pulled me to the other side of him at my waist. I were fair certain I didn't need the help, so I didn't know why he did it. "Be careful, Scar. He nabs you and I'll go after you, and there's more of them so I'll die doing it. But I'll still do it."

"Don't be stupid," I hissed, moving past him.

I walked around the outside of the market square, catching glimpses of Gisbourne taking a local villager and putting a knife to his throat. I saw a longbow drawn taut, and I sidled up beside Robin. He nodded to me, never shaking a muscle. "Go up," he murmured. "Cover my shot."

I nodded, scaling onto the roof of a little house right quick.

"Now," Gisbourne continued. "I know you good people know who the Hood is. You love him. You protect him. But will you die for him? I don't think so." He looked to his first captive. I weren't sure, but he might have been the dyer. Worksop did a lot of clothwork. "So what can you tell me about the Hood?"

"His name's Robin," he blurted. "Robin of Locksley."

Gisbourne looked right shocked, and his arm loosened an inch. "Earl Huntingdon?"

The man nodded, and Robin took his shot, sending the arrow whizzing over Gisbourne's knuckles. It were an impossible shot, skimming Gisbourne and missing his captive altogether when a hair either way would have sent it off, but Rob made it. Rob's like that. Gisbourne dropped the man and roared in pain.

"Something to discuss with me, Guy of Gisbourne?" Rob called. The people scattered at this chance, the second captive forgotten.

"Guards!" Gisbourne called, drawing his sword.

I couldn't resist. I'm a thief; we weren't never good with temptation, honestly. I pulled a knife out and flicked it; with the clear angle, it sliced a deep line into his left cheekbone. Blood began to drip fast, I noticed with a grin.

I flattened to the roof as he held back from chasing Rob, looking around for his attacker. He didn't see me, but he did see my knife in the ground. I hadn't put a ribbon on it. Small mercies like that are the only reason I tend to go to church.

He picked up the knife and tucked it in his belt, going after Rob. I looked around, and I saw Rob on the roof next to me, looking at me like he knew why I threw the knife. I hated that look.

Gisbourne sent his men round the village, leaving the dyer to grab his wife and hide inside their house. Fact, most people did the same, and soon Much and John were hidden in someone's house and Rob and I were hidden on separate roofs, huddled against the chimneys. It weren't long after that Gisbourne sent his men into the forest to search for us, leaving a few in the town square to wait.

We stayed separate until the farmers came home and people came out of their houses so we could fade into them like shadows. The four of us met up in the forest and headed back to Major Oak.

"Rob, did you hear about Scar's new lover?" John crowed.

Rob looked sharp to me. "Was there an old one?"

"Jenny Percy!" Much said, pleased with himself.

Rob smiled. "Of a band with three actual boys, why is it that all the maids lust after the fake one?"

"I had nothing to do with it! I were right in the middle of telling her off and she kissed me," I grumped.

"Thought all you girls liked to be insulted," John told me, pinching my side.

I hit his arm. "Don't touch me, and don't lump me with that kind. She said everyone heard 'bout Freddy, Rob. If townspeople are talking, things are going to get worse."

He looked at me, still smiling. "For us, maybe a little. But when they talk to each other about us, they're passing on hope, Scar. The girls love you because you give them their hope back."

I spat on the ground. "And if they ever knew it were a girl giving them hope back, they'd hiss at me on the way past."

"Some of them know," Rob reminded.

"Only them in no position to be judging."

Rob shrugged. "None of us are in a position to judge anyone unkindly."

"I'll not put that to the test, thank you."

"Good," John said with a broad grin. "Because then what would Much and I do for amusement?"

He slung his arm around my neck, and I pulled away. "Wait, do you smell that?"

John lifted his shirt to his nose and sniffed it, but I took a deep breath.

"Smoke," Rob said.

"Something's on fire," I agreed.

I set off running and the boys followed, heading up the crest to higher land toward Major Oak. When we breached the ridge, we could see it, even from far away. Smoke were starting to curl through the trees, blurring out the orange tongues that were lapping up our hideout.

They set Major Oak on fire.

—⁊〇⁊—

We stood frozen to the spot, and it were then that arms came around my back. "We've been waiting for you lot," a voice growled in my ear.

I didn't hesitate. I slammed my foot down hard on his foot and drew my knives, twisting behind me to wedge them both in his stomach. "If you're going to hold a thief, you might want to try the arms," I snapped, pushing him off me. I felt hot blood on my hands and saw him fall down the ridge, sliding into a pile of leaves. He were dead, I reckoned, and it turned my blood to ice.

"Gisbourne!" one cried, hollering loud as possible. Gisbourne were close, then, hunting for us in the forest. I turned to see three men on Rob, and I felt the sting of insult. Honestly, I were just as much a threat as him. Why did I only get one?

One grabbed Rob round the neck while the other two came at him, and I skittered into action. I slid to my knees and cut the heel on one of Rob's attackers. He fell to his knees, howling. Rob had his sword out, his bow strapped 'cross his chest, and he pushed off the two men, fighting them back.

I looked to John, who were getting punched in the face, but Much took my attention. Someone punched him down and got out a knife, the blade wicked and long and closer to his chest than I were fair happy with.

"John, duck!" I called. He took a punch and obeyed me, ducking down long enough for me to step on his back. He started to stand as I launched off, and I flipped in the air to bring my feet down hard on Much's attacker. I threw him to the side, and his blade grazed my leg but I weren't bothered. His head hit the ground hard, and I didn't 'spect him to get up anytime soon. I held my hand out to Much, and he pulled himself up.

"Scar!" he said, pointing behind me.

"Hold on," I told him, holding his good arm tight and turning us both around. I gripped his arm and jumped, kicking the guard's chest and snapping my foot across his face. Much held on and pulled me back so I didn't fall as the guard dropped.

I let go of Much and went back to Robin, charging into a guard from behind and pushing him to the ground. He were quick and threw me off his back, scrabbling on top of me before I could get up. I kicked sharp between his legs, but my knee met with some kind of armored codpiece.

He chuckled, and a thread of panic shot through my body. One of his hands pinned my arm back and the other pressed my chest to the ground. My fingers searched out a knife on my hip as his hand on my chest moved around too much for my liking.

His eyes narrowed as he pinched my bits. I caught a knife with my free hand and hit the hilt into the side of his head where the helmet didn't cover.

He fell deadweight on top of me, and I shook a little as I tried to push him off. Rob threw him off and John caught my hand, pulling me up against him. He caught my waist, keeping me there. "You all right, Scar?"

I nodded.

"Let's get to the cave. Scar, take the high road and be a lookout," Rob told me.

"Rob," I said, pulling away from John. "Rob, please tell me you and John took the chest to the cave."

"What?" His head whipped toward the tree, and every muscle he had jumped forward.

"Please tell me you didn't just leave it sitting by the oak."

"Of course we didn't," John said. He lifted his shoulders and his jaw were tight. "I kind of put some leaves around it."

Robin swore.

"You lot stay here," I ordered. "I'll see if they nicked the chest." I jumped fast into an old pine tree. I scaled it quick and began running through the crisscross of branches, going toward the thickest bit of the smoke. Major Oak were hidden just beyond.

Close to it, I dropped to the ground. The tree were most ember and smoke now, and there weren't any guards or Gisbourne's men. The smoke stung my eyes like a whip and I covered my mouth with my sleeve, coughing hard. I went by our little fire pit, and my stomach wrung out like the washing. The chest—and everything in it—the baubles and riches that were to buy a bare slice of time for the people of Nottinghamshire—were gone.

I climbed back into the trees. My arms felt heavier now, and climbing were fair hard, but I made it back to the lads and whistled.

They looked up, and I shook my head, pointing them on to the cave. I stayed high, watching over the lads as they ran on the ground. The smoke were getting thicker, like it were chasing after me, and it were harder to run 'cross the branches. One snapped beneath me and I lurched forward to grab the next trunk. I looked down, my heart drumming in my chest.

Pushing my cheek against the bark and holding tight, I waited for the boys to catch up before moving ahead.

I whistled twice for the boys to hide as more of Gisbourne's men came plowing through, and we all met at the cave without running into more trouble, going in and all the way to the back.

"Best for us not to light a fire tonight," Rob told us. "Who's injured?"

The cut on my leg already stopped bleeding, but John's knuckles were torn up and Rob had a slice on his arm. Much were going to have a bright, shining eye the next day; the skin were already closing over. "Sit," I told Rob, going to our kit to get some bandages and water. When I came back he had taken his shirt off, and it made my mug feel a little hot.

Honestly, it's not like I've ever lied about the fact that Rob's fair enough to look at. With or without shirts in the mix.

I chewed the skin off my lip while I rubbed the dirt and blood and bits out of the slice with the water, then lifted his arm gentle and tied the torn bits of muslin around the wound. I pressed my hand to the wound when it were done.

"Why do you always do that?" he asked soft.

"What?" I tucked my hands back around myself.

"Put your hand over the wound like that."

I shrugged. "Habit. Someone told me that hands can heal. I figure if they can kill, it ain't much of a stretch that they can heal too."

"Someone tell you that around the same time you got this?" he asked, putting his hand on the scar on my cheek like I had with his arm.

I swallowed. "Yes."

His hand dropped away. "You did well today. Like a warrior woman," he told me.

"More like a warrior squirrel," John threw in. "Hopping and twitching about like that."

"You saved my life today, you know, Scar," Much said. His voice were graver than the other two.

I nodded. "We watch each other's backs." I didn't want to fuss about it much more than that. "But we lost the chest. We lost the baubles, the coin, all of it."

Rob sighed. "It was Lady Luck that put that in our hands in the first place, and she just took it back. It was too much to hope for."

I looked around. Our stockpile were fair meager. "We won't make it, Rob. We won't have enough to pay the taxes, and he'll string up as many as the gallows will hold."

Rob looked around too. "We'll find a way. We have to find a way."

—⁂—

Later that night, after a cold supper, we all went inside the cave. We kept some mats there for sleeping on, just burlap stuffed with hay and some bits of wool when we could get it. It were dark as pitch in there, and I could hear the boys breathing and the cats scratching around.

"I can still smell the smoke," Much murmured.

"Me too," I told him. "Can't believe they killed Major Oak. What did the tree ever do to them?"

"Several," John said. "Looked like a few around it caught light too."

"It were our home," I said, soft as I could manage. I didn't know if the others heard.

"She's a tough old tree," Rob said, his voice rough and farther away. "She might last."

"Unlike that guard that tried to grab Scar." John laughed. "You know, I've heard all the sayings about the wrath of women, but whew, Scar, you have a temper."

The others chuckled.

"Keep it in mind, John Little," I warned him. I didn't feel much like chuckling.

He laughed. "I'll be sure to inform Jenny Percy," he said.

I rolled my eyes, but this time I heard a small laugh come from Rob's distant corner. "So she really kissed Scar?"

"Should have seen it, Rob! Scar's right in the middle of giving her a talking-to, and Jenny lays one on her," Much crowed.

"So that's how we shut her up," John said.

I knew he were fair close to me so I tried to kick him. It took a few attempts, but one finally hit something and I heard him whine, "Ow, Scar!"

"And none of you jumped in to defend—her—her honor?" Rob asked, but it got broken up with laughs.

"The lot of you are stupid blighters," I snapped. "It ain't for laughing."

This made them crack apart with howls. After a day where another home got ripped away from me and the smell of smoke were still wrapped around us, I could play at being fair grumpy—but honestly, it felt better to hear them around me.

Their laughing even made me smile a small bit, and it felt like a gift.

We piled up all the blankets we had and turned in for the night. I don't know what it were; I were used to sleeping outside, which should have been much colder than the cave, but I were shivering cold. The scent of smoke had snuck into everything—the blankets, my hair, my clothes—and it made me feel colder, hollower. I called for the kitten, but even he wouldn't go near me, like death and sin were hung round my neck. The shivering got worse, until my breath started coming in harsh shudders.

An arm with an extra blanket wrapped around me, dragging me back against John's chest. I went stiff.

"Easy, Scar. You crying?"

He thought my shakes were for tears? "No," I snapped, offended.

"Then you're cold, and I'm warm, so just hold on to me and go to sleep, all right?"

He were warmer than sitting next to a hot fire, and I felt him like a blaze all along my back. His arm wrapped over my arms and held me tight against him. It were passing strange, but I stayed still and warm against him. The shudders began to ease. I felt his breath on my neck, his nose against my head.

"Your hair's longer than I guessed," he said.

I killed a man today. It were the first response that bubbled up out of my head, but I didn't open my yap. I didn't know what that had to do with my hair or him pressed against me, all warm and alive and very much not dead, but it were all I could think. I couldn't say it, and it settled down like a rock wall between my head and his, even though his breath were on my neck and his nose were against my head.

—〰—

I woke up feeling warm, but my head were ringing with alarm. I were still tucked against John, both my arms behind his one like it were some shield, and the light were snaking into the cave. I looked around, trying not to move till I knew what were wrong. I saw Rob, sitting up a few feet away and looking at me, and looking at John, and looking at the way me and John were wrapped together.

He met my eyes, his face grim and his eyes stormy blue black. He didn't say nothing and stood and walked out of the cave.

I pushed away from John and pulled the blanket around me, cold again but for my cheeks, which were blushing hard. He were walking away fast, and I moved faster to keep up.

"Rob," I called. "Robin."

He stopped.

"I just—" I stopped, and he turned to me, his eyes dark and hard. I felt shaky again. "I killed that guard yesterday."

He nodded, like he got why I just blurted that out. Which must have been fair hard, since I didn't know, myself. His ears were red and his jaw were clenched, but he nodded again and turned away from me, walking deeper into the forest.

I turned back to the cave. I couldn't go back to sleep, but it were right enough; it were Sunday, the Lord's day, and I went deep into the cave, looking for the small parcel I tried to keep hidden.

Staying in the darker bits, and watching John and Much, I changed quick into the gown, untwining the muslin that I used to pin my bits back. Couldn't very well be running for your hide with bits jiggling all over the place, could you? I combed through my hair, tying it out of the way, and pulled on the hooded ladies' cloak. Looking very much like a girl, I went out of the cave.

I know it's fair strange for a girl who turned her back on the wishes of her father and mother (fourth commandment) and steals (seventh commandment) and lies a fair amount (eighth commandment) and even killed a body (fifth commandment) to feel so particular about going to church. But I went every Sunday I could, and I figured that, black as my soul were already, the one person I shouldn't be making falsehoods to is God— and most times, that's what wearing my usual clothes felt like. Besides, I couldn't wear a hat in church, and I couldn't very well wear my hair down and look like Will Scarlet—that way were faster than wildfire for trouble.

There were a small little abbey in the middle of Sherwood run by the Franciscan friars (it's where Tuck got the name for his house), and they always let me come in to their masses and confess to their priest. They weren't much popular with the local folk, but that suited me just fine.

"My dear lady," Brother Benedict greeted. He and I were friends, I think. I handed him some money I had collected that week, and he pressed it to his chest, treasure-like. "As always, your generosity astounds me."

I looked down. "Well, you know how I come by it," I reminded.

"Come, daughter, and walk with me before the Mass."

I nodded, and we walked over to the animal yards. The Franciscans loved their animals dear, and they had the oddest collection in the shire. A spaniel that favored Benedict bounded over to me, leading a baby duck and three kittens like a piper. "Gisbourne is here," I told him.

"Ah," he said.

"He's going to make it worse. He'll kill people. He'll gouge their hearts out to get what he wants."

"Is it you he wants?"

"If there's such a list, I'm more than like on it. He doesn't know I'm here yet."

"And can you stop any of this bloodshed?"

"Yes. We'll stop as much as we can. We protect our people."

"And if you turned yourself over to him?"

I shook my head. "I can't. It wouldn't stop him, and it won't help me any." My mug filled with shame, and I searched the sky. "Besides, I reckon he'd kill me."

"You and your fellows are charged with a most difficult task, my lady. You protect the people, and no one will imagine it to be easy for you, or your souls."

"I killed a man, Brother," I told him. "Yesterday. He attacked me."

He sighed. "These are strange days. I've said to you before that if there were any time the Lord might forgive our darkest transgressions, it may well be these equally dark times, but we both know the peril your soul is in."

I nodded. "I don't have much hope for my soul."

"You've sinned, my lady, but if anyone ever did it for the right reasons, it's you and your fellows. It will be for God to judge such a tangled web, not I." He touched my hand. "And as for Gisbourne, stay far away from him. If he knows you are near, he won't stop until he possesses you. We would all be loath to see that happen."

I bent and let the spaniel lick my hand.

"Come. You must pray, and confess, and cleanse your soul if you have any hope to defend its righteousness."

I nodded and let him lead me back to the small chapel. I started to move toward the back, but he tugged me frontward.

"A lady of your caliber does not sit in the back, my dear."

CHAPTER

SIX

Iwalked back to the cave, feeling jittery with every step. I didn't like looking like a girl, and without my knives—you certain can't bring knives to church—I rather felt like a girl. If I came 'cross a guard, I wouldn't have much of a chance. And worse, I weren't sure if the lads would be back at the cave or off and about. Robin never went to masses since he came back from the Crusades, but he still seemed to feel like Sundays were for reckoning anyway, and he were fair hard to find come Sunday mornings. John and Much tended to go over to Worksop to go to church with Much's father, and it were passing rare for us to be at the cave instead of the oak. I never had to risk them seeing me in a dress before, but with all the muck about the tree burning and such, I knew Robin wanted us sticking together; I just weren't sure where they would be.

I got back to the cave and halted as I saw Much and John talking to each other. They stopped and turned to me.

Much looked confused, and John stepped forward. "Wait . . . Scar?"

My mug got hot. "Stop gawping, John. Let me pass."

"I'll tell you one thing, Scar—Miss Percy wouldn't be after you in that getup."

I scowled at him.

"Where'd you get that dress? And when'd you start filling it out?" John asked, following me into the cave.

"Bugger off," I told him.

He didn't; he kept coming closer. "You look good in a dress."

"Go, John."

He grinned at me and turned, going back out to the front of the cave. I didn't like his eyes on me like that.

I changed quick as I could, sliding the dress back into my hiding place and going out front to the lads. I sat on the ground and tucked my legs up.

"I could get used to you in a dress," John told me.

"Don't."

"You looked nice," Much told me.

"Thanks, Much," I said, even though I didn't really want him thinking I looked any which way. Better him than John, though.

"So where were you going in a dress? Meeting someone?" John asked.

"Leave off, John," I said, scowling.

"Can't. Who were you meeting?"

I stared at him.

"Fine, maybe I'll guess. Secret love? Lad from one of the villages?" He studied me, then shook his head. "Are you running something? Show 'em some chest and they'll let you get away with anything, I'll bet."

I snorted. "Please. If it were so easy, I'd gussy up every day."

"Trust me, I think you're not putting enough faith in how you look in skirts. Now, who do you think Scar would actually want knowing she was a girl?" John asked Much.

I looked away. "This is why we near get pinched; you lot pay too much attention to the wrong things."

"Like what?" Rob asked, coming down over the ridge above the mouth of the cave.

"Scar was in a dress," John reported.

"Looked pretty, too," Much added.

Rob didn't look at me. "She's right—there are more important things to discuss."

We all looked at him.

"Someone told Gisbourne we camp at Major Oak."

"Who?" John growled, stepping forward.

"Hey," I interrupted. "Settle back. If someone sung, then I reckon they had real good reason."

He shot me a look.

"She's right, John. I'm worried that whoever it is, Gisbourne has some heavy leverage on him. Or her." He sighed. "It also means that we can't put that burden on the people. If no one knows where we are, how we work, Gisbourne can't torture anyone to get to it."

"He can torture anyone, knowing or not," I said.

"Well, we can't risk it either. We can't help the people if we're dead." He rubbed the narrow bit of his nose. "Much, you go into town today and talk. Take John with you. I'll go with Scarlet. No one goes anywhere alone today. We need to find out who told and if they're all right. Meet up at nightfall at Tuck's."

John held out a hand to help me up. I looked at it but stood on my own. He frowned.

"You two cover Worksop; we'll go to Edwinstowe," Rob said. We all nodded. The lads set off, and Robin started walking in the opposite direction.

"You know who told, don't you?" I asked him as we went.

He nodded. "I knew John would react like that, but I wanted you to come with me."

"Why? Who is it?"

"Edward Marshal."

That weren't good. Edward Marshal were the marshal for Edwinstowe, a position that came with some land and money and reported to the sheriff. Edward himself had always been an ambitious man, but folk made sure they didn't tell him nothing. I also reckoned Lady Thoresby were in the habit of protecting us, for she talked fair often to Marshal and whenever he had some misinformation that I couldn't account for, she'd been to see him fair recent. There weren't too much she could do as the wife of a weak lord, but I liked to think she tried best she could. Anyways, for someone to tell Marshal something meant less helpless motives. He wouldn't torture no one, so that left a volunteer.

"What do you need me for?"

"He's clever; I need you to cover me with those knives."

I looked at my hand, still a little swollen. My aim were just a lick off, but we'd be in close quarters. I nodded to Rob.

He were silent for a long stretch, and I didn't speak, crunching leaves as we walked.

"About John," he said at long last.

I blinked.

"I don't want to know how you two are fooling about, but if it interferes with the band I'll kick you out myself."

The breath stopped in my pipes. "What?"

"I won't repeat myself. And I don't want to talk about it more than that."

"But—"

"I'm not joking, Scar. I don't want to know."

I snapped my yap closed. Fooling about? Did he think I were John's bit of fun for the day? My belly twisted and I didn't like the feeling. Worse, were that what John thought? It weren't like we ever snuck kisses or nothing like that. I never even got an inkling that he might like to kiss me, and I certain didn't want to kiss him. I didn't think. He weren't bad looking or nothing, but he were in my band. I fought with him; I watched him gut deer. Most days I wanted to smack him more than anything tender.

And he weren't Rob. But then, maybe that weren't such an awful thing. Rob's sort I could never deserve.

Rob didn't speak the rest of the way, and thoughts of John and Rob kept wheeling over in my head.

—⁂—

I sat in the window, spinning a knife on my finger while we waited for Edward to enter his bedchamber. He wouldn't have a guard or company of the male sort in there, so we waited for him to appear, knowing we could hold him back.

We didn't have to wait long. He came in and shut the door before turning with a start. "Robin Hood?" he asked.

"I heard you've been singing Gisbourne a song, Edward," Rob said, his eyes black.

"Oh Christ and the saints," Edward swore. "Of course I told the thief taker. Why shouldn't I? Quicker I'm rid of you lot, the better."

"There are a few reasons," Rob said, nodding toward my knives.

"What, a whip of a lad and a few pin sticks?"

I smiled at that, and Rob chuckled. "You don't want to know what those pin sticks can do."

"Well, you ain't going to kill me, and you ain't going to hurt me, and I ain't going to stop telling the thief taker or the sheriff what I hear. So what do we do now?"

"We don't want you, Edward. You're a fool if there ever was one. But you didn't know where we live, so who told you?" Rob asked.

"Informin' on the informant, eh? That's the game today?"

"Just tell us the name. You shouldn't be shy to reveal your source."

"Can't imagine what you want with him. You ain't going to kill him neither. And if I don't tell you, he'll keep on keeping me on—isn't that right?"

"Rob's got more principles than me," I reminded. "Me, I know that you pay taxes like the rest of us, and I know where you keep your collection money. What would your sheriff do if you couldn't pay?" I shrugged. "I like shiny things like that, but the sheriff likes softer bits. Like your wife, or your little son."

He looked more worried. "You wouldn't never hurt my wife or son."

"Wife and son, no, no. I told you, I like shiny bits."

He grimaced. "Everyone says you lot are so honorable."

Rob shrugged. "Can't hold a thief accountable."

"It was Godfrey Mason what told me."

Robin's face went white like someone stole his blood, and I stood up.

"You're lyin'," I said.

"'Fraid not. The sheriff is awful insistent that we should help this thief taker, and once the sheriff sends me up, Godfrey wants my seat. Thought to grace his way in."

I shook my head. "Sheriff's not sending you nowhere, Marshal," I told him.

"Is so. Promised me Constable of the Royal Horses in Nottingham."

"That station's filled," Rob told him.

"Things shake up round here fast, Hood. It'll shake up and we'll shake you right out."

Rob frowned. "Not likely. Will, let's go."

Rob looked toward me and I saw Marshal go for his belt dagger. I pushed forward in front of Rob. "Settle back there, Marshal," I told him, putting two daggers on him.

He sighed and moved backward, holding his hands away from his belt. Rob went out the window, and I backed my way over to it, tipping my hat to Marshal and hopping out the window.

His house had two levels, so we went across the lower roof and then jumped off the end of it, walking farther into town.

Rob put his hood up. "I can't believe it was Godfrey."

"Honestly."

"I doubt Ravenna knows."

"She's his twin; how could she not know?"

His jaw worked. "God knows you can be right beside them day in and day out, and sometimes you don't know those closest to you at all."

"Should we talk to him?"

Rob's face were all kinds of sad, but he shook his head. "No. Let's get to Tuck's."

"We need to make a stop first," I told him.

He just nodded, following behind me.

I went almost clear to the other side of Edwinstowe, knocking on the door of a small house. A tall man that almost had to hunch over a bit greeted me and smiled. "Scarlet—and Robin Hood!" he realized, bursting into a big grin.

Rob looked at me. "Scarlet?" he asked quietly. "Not Will?"

I shrugged at Rob and smiled back to the big lug. "Hullo, George," I greeted. I produced a small ewer of milk that I nicked from Marshal's dairy. George took it and picked me up and hugged me like a bear, setting me down inside the house. He greeted Robin, but I went in and went over to Mary, who struggled to sit up. I put my arm on hers, stopping her, and kissed her cheek.

"You look right as rain," I told her.

She smiled. "Almost," she told me. "We've both been a little weak."

The bundle in her lap started squirming and began to keen, and I picked up their newborn son, curling him in my arms. He looked up at me and stopped fussing.

"Look what she brought," George said, pouring some milk into a cup. Mary drank and then held it out to me.

"Rob," I said. "Dip your fingers in the milk and give it to the baby." I looked up at him as he did what I said. He were focusing hard, but the sadness in his face were gone. I smiled.

"What's his name?" Robin asked as the baby started to drink the little drips of milk.

Tears sprung into Mary's eyes. "Scarlet didn't tell you?"

He shook his head.

"We named him Robin. He's given us hope, the same way you have."

"Hope," Rob repeated, touching the baby's cheek with his fingertip. "I'm sorry if it's been in short supply lately."

Mary's lip trembled, and tears darted down her cheeks. "Oh Robin," she whispered. "We'd have nothing left if it weren't for what you do for us. If giving him your name means our son will have just a bit of your courage and heart, I'd be the proudest mother there was."

To my surprise, Robin looked to me, his eyes bigger and bluer. "You knew? About the name?"

I shrugged. "Thought it might buck you up."

He smiled, a big, generous hero smile. I held the baby up and Robin took him, holding him against his chest.

"Scarlet near saved his life," Mary told Robin, wiping her eyes.

"Did she?"

"A week and a bit ago. The birth was hard, and I was crying out," Mary said soft.

George nodded. "Scarlet wanted to help, but I wouldn't let her in; no one told me he was a girl, after all. Her. She, whatnot. And she climbed into the window instead."

"She told me right away the boy was twisted, and she went and got Lady Thoresby. I never even knew the lady was a midwife."

I were blushing hot, and I couldn't even fuss with the baby. Honestly, I didn't bring Rob here so he could hear them fawning on me. He were holding on to the lad like he were gold bars, though, so I reckoned my plan worked.

"She's resourceful like that," Rob said with a chuckle. The baby squirmed and twisted against his neck, and he beamed. Something in my belly flipped over a little bit, seeing him hold the baby.

"I'll try and get you some eggs tomorrow, Mary," I told her.

"We're all right, Scarlet. You don't need to dote. We just finished the harvest, and we'll take it to market tomorrow."

Rob looked to George. "How much did the sheriff collect?"

He sighed. "Near half. We're still better than most, though."

Rob nodded. "We'll help as best we can. Can't let my name-sake go hungry."

Mary rubbed my arm. "We thank God for your help. We all do."

A bit of the shadow came back over Rob at that, and I knew he were thinking of Godfrey. He dipped his fingers in the milk again, though, continuing to feed the baby.

"You warm enough?" I asked Mary.

She nodded, and I tucked her feet into the blankets; I could feel how cold they were through her stockings.

"He's a handsome lad," Rob said, holding the baby out to look at him.

"Takes after his father," I told George, and he puffed his chest up.

Mary laughed. "He thinks far too well of himself after you come, Scarlet."

George chuckled, coming and sitting beside his wife on the

small bed. "I've only eyes for you, my love, but I'll take pretty words when I can."

"I think he's nodding off," Rob said, watching the baby's mouth open and his eyes close.

"I'll take him," Mary said, and Rob put the babe in her lap gentle, wrapping him up tight in the one fur they had.

"We won't wake him, then," Rob said, nodding at me. "But thank you, Mary, for letting me meet him. He's a good lad." He patted her shoulder, and she covered his hand.

George led us out, shaking Rob's hand and hugging me again. When the door closed, Rob looked sharp to me. "You planned that?"

I lifted a shoulder. "After hearing 'bout Godfrey, seemed like a good time to remember why you're doing all this."

His eyes looked into mine in a way that made my breath suck out of my pipes. "You're every kind of surprise, you know that?"

I shook my head.

He put his hand to my cheek, just touching the fingertips to my skin before pulling away. "You are."

He looked away and started walking down the lane to Tuck's, and it were a few paces before my breath came back.

—⁂—

Inside Tuck's, we didn't go straight for the back room. Keeping his hood up, Rob pulled Tuck to the side.

"Who was it, then?" Tuck asked, his face sour.

"Godfrey Mason," Rob told him.

Tuck pulled back. "Godfrey? No. Wasn't him, Rob."

"I wish it wasn't, but it was."

"But he's such a good lad. Always been right awed by you too. If he did—and I'm not saying so—he must have done it for Ravenna. Maybe they're in trouble."

Robin shook his head. "No. Perhaps, but I don't believe so. Until I find out otherwise, I need to be sure no one passes him information about my lads."

Tuck nodded. "I'll make sure of it. You and Scar head on back. I'll get you some food."

"Thank you, Tuck."

We went into the back, and Rob sank onto the bench. "Do you think it was him, Scar?"

I slid in beside him, putting my hands on the table. "Yes. He's a good kid, but he's got a rotten father and a silly mother, and he's got his sister depending on him—if she's not married off soon."

He nodded, reaching forward and flipping my hand over. "I think even in these times they want more money."

I tried hard to swallow, staring at his hand touching mine. "Working for the sheriff would be good money."

"Most likely." Quick and sure, his thumb pushed over each finger, dragging lightning over my hand. "We played together as children, you know. My father hired his father to build half the Locksley estate. I'd been gone for those few years for the Crusades, but I always thought we were friends."

His fingers slid into mine, locking into a grip. I were staring at the hair on the knuckles of his big hand. "Everyone thinks high of them. Ain't no one doesn't like the twins."

"But to betray us?"

I hesitated. I knew I tended to see things different, but this were still hard to say right. I squeezed his hand and pulled my eyes up to his face. "As far as betraying goes, he didn't get us pinched. It weren't a trap, but Gisbourne thinks he got victory."

Robin scowled. "That's true. Why didn't Gisbourne ambush us instead of burning the tree?"

"Maybe Godfrey will know."

Robin pulled my hand under the table and didn't let go till the lads arrived.

—⚉—

Godfrey made a bit of a mistake that night. Tuck told people to keep their traps shut, of course, and he had to tell them why. John heard, and so did all the customers of Friar Tuck's. Godfrey showed up well into the night, which meant most of the men were more than a drink down.

When Godfrey appeared, the place busted open, attacking Godfrey and launching into a drunken brawl. I understood that. It made big men feel better to hit someone when they were scared, and God knew everyone were scared these days.

He took a few punches, but I managed to squirrel him out while the bar were heaving without anyone noticing him gone. I tugged him around the building to the back door.

"What in God's name was that?" he demanded, spitting out some blood.

I crossed my arms. "You know."

His face went white. "They all know?"

I nodded. "You want to be marshal?"

He sighed. "Look, my parents want to marry Ravenna off to a Frenchman. A *Frenchman*. If I can start my own household, she can live with me."

"You near cracked Robin."

He hit the wall. "I figured."

"Maybe you should be talking to him," I told him.

"I'm listening," Rob said, coming from behind me. He must have followed us out.

Godfrey's face went all kinds of mournful. "No one got hurt, did they? I told them that's where you pass messages with the townspeople, not that you live there."

"We're all right."

"I'm sorry, Rob. Gisbourne wanted the information or he said he'd throw me in the prison."

Rob nodded. "It's all right. We just can't tell the townspeople anything anymore. And that will include you, Godfrey, but I'm not singling you out."

"I know. And I suppose I'll get a rough shake from the townspeople, then."

"Probably. But come on, we'll see what we can do to fix that."

Rob put his arm around Godfrey's shoulders and brought him in through the back door. It weren't a moment or two that John appeared, kicking a bucket so hard it split in two.

"Unhappy?" I asked him.

He spun around to look at me, and then kicked a bucket bit again. "He betrayed us and Rob's welcoming him back. He's a rat!"

"Thought I were a rat."

He wedged his hands onto his hips and looked at me. "Different sort. Your kind of rat isn't so bad."

"He did what he thought he had to, John."

"Christ, I don't get you, Scar. You spit with venom at the likes of the thief taker and the sheriff, but other than that, you can't judge a living soul."

"I'm a thief. Ain't got so much moral ground to stand on."

He gave me a little smile at that. "I suppose. I still think Robin's a fool."

"We both know he's no fool."

He looked at me, his eyes running over my face. He came closer, and I were against the wall, so my heart started to flutter-beat in my chest. I didn't much like feeling trapped. He palmed my hat, pushing it back.

"What are you doing?" I asked, pulling away.

"I need to see your eyes when I ask you this."

"Ask what?"

"Are you in love with Rob, Scar?"

I hesitated. Sometimes, like with the baby, or the strange way Rob touched my hand, I kind of thought I might be. But then he would yell at me or shut me up with a glare and an insult like he had that morning, saying I were fooling with John. John, who were in front of me, asking if I loved Rob, looking at my weird eyes without looking away. "No," I told him. It were the truth, I think. Or as much of the truth as made a difference.

"Good."

He leaned forward, his eyes looking right into mine, and his mouth came so near I felt the skin of his top lip on mine. His eyes stared into me, and he just waited there, looking for something, or waiting for me to do something, but I didn't know what. I looked down, not sure of myself.

He chuckled, and his thumb ran over my lips. The touch made me jump, made everything stranger, and I pulled away from him.

"See you back later, Scar," he told me.

I didn't look up until he left, and then I sat on the ground and hugged my arms about my knees. I didn't know what to make of that at all.

CHAPTER

SEVEN

—o—

The morning were rough. It were our first day on the road since the chest were taken, and it felt like rolling thunder in the distance. With just a fortnight to get enough goods and fence them again before tax day, we all knew how much more gold were needed now, but it felt like all our luck had pure run out.

I kicked at a branch and stared at the empty road like travelers would appear if I wished it. I kept glancing at Rob and John, and the rough feel of John pushing his thumb over my mouth jumped into my head.

I stood. "Rob!" I called. He stepped out onto the road, looking up at me. "I'm going to Nottingham, see what I can steal there. This isn't helping none."

He nodded. "Fine. Meet back at Tuck's tonight, all right?"

"Sure." I skittered across a tree branch, heading to Nottingham Castle and away from John and Rob. 'Course, going to

Nottingham weren't getting away from Rob, in truth. It had been his home once, and walking there felt like he were walking 'longside me.

I nabbed some silver and food from the keep and were leaving at dusk when I heard someone making an awful racket. I ducked down one of the alleyways of shacks that made up Nottingham's town, and sure enough, right by the castle wall, I found a girl in a pretty red dress crying her eyes out.

I came over to her and looked down the way, making sure there were no one to bother her. "Come on," I told her soft. "I'll get you home."

She looked up at me, and my heart kind of stuck in my throat. It weren't Joanna by any stretch, but she had yellow hair and blue eyes, and for a second it looked like her. My hand were already out and she took it. "Thank you, sir."

I helped her stand up, and she leaned on me. "What's your name?"

"Alice."

"Where's your home?"

She shook her head. "I live inside the castle. I'm one of the maids."

"Why you crying, then?"

She burst into tears again, and I didn't know what to do. "S-s-sh," were all she managed.

"Hush," I told her. I pulled out a roll from my pouch. "Here, eat something."

She took the roll and managed a few bites of it. "'S terrible

work," she said. "Me and the girls all know. It's better if the
sheriff takes a shine to you, you know? He's kinder then. Gives
you money and lets you skip some chores and feeds you more
too. It's not so bad. And he was so nice to me—I thought he
really loved me. But I t told him it's his baby," she said, pressing her hand against her tummy. The breath whooshed out of
me. "And he hit me!" she wailed, fizzing up into tears again.

"Listen," I said, thinking quick. "I know someplace you
can go. The keep won't mind you having one on the way, and
the work's not too bad. You'll be right as rain."

"Are you mad?" she cried, pushing away from me. "You
think I can leave this place? I can't, not ever. He'd send
Gisbourne to kill me, he told me."

"Gisbourne's a thief taker, not a hireling. The sheriff can't
order him about as he pleases."

She shook her head, turning back to the castle. "You're a
stupid boy. You don't know anything of how the world is."

I shook my head too, watching her scamper back into the
castle.

—∞—

I waited as long as I could to meet up with the lads, going up
by Thoresby Lake and waiting till stars popped out overhead.
Too many thoughts were rolling inside me, thoughts of Joanna
and London and those last final days that I never liked to think
of much.

When I thought of Joanna, there were days I wanted to

remember. When we first ran away to London, we still had money in our purses, and it felt like the world were opened up wide to us in a single breath, like we never had to listen to no one again and everything would be perfect. Like we had cheated fate.

'Course, fate were right around the corner, waiting. Fate never stopped following me—not now, when just as I thought I were free Gisbourne came blazing back into my life like a hell beast, and not then—in those terrible days in London when the money were gone and Joanna and I both turned our own kind of desperate.

That were why it were no use to think on Joanna. Everything ran back to London, to those last days.

I were right tired, that were all. The sheriff's poor Alice weren't no Joanna and I couldn't fix neither of them, and I had no business thinking of such things anyway. People who wanted my help needed it tonight.

I saved one roll for myself, chewing on it slow. Maybe if I could just eat I wouldn't get stuck on the past quite so much.

The quiet night were falling, so I went to Tuck's, but it were a slow sort of going.

I walked straight into a storm.

The boys were waiting for me outside Tuck's, and Rob nodded me forward, walking off into the night toward the cave.

"The sheriff caught Godfrey and Ravenna," Rob told me.

"Caught?" I asked.

"Lady Thoresby told us they're accused of trapping a rabbit."

"That's not poaching!" I protested.

"I think the sheriff is punishing Godfrey because he didn't get us. Sheriff thinks he lied to him."

"He didn't promise them us," I argued.

"The sheriff doesn't give a damn!" Rob snapped at me. "And he's going to hang them with whatever thieves Gisbourne can round up."

I felt my cheeks blush. I hated when he yelled at me.

"We'll have a few days yet if he wants a big hanging," John said.

"Possibly even a week or so," Much agreed.

"I'm sure we can wrangle something up to keep him busy for two weeks, can't we Scar?" John asked with a smile.

I looked away, and I felt Rob's eyes burning holes in me. "Let's just break them out of the prison tonight and make no bother of the lot."

"Get it done. I want this done," Rob said. He rubbed his head. "And we all need sleep before we do anything. Even you, Scar."

I shrugged. I were fair tired, anyway. We stayed quiet till we reached the cave, and once there, Much handed out some bread to all of us. I took mine and went to sit on top of the ridge above the cave.

"Scar," John called. He bounded up the ridge and sat beside me.

"You aren't fixing to watch me eat, are you?"

"No," he said, biting into his bread. I bit mine. "How you feeling, anyway?"

I lifted my shoulder, not bothering to talk. Awful. I felt awful.

"What's your plan for the prison?"

"Don't know. Need to think on it. Whatever we do, we can't never use it again, because Gisbourne will figure it out and fix it. Think maybe we should save the tunnel for later."

"How do you reckon to get in, then?"

I grinned. "I got ways, John Little."

His eyes looked me over in a funny way. "You don't need to tell me, Scar."

My cheeks went hot without me knowing much why, and it were light enough that he could tell, which made the whole matter worse.

"You ain't half bad when you blush, Scar."

"What happened to me being a coward?"

He shrugged. "I think I'm starting to figure you out. You steal all this food and eat none; you had a friend that you loved. Really, I'm starting to think you're pretty tough—but with a bit of a soft belly."

"What friend?" I asked. I never loved any friend of mine. Never much had a friend.

"That Leaford girl. When you talked about her, it was obvious how much you cared about her."

I felt the blush slide right off my mug.

"You don't like to talk about much, Scar, and don't worry, I'm not asking. You don't have to talk about your friend. But yeah, I think I'm figuring you out. Slowly, of course."

I smiled a little, but not a real sure smile, and stared off into the night. I waited until everyone else went to sleep, and when I went into the cave, I mounded my bed far from John. Were this his way of shining on me? After all this fighting?

I slept, but it weren't a real restful sleep.

—⁂—

I went to have a lookabout round the prison the next afternoon, and Rob said he'd come with me. I nodded, waiting for him to run up 'longside me. He had his dark hood up, and I had my hat down low.

"You angry at me for something?" I asked him after a little bit.

"What makes you say that?"

"Usually you talk. And you yelled at me last night."

He turned to look at me, but I didn't look back. "I hate what's going on. Can't believe they arrested the twins; Godfrey was only trying to keep his sister safe, and they throw him and his sister in prison—and she had nothing to do with it."

"I'll get them out," I told him.

"It'll be years until Richard's back. It took him as long as I was there to conquer the city of Acre, which is miles outside the Holy Land, and he won't come home until he takes Jerusalem. How can we fight back this flood for years more? How can this situation continue?"

I crunched a branch underfoot, sneaking a look at him. I knew my heart weren't never too sure 'bout many things, but if I ever could, I wanted to be sure for Rob. That way when his heart stumbled, I could be sure for the both of us. "It's like you said, Rob. We do what we do because there's something we *can* do about it. Things like 'how long' and 'what if' aren't part of that. It's about the hope, not the horror." Thoughts of London welled up in my pipes but I kept going. "And for that matter, you know all about the horrors, just like I do, just like John does, just like Much. We shoulder it so these people don't have to know it too. And I know this because that's what you say. And when you say it, I believe you. And when I believe you, I'll follow you anywhere."

His eyes closed, and he nodded. "You have more faith in me than I do for myself sometimes, Scar."

"Well, that's right as rain," I told him. "You don't need to be sure of yourself all the time. Fact, it's a little more bearable when you ain't."

He smiled a little, looking at me. "You think I'm unbearable?"

I shrugged. "Sure. You ain't like nobody else. Sometimes I don't know what to make of you at all."

"This coming from the thieving, knife-throwing outlaw girl. As if there were anyone like you in the wide world."

"Yeah, but you see right through me."

"It's not that I see through you," he told me. "It's that I see you. You don't want anyone to see you, but I do."

I nodded, and my old bruise started beating under my hat. "Wish you didn't, sometimes."

He sighed. "Sometimes I wish I didn't too. It would certainly be easier," he said soft.

That knifed into my belly like a hot ax. I knew that, as far as souls went, mine were black as tar and, like my face, it were strange and scarred. Somehow, some part of me always thought Rob saw me as different than all that, though, saw the good bits of me as better than the ugly bits.

That weren't the way of it at all, clear as day. Rob saw the tar and the scars and wished he never peeked at all.

I didn't look up or speak the rest of the way there.

—⁓—

We spent several hours in Nottingham, which were tough for Rob. People could recognize him there, so he stayed out of the castle proper while I found a way in.

When I met up with Rob again, it weren't with good news.

"Gisbourne is fussing with everything. He's changing the guard shifts—he's doubling them on the prison and on the gate and ordering them to move around at night. He knows I can get in but he don't know how."

"How many ways do you know?"

"The tunnel's my best way in. I can get over the wall in a trice without them seeing me, but the tough bit is getting others over." I stopped, my eyes going wide. "I know what we can do."

"Tell me."

"Well, they'll be expecting us to break Godfrey and Ravenna out, won't they? They'll be guarding the prison extra just for it."

"So?"

"So let's give them what they expect."

His eyebrows pulled together tight. "You want us to walk into a trap? Or, rather, a heavily guarded prison that might as well be a trap?"

I grinned, setting off. "Nail on the head, Rob!"

"Wait, Scar, that makes no sense."

I kept walking.

"Scar!"

—⚏—

"You've gone completely mad," John told me, again. Again and again. And again. Rob and Much said nothing, but they were with me too.

"Stop saying that. It's bad luck."

"You don't need luck—you need to not go in there."

"Since when are you antsy about scaring up some trouble, John?" Much asked.

He glared. "Since she's taking far too much risk on her shoulders. They're little shoulders, if you lot haven't noticed."

"She'll be fine, John. It's a good idea," Rob said, rougher than I would have thought. Honestly, the lug were just worried.

"I'm holding you responsible, Huntingdon," John snapped. "Remember that you're the one who agreed to all this."

I slapped John's stomach. We never called Rob by his title. "In case you forgot, John Little, we don't look back once we agree on a plan. Stop casting bad luck round." I spat on the ground; it were supposed to send off bad spirits.

I looked up at the sky. It were a dark, clouded sky without a moon, like a better thief than me stole the light to help us hide. We climbed the wall, scaling the rough stone by moving quick and never searching out much of a foothold. Only Much couldn't fair get it, and John climbed back down and did it again with Much on his back, like he'd done Freddy the other time.

Rob and I went over the wall to the parapet, looking for the roving guards. One came through and we separated, each flipping over the side of the guard's walk at the top of the wall to hide in the dark. The side I flipped over, of course, left me dangling above the castle residences. I lowered myself onto one careful, hiding on the back of the roof.

Rob came down, and then John and Much came a few minutes later. Once we were all there, I dropped down into the central courtyard, looking straight into Gisbourne's chambers. The room were lit, but he weren't there, and that chilled me a little.

One by one we dropped down, then ran across the upper bailey and down through the gauntlet. There were more guards on, and they were moving, but they still tended to group together and leave areas unprotected. We knew how to move in the darkness unseen, but I knew the Mason twins wouldn't be so good at it.

Once we got to the prison, I went round the side of the lads while John came in from the front, bumbling like a drunk. The two guards from the front threw their gaze to him, and I slid in behind them. I heard John shouting at them as I ran deep into the prison.

The rough rock walls gave way to cells, a lone candle guttering in the front to cast light over the place. I could see the cells and the people within, and I stopped dead.

Something were wrong. 'Ever I set foot in the prison, they'd all be whispering and calling to me, begging for help or helping me find who I needed. They were all dead quiet, and I didn't flatter myself that they couldn't see me.

I stopped at Jack Tailor's cell. We had tried once to help him get out of there, but he wouldn't go; he didn't want no backlash on his family. He said it weren't worth the price of being free. That were a few months ago; I wondered if he might change his mind if he thought there'd be some hangings soon.

He came to the front of his cell, meeting my eyes and then looking over toward the back of the prison. I drew my finger down between my eyes, trying to ape the nosepiece that were on the guards' helmets.

He shook his head.

I nodded. It weren't a guard, then. That meant it could be someone I didn't need to bother 'bout none—or Nottingham. Or Gisbourne.

Either way, I had to move quick. "*Mason?*" I mouthed. Tailor pointed to a cell farther down. I would have to be quicksilver. I nodded my thanks and moved into the darker end of the prison.

I could feel someone there. I could hear soft breathing, measured and even, and, worse, I could feel his eyes on me. Watching me. Hunting me. Somewhere in my gut, I were sure it were Gisbourne, standing in the shadow just beyond me like he'd always done.

Didn't matter none. Couldn't turn back now.

I slid the package from my back. It would fit through the bars. I moved quiet along the cells, looking for the twins. My heart were drumming up a storm. I just had to be steady, I kept reminding myself.

It were nineteen paces and six cells in that I found them. They rushed forward and I pressed the package through the bars. "Have faith," I whispered, gripping Ravenna's hand on the bar and meeting her eyes, trying to somehow show her everything that I couldn't tell her and her brother.

A huge hand came out and grabbed my neck, ripping me back from the bars. I fell back against the other cell across the row, and even in the dark I knew the Devil when I saw him.

"Gisbourne."

He pulled back, surprised that I knew his name, and I didn't sit around gawping. I bolted. "John!" I barked as I cleared the prison gate. He threw off the guards and snapped a couple quick punches, and we set off running.

Rob were running ahead of us, and Much were on the roof, waiting to grab him with his good arm and toss him up. Then Rob hauled John up while I scrambled up the wall. We were over the wall as archers started setting in.

The archers shot, but there were big brass bowls full of fire right on the parapet, and they couldn't see into the dark beyond that. We skittered right down the wall and scampered quick into the forest.

We ran for a while, and Rob called us all to stop by a stream. We drank, and I pulled onto a tree branch. "Well?" Rob asked.

"Went perfect," I told him. "Now that they think we've tried and failed, we'll be set to get them out tomorrow. Got the package in, so they'll think we've been getting people out dressed as guards. And they did keep a man inside, like I thought they might."

John sighed. "Christ, you had me, Scar. When you came running hell for leather, I thought everything was done."

I shrugged. "It were Gisbourne. But the twins looked hale and hearty, and we'll get them out tomorrow."

Rob nodded. "So far, your plan is flawless, Scar."

I started to smile, but him saying he wished he never saw me popped into my ears. I looked down instead. "We'll know tomorrow."

He nodded again. "We should all get some sleep. Tomorrow will be complicated enough."

—∞—

When we rose, my heart were unsteady. Seeing Gisbourne's face so close had rattled me sure, and though it had been dead dark, there were some tiny terror in me that he'd known me.

He couldn't have known me. It were too dark, and besides, I've changed.

'Course, there were the eyes. He could know the eyes. And the scar.

But the light were too low for him to get a fair look at either. He couldn't have known me.

Every bit of me hollered to run away and go nowhere near the castle, and I did nothing of the sort. It were unbelievable foolish to not trust one's own bits; this were the sort of stupid muck that you got into by caring 'bout other people. I were haunted by the feel of my hand on Ravenna's all night through.

I waited by the side of the road until I saw Tuck's wagon round the corner, just like we planned. I hopped up beside him when he slowed. "Robin thanks you for this, Tuck," I told him.

He nodded. "I do love Robin, but I'm doing this for those twins. You just make sure it runs like sunup and sundowns, Scarlet."

My stomach pushed into my pipes. "Yes."

"And I'm sorry already for having to hit you around in a bit."

I nodded and put up my hood, and we rode to the castle in quiet. It were strange; the pitch of the wagon were gentle and fair even, and for a breath I felt like this might have been the way of my life, if I were a boy in true, if I hadn't had the cursed luck to ever be born a girl.

The guards stopped us at the gate, and they inspected Tuck's barrels. This weren't the hard part, 'course. This were the "no yap, no trap" part, and all I had to do were keep my mouth shut.

They let us pass, and the slow and easy pitch of the wagon continued. We rolled through the lower bailey, and there I slid off the wagon. I went quick to the air vent, trusting that Rob, Much, and John would uphold their own parts.

With a twist and a jump I slid down the vent, bringing dry dirt in behind me. I dropped to my feet; my knee hit a touch hard and smarted, but it weren't broken. I stood, running for the twins' cell.

"You're too late," Godfrey told me, his voice something mournful.

Ravenna were gone.

CHAPTER
EIGHT

—o—

Godfrey, what have they done with her?"

He hit the bars. "Nottingham came down here after you left, and he saw her. He said she was pretty and then she was just gone. Goddamn you, you coward! You could have fought him off last night; you could have taken us then. This is your fault!"

My hands shook as I picked the lock. Tears were pushing at my eyes and I felt like retching. "I'll get her free," I promised him. My voice were a bare squeak. Christ, and the sheriff just lost his mistress to the birthing chamber, if that Alice lass the day before were such.

The door swung open and he charged at me, slinging a punch across my face. I didn't even bother fighting back. I hit the bars and he hit me again. I fell, and he kicked me. "Goddamn you, Will Scarlet!" he spat.

He stepped back, and I reckoned he were done. I got to my feet. I could bare see straight; my eyes felt like they were rolling loose, and every time they rolled, gunpowder went off in my head. I went to the next cell, and it took me a few minutes too long to pick the lock on that.

"What're you doing?" the prisoner asked. "Get the lad out of here!"

"We can take six," I told him. "So we're taking six."

I opened four more cells, and by then the pain didn't feel so god-awful. On my face, at least. There were a sickness I felt that retching wouldn't cure. Godfrey were right. It were my stupid plan, and I failed them both.

Rob and John came into the prison to meet me. "What's taking so long?" Rob asked. "Where's Ravenna?"

Godfrey shoved me from behind, and I fell to my knees. "Ask this miserable vermin!" he roared.

Rob picked me up. Not by the arm, like he'd do with a lad; he took one of my hands in his and with his other arm caught me up by my waist, pulling me to his side and a bit behind him. His voice were steel and his arms sure felt like it. "Do that again, Godfrey, and I'll lock you back up myself."

"Nottingham has her," I told him. My voice felt like I swallowed rocks. "Nottingham wants her."

"Which one of you is actually the Hood?" one of the prisoners asked, confused.

"Me," Rob said, lowering his hood.

"Your Grace!" several cried.

John started tossing out the robes he and Rob were wearing. "Let's go."

"Like hell," Godfrey snarled. "I'm not leaving without Ravenna."

"We'll get her out," Rob told him. "We need a plan first, though."

I shook my head. "I'll stay. I can't leave her here. You lot get them out and get back in to help, however you can."

"Not a chance," Rob told me, his hold on me tightening, his ocean eyes locking on me and washing out the rest.

"Don't be a fool, lad!" one of the prisoners told me. "You took too many blows to the head already."

I glared at him from under my hood, but Rob just held on to me and pulled my hood back, looking full at what Godfrey'd done. Rob's grip felt full to bruising, and for a moment I didn't stop him. Any pain at that moment made the sickness feel a little less sick.

"You need to get them out of here, Rob," I reminded, trying to shake loose of him.

"Not before I kill him," Robin growled.

I saw Godfrey step back.

"You did this to her?" John roared, pushing Godfrey back from me.

"Her?" Godfrey cried. "That's a bleeding girl?"

"We need to go!" I yelled, pushing at Rob's chest.

Rob didn't budge, his fingers iron bands strapped round my own. "Only if you're coming too."

"Fine!" I snapped. I turned to Godfrey, shaking Rob off. "I'll get her out or I'll die trying, Godfrey."

Godfrey's face twisted but he nodded, and he finished putting on the robe.

I broke away from them like I were supposed to. The only reason I didn't run hell for leather were because I knew Rob would get pinched coming after me, and he wouldn't even care. My face felt wet in the open air and I weren't sure if it were blood or tears.

I kept an eye on them, moving at an equal pace but staying far ahead. When I got to Tuck delivering barrels in the upper bailey, he started yelling at me for running off. He slapped me around, making sport of it when I tried to defend myself, and everyone were watching, never noticing my boys climbing into the empty barrels.

When he pushed me back to the wagon, I sat there, letting the pain wash over me again and again. We got to the guards and I were only a bit aware of Tuck passing them a small barrel of wine for their enjoyment, for which they waved us through 'stead of checking barrels.

Once we hit the woods, I jumped off the wagon and bolted. I went to the only place I knew for sure that no one could follow me, the one place only I could climb to.

I went back to Major Oak. She were covered over with ash and black, but then again, so were I. I climbed up careful, staying to the thick roots of the branches, like the tree were glass and snapping a twig would bring the whole thing down. I hid up high in the cluster of branches where my hammock used to be, high up and alone in the sky, and I curled over my knees and let rivers spit from my eyes. I failed Ravenna just like I failed that crying girl at the castle, just like I failed Joanna. I wanted to help, and all I did were push more girls into horrible scrapes.

—∞—

I stayed at the treetop for hours. When I ventured down, I found Rob and John both sleeping as high as they could get. Whether it were to protect me or cage me in, I weren't sure. I tried to move past them, but Rob woke up.

"Scar, you can't go alone."

"I can."

"Let me look at your face, Scarlet."

I turned toward him. "There. Look." I knew it were bad, but it weren't like he fancied my face anyway; might as well let Godfrey muck it up.

"Christ, Scar. Why didn't you fight him? He said you didn't even fight him."

I shrugged. "It's my fault his sister's suffering a fate worse than death. Me taking a punch makes him feel better, so be it."

"You didn't deserve it, Scar."

"Yeah I did."

"Why, because we stuck to the plan? Many things you can do, but seeing the future isn't one of them."

"I should have known better. Shouldn't have let them stay

there all night. You're coming up with the plans from now on, you know."

"You saved Godfrey, Scar."

"And I might as well have killed Ravenna."

"You think I haven't made mistakes?"

"Not like this."

Rob swung closer to me. "What do I have to do to convince you you're not some gutter rat, Scar? You deserve better than all this."

I shook my head, slipping down through the branches. He shouldn't say that to me. I were a rat. I were a thief, a liar, a no-good sort. Even Rob, a hero to be sure, looked at me and saw nothing but tar and scars. He shouldn't make me believe he thought different when he already said his piece.

"I'm coming with you."

"No one's coming with me, Rob." I dropped to the ground, and he dropped right behind me. "I'll knock you out if I have to."

He kept on, and I swung around to backhand his mug, but he caught my arm, grabbing the other arm and hauling me against him, my back to his front. "And I'll truss you up if I have to."

I whipped my head back but he dodged it, and I tried to kick him but he moved.

"Christ, Scar, quit fighting me!"

I stopped, but angry blood were roaring through me.

"This well may be one of the worst nights you've had, Scar,

but we can't win all the time. If we could, we'd be the ones in the castle."

"I will make it right!"

"Scar, you can't—"

"Do you know what he's doing to her?" I snapped, bucking his grip again.

"Do you?" he asked. "Do you? Is that what all this is about? Some London lord hurt you like he's hurting her?"

Joanna's voice saying good-bye and shutting the door rattled through my head. Never since had I felt as awful and helpless as when she left on her own two feet, night after night, to do the things I wouldn't never speak of. Not to anyone. Never to Rob.

I shook my head, more to get it out of my head than to answer him. My eyes squeezed tight, and water slipped out. I hit him in the gut. "Stop guessing things! You know nothing 'bout my life, Robin Hood, and you know nothing 'bout me!"

"Scar," he murmured, soft in my ear. He pulled me down to the ground, still holding me vise-tight. "Scarlet, what happened to you?"

"Nothing," I fessed. "Nothing never happened to me. It all happened to her. She took it all on and I didn't help her none."

"Who, Scar?"

I shook my head again. Her final good-bye were the worst by far, when she didn't want to go willing, when she were taken from me, hurting and in pain. I could see Joanna, pretty blond hair and happy blue eyes, and it were like the vision turned to ash in my head. Her skin went gray and pale, her hair lost its light, and her eyes went dark—blood on her sheets and her mouth and her hands from all her coughing.

"I left right after Richard conquered Acre," Rob whispered against my head.

I stopped moving, confused. "What?"

"When I got the news, about my father. It was right after Acre, and I wanted any excuse to leave." He shook his head against mine, and I were quiet, waiting to hear. "We had thousands of prisoners. The negotiations had gone on too long, so they weren't the enemy anymore. They were our prisoners, but they were men and women and children that we spoke with. We ate with. And then Richard ordered us to kill every last one of them, and we did. I played dice with a boy not much younger than myself one day, and the next I took his head off with one stroke of my sword."

He paused, and our breath huffed hard from tussling.

"When I left on Crusade I was fifteen. I was a boy, responding to Richard's call for holy soldiers. I went with him, campaigning for funds through Europe on the way to the Holy Land. I was a boy up until the moment I drew my sword. And then I was a man, and I had already done unforgivable things." Rob's head pressed harder against mine. "I know what it's like to look into your past and see nothing but your mistakes," he said.

My fingers crushed tight into his skin, clawing him like if I could break the skin we'd be connected by blood, and I could comfort him and he could see into me without me having to speak out loud. "They were your orders, Rob. You were a soldier for the King's Crusade. It can't be a mistake if you didn't have a choice."

"Yes it can. Because we always have a choice, even when it feels like we don't. Isn't that what you're torturing yourself over?"

Memories of Joanna bubbled up so hard in my throat I weren't sure I could breathe, and they choked out as tears instead. "She were protecting me, Rob. She did awful things, things I should have stopped, to protect me. I didn't protect her, and she needed me to."

"Richard liked me. If I had said no, if I had refused, he might have listened. I might have saved those people."

A hiccup jumped from my throat, and Rob twisted me somehow so I were tucked against his big chest, restrained like a dog. He held tight, painful tight, my breath rushing out over my teeth, and I wondered if it were me holding him or him holding me. I wanted to tell him he were a fool and Richard wouldn't never have listened to him, never gone back on his word or his orders for Rob. But he knew that. He knew, and it didn't help. I knew it weren't my fault Joanna were dead, but it didn't help none at all.

Rob's breath were pushing over my ear, his chest puffing up underneath me. His heart were beating so close to my own that it calmed me for sheer distraction.

"I have to help her," I told him.

"I know. Let me help you."

"Can't. The plan I have is for one."

"How are you going in?"

"Wall."

"And out?"

"Wall."

"She'll be in no health to climb."

"She'll manage. I'll carry her if I have to."

"I'll carry her. I'll go to the wall with you and wait there. You send me a signal if you need me, and I'll come."

I swallowed. "We watch each others' backs."

He nodded. "Precisely."

Standing up were strange. I stood first and looked down. I had been all tangled with him. He had been holding on to me. It felt like something changed before I stood up, but on my own two feet I didn't want nothing to change. It felt like something had shivered loose inside me, and all I wanted to do were keep it in, keep it hidden and deep.

I pulled away from him. I could see John still sound asleep in the tree and it made it all the stranger. Rob and I grabbed some weapons from the cave and set off on foot.

—⁂—

There are many things that I never bothered to guess at. Things like weather, or farming, or feelings—I'm fair useless for those sorts. The one thing I know is sneaking—and knives, I reckon—and that night I focused on all I'm good for. We moved double-quick to the castle, and once there I told Rob where to wait.

On my own, everything gets clear. I don't worry, I don't

think, I can just sneak. I fade right back into the black darkness and no one sees me. A guard can walk a foot from my mug and he won't never know I'm there.

The hard bit were finding her room. There were so many in the residence that I knew it would take me most of the dark hours to look for her. I went through real careful, and I reckon it must have taken me hours, but I didn't feel it none. It felt pure and simple. It were the only thing in life that were such.

I found her up on the top floor, sleeping. I swung into her window quiet, going to check the door before I woke her. I creaked it open a sliver and saw a guard blocking the doorway. Window it would be for escape. Just hoped she weren't too rough off.

I went over to her, covering her mouth and pushing her a bit. Her eyes shot open and she screamed under my hand.

"Hush!" I hissed, squeezing her mouth. Had to make sure she minded me.

She stopped moving.

"You know me?" There were a fair bit of moonlight coming in; I could clap eyes on her, so she must have been able to do the same at me.

She nodded.

"You'll hush?"

She nodded.

I let her go and sat back. "Are you all right?"

She nodded.

I swallowed, and my hand fell on hers like dead wood. "I'm

so sorry, Ravenna. I should have gotten you both out last night." The words rolled over one another. "I'm going to get you out of here right now."

She shook her head. "I'm staying here."

Not another one. Christ at the crossroads, not another one.

"They won't hurt your family. We can get all of you out of Edwinstowe, Ravenna, I promise."

She ripped her hand back. "You promised to get us out last night."

If all were fair and good in the world, I would have told her that I never promised nothing to her last night. I said "have faith," and it were only because I couldn't explain the full plan to get them out today. As it were, her words cut like the truth anyhow. "This is different. We'll move your whole family if we have to."

She shook her head. "I have another plan. I told the sheriff if he wanted me, he had to marry me. And he said he would." She pushed her hair off to show me the gold necklace like a shiny collar round her white neck. "He gave me a betrothal gift and he's calling for my father in the morning. In a month's time, I'll be the Lady of Nottingham, and my family won't just be safe, they'll be nobles."

I felt like stone. "But Ravenna, to marry him?"

"You may live like an outlaw, Scarlet, but to save yourself from shame you let everyone think you're a boy."

My mouth gaped.

"Of course I knew—don't be stupid. You're too pretty by

half for a lad. But I'm not like you, and I don't have those sorts of choices. I was going to be married anyway, and my father was fishing high, so it might as well be him."

I shook my head. "He'll hurt you."

"They all do. At least he'll be my husband."

I grabbed her hand, settling my mind on Robin and John and Much. Even Tuck, with his wife that never minded him and always raised a ruckus, which he seemed to think of as endearing. "They all don't. There are good men out there."

"There are poor men out there," she told me. "And rich ones. Rich men never wait for nothing, so why would they be good? Good men are poor, because they have to count on others' kindnesses. And my father said clear as morning that I'm for a rich man."

"Godfrey will kill you."

She shook her head. "Father wants him to protect us all. Godfrey deserves some rest from that task; I can carry this burden now."

Stupid, foolish, moron tears were in my eyes. Ravenna and me weren't never kindred. It shouldn't matter none who she tied herself to. "I can save you. Let me save you."

"I don't need saving. It's my choice. For once, something is my choice."

"It's no choice when you think you're saving your family, Ravenna."

She leaned back from me. "Leave, or I'll call the guard in. If you see Godfrey, tell him what I've told you."

"I'll stay close. If you change your mind, if he hurts you, I'll stay close."

She swallowed but didn't look at me. "Go."

I went. But I weren't going far.

I didn't go back to the camp. I signaled Rob with two daggers, meaning I didn't need help, and he left. I waited until he were long since gone and went down to collect the daggers, and then I slept in the tunnel. There were tears on my face, and I didn't scrape them off. This were my fault, and I would be there when she needed me.

—⁂—

There were a dark crook in the roof between two eaves, and when dark fell the next night I sat there, hidden, listening. I stayed close as quarters to her, just to make sure she were safe. It occurred to me that Rob and the others were fair worried 'bout me, but it didn't matter. If I left, he might hurt her and I wouldn't be there to save her.

I didn't let the time go full wasted, though. I started a little collection, nicking some gold and silver and jewels where I could. If I weren't going to be on the road with a bare fortnight till tax day, I had to get enough to sell to make up for it. It weren't as if I could walk into the armory, but guards left their weapons without a watchful eye fair often, and I nicked an armful of swords and a whole new set of knives. I kept a stockpile down in the tunnel.

And I watched. I watched the way the guards moved round. I watched what they were guarding, and I watched what they weren't. It were awful strange; during the night, guards and work-men were centering around the top bailey. There were only resi-dences and a few workshops up there, but the men all clustered round the old guardhouse. They hadn't used the guardhouse since they built a bigger one down in the middle bailey. What were they doing?

I watched Gisbourne come in and out; I stayed by his win-dow and listened. I were drawn to Gisbourne in a way that made me want to retch out my innards. He scared me, that were right sure, but when I were in the dark, I felt like I could look all I wanted, and part of me were nosier than a kitten. This were the man who had wrenched my life off to the side, and I were curious.

He carried himself with the arrogance I first feared him for, and his face never changed. He had dark eyes that had hate in them, and everyone could see it. I thought of Rob's eyes, deep like the water and quick to show how much people meant to him. How much I meant to him.

The middle of my back shivered. It were getting colder. My legs felt stiff, and I couldn't remember when I last moved. I stood to go for a walkabout, scaling the wall and walking the parapet. I got to the middle bailey and I caught a glimpse of metal in the woods. The sight grabbed at my heart like a hand would my arm, and I began to run. I launched from the parapet to the outer stonework that kept the portcullis, and from there I jumped to the ground in time to stop Godfrey with John Little behind him.

"Move," Godfrey snapped at the same time John pushed forward and grabbed me off the ground in a crushing hug.

"Christ, Scar, you're all right," he said, his voice hot with breath and right next to my ear. His head turned a hair and I felt his lips on my cheek. "Where were you, Scar?" He let me loose a little and my feet hit the floor again, but he didn't full let go.

"Here. With Ravenna."

Godfrey pushed John off of me, and when he looked at me he swallowed and stepped back. I wondered what my face looked like. It were still fair sore and overtight. "Where is she? Why haven't you got her out?"

"She won't come."

They both stared.

"She's marrying the sheriff."

Godfrey surged forward, drawing his sword. "Come off it! Where is she?"

"She's in there." The truth were putting a shake in my bones. "Godfrey, she's not a prisoner anymore, which means neither are you. She's there of her free will. You can go to the gate and ask to see her. I reckon they'll let you in."

He stepped forward again, and John pushed him back, stepping in front of me. "Why would she do that? Why marry him?"

"She says she were to be married anyway. Sheriff will give her a position, and favor in the court besides."

"I don't believe you."

"You don't have to. Like I said, go to the gate. The sheriff will let you call on her. Your father knows already."

He looked to John, and then he lurched forward. John pulled me out of his way and let him go to the gate. He pounded the gate and the small door opened. He spoke to the guard, and his body lost its anger. The gate were opened and he were let in.

"You weren't lying," John said soft.

I turned to walk away.

"Scarlet, where are you going?"

"He's with her now. I can go."

He grabbed my arm with a smile. "You're coming with me, love. I never buy your tough act. Where would you even go?"

"Wherever I damn well please, John Little." I needed cold and quiet—and some good darkness. My head were full of Joanna and London and even a touch of Gisbourne, and it felt overfull.

He pulled me against him. "Don't go, Scar," he said in that voice he used with Bess. "Come back with me. Much is frantic as to where you might've gone."

I didn't know if he were or Robin were, but I were fair certain that John didn't care if Much were worried for me. "He'll last a day or two longer."

He nudged his nose against the side of my face, and I pulled away from it a hair. His hand came along my cheek and it tugged my face over to his. "Maybe, but I won't."

His lips pressed against mine, strong like the rest of him and a little wet, pushing my lips into a fair good kiss. He caught me up 'bout the waist and kissed me deeper. I shut my eyes, and Rob's face popped into my head.

I pulled my head away, flushed and not sure what to do, or say, or think.

His nose rubbed mine. "Scarlet."

It tickled and I sniffed. "What were that for?"

He tilted his head a bit. "You."

"Why you kissing me?"

"'Cause I like you, Scar."

I shook my head. "You like every girl, John." I smiled a little. Something 'bout a kiss makes you feel silly, and a kiss from John somehow felt more silly than most. "I'll be back in a day or two."

His arms went looser. "What does that mean?"

I pulled away from him. "I'll let you know. If you go to the tunnel, there's a fair bit of loot." I walked a few paces and stopped, looking back. "And thanks, you know, for the kiss."

He just stared so I kept walking. Might as well be polite.

CHAPTER
NINE

I didn't get far. I went east through Sherwood to Worksop and stayed there during the day, helping Much's father and checking on Freddy Cooper. He stayed when the rest of his family went on to Dover, making what wages he could till they were settled. The miller were at the grinding part of the harvest, and he always needed extra help, and Freddy were taking to it like a duck in water. Much's father didn't talk a lot. Freddy talked enough for the two of us, and that were a whole different kind of silence that my mind knocked around in. When night fell, Freddy and Much's father wheedled and begged till I stayed for supper, and they set up a bed for me to sleep in. I nodded, because it were easier, and then when they went off, I left the house.

I liked wandering the night. The animals were different. They talked to each other in soft twitters, little whistles, hoots, and such. They had a nighttime way of talking.

There were an inn at the edge of the village that I liked. The innkeep were a woman, which were fair unusual. It used to be her husband's, but he keeled over and she took it on. She were always good to me. Sometimes girls had troubles that boys weren't meant to know nothing 'bout, and she helped me out once or twice.

I went in and she nodded to me. I slid into a table in the back. She sent over an ale and I nodded to her again, settling into the corner to watch and listen. There were a few travelers eating their supper, but most were locals sitting for a drink. I recognized many of the men, most farmers and craftsmen, and a few farmhands.

"Lena!" bellowed a gruff voice. Three of the sheriff's personal men walked in, dressed all in the sheriff's black and silver, like death and metal. I looked to Lena; she were smiling, but it weren't one of her big wide smiles that I got. She sent one of her girls to get some drinks and ushered the men to a table. They sat and took the drinks, and the ringleader grabbed Lena's wrist and dragged so she leaned hard over his shoulder. "You know that's not why we're here, Lena."

She shot a look to her muscle, a hulk of a lug everyone called Pea, but he were already on his way. He stood over the men and the ringleader let Lena's wrist go. "I don't have the money. I'll have it next week."

"Sheriff doesn't believe you. Sheriff thinks you're holding out."

She flushed. "Well, what does he expect me to do? I don't have any money. I can have it next week."

"Lena, the sheriff gave you meat for your customers when you needed it. He expects his investment returned."

She crossed her arms. "If I had known his 'gift' came with such a price, I wouldn't have taken it. You'll get your money when I have it."

"Sheriff's cracking his whip, Lena." His fellow took the candle from the middle of the table and held it underneath the wood table. The other two men grabbed Lena and Pea as she screamed at them.

I whipped a knife at the candle, pushing it from his hand. The flame doused before it hit the ground, and the table were black but not burning. The ringleader whipped his head round to see who did it. "Someone bein' a hero, then, eh?" he asked, drawing a knife and turning toward Lena. She screamed again, and as I drew another knife, a customer tackled the guard. The place split open into a brawl.

Lena began yelling for people to get out, and sent one of the girls upstairs to warn the travelers. If they meant to burn the place, they wouldn't stop there. I ran outside with a nasty feeling in the pit of me.

Sure enough, I heard a horse's scream and saw another set of guards lighting the barn on fire. They put a torch to the hay, and the animals started to fret something awful. I ran at them, taking five knives in my hands and starting to throw. I hit two guards with the hilt of a knife tossed to the back of their necks, which dropped them to the ground. The third turned to face me, which were a stupid move on his part.

I jumped onto my hands and flipped to kick him square in

the chest. He went down. I didn't much care if they stayed down or not; I needed to get the horses free. The fire were spreading quick with so much hay, and they were kept in by ropes across their stalls.

With a knife in each hand I sawed the ropes loose one by one, letting the panicked horses run out. I had two left to do when one of the guards pushed me hard against a stall wall. I grabbed the wood of the wall and slammed my head back, connecting with his nose—including the nosepiece, which set my head to ringing—and stepped hard on his foot. He scooted back enough for me to cut another rope and grab the last one. The horse were rearing on his hind legs, and I did my best to forget I might well be trampled soon as I loosed him.

I ducked to miss a kicking hoof, sliced the rope, and curled off to the side. The horse bolted and the guard grabbed me by the throat, pulling me off the ground and ramming me against the wood. Black smoke were billowing and it swallowed the horse up whole. The whole barn were popping and cracking like a heaving giant.

"And you must be the famous Will Scarlet," he said, spittle flying at my face. "Sheriff's been dying to meet you."

I sent the spit right back with a fair helping of my own. He cocked his arm back to throw a punch.

An arm shot out and hooked the guard's, sending him off me. Robin stepped out of the smoke like a god and delivered a sound punch to the guard's face. Without a breath he turned, grabbed my hand, and ran out.

The night were much, much colder than I remembered. Robin were holding my hand tight and I clutched at him like he were a handhold on a cliff and I were slipping off, like he were the difference between life and not.

When the smoke let us go Rob dragged hard on my arm, enough for me to yelp and twist back, which landed me fair square against his chest. His arms latched round me like iron bands, and for a stupid second I shut my eyes and squished my head to his shoulder. His face pressed to the side of mine, and hard breaths huffed out over my hair. "Thanks, Rob," I whispered.

Guess it were the wrong thing to say. He pushed me back, pulling his heat away from me, and my shoulders hunched against the cold. He nodded.

"Christ's bones, you saved the inn, Scar!"

I turned to see Lena fair flying at me, wrapping me up tight in her arms.

I looked over her shoulder. It were still standing, not even scorched. "Sorry about the stables."

"Don't, my girl," she said soft. "You saved me and the horses."

"Here," Rob said, pressing a purse to her hand. "Money for the sheriff. When those guards come to, just pay them."

Lena didn't like charity, and her face showed all its wrinkles and age that weren't there when she smiled. "Take a horse, Robin. I'll tell them one ran off."

We looked to the travelers huddled in the grass, watching the barn burn. She turned to call them all back into the inn, and Robin held me tight by the waist as he steered me to a horse that had wandered behind the inn.

"I can walk."

"I'm well aware. But right now, I don't want you to walk away," he said.

That were fair enough. Right then, I didn't have no clue what I wanted, so it worked fine. He mounted the horse and held an arm out, and I jumped on behind him, ringing my arms round his waist. I shivered, feeling like all the awful things in my head just left in one quick rush. He were like that. Rob could change anything in an instant.

He didn't take me to Major Oak but to Thoresby Lake. "You're covered in soot and smoke," he told me. "And a fair helping of dirt. Were you sleeping in the tunnel, then?"

I nodded, jumping down off the horse. Rob came off as well and sat down on a rock facing away from the water.

"You ain't gonna turn round, right?"

"Scar."

I took that as a yes and skinned out of my clothes real quick. The difficult bit were the muslin I wrapped around my bits in front. Once I got it off, I dove into the water. It were ice cold and I scrubbed hard before my hands went thick with the cold. I liked the cold. It made Joanna and Gisbourne seem farther away, and that were good.

I scrubbed through my hair, and I remembered Joanna sitting up late with me, brushing out my hair. *What a cabinet we could make together*, she said. I thought she were gone madder than a marmot. *You have rich mahogany and I have burnished gold; it would be a precious chest indeed.* She braided our hair together to see the difference. *Good English hair,* she told me. *None of my Saxon color.*

I took her tie and banded our hair at the bottom, and I snuggled against her as we went to sleep. Those were the days when she started going out at night without me, making me feel littler for not knowing what were going on. Seemed to me then that Joanna and I were as distant and separate as our hair, and if I could only braid us together, we'd never part. I had fallen asleep thinking it were as easy as that.

'Course, I'd woken up alone in the bed, night fallen in full and the hair tie loose around my single tail, her gold hair gone.

I pulled out of the water and twisted my hair up, tucking it under my cap with the good memories of Joanna. That's where I liked to keep her, secret and safe.

My clothes were sooty, but it were cold so I wriggled back into them and then came beside Rob. He had already taken his cloak off, and he put it on my shoulders. His arm dropped to the rock behind me so he were caging me.

"I missed you."

I got that funny, twisted feeling in my stomach. 'Course he missed me. I were a member of the band and they didn't work well without me. It weren't nothing more he meant, and I were a ready fool to have my heart lurch with other hopes. "But you knew what I were 'bout."

"I knew that you were atoning to yourself, however you meant to do it."

"I stole things from the castle to sell," I said.

He smiled. "Never idle. John thought you'd been collared."

"You have more faith in me."

He shook his head. "I don't, really. You scare the hell out of me."

"Tonight were good timing," I admitted.

He nodded. "You would have gotten out anyway."

"How'd you know I hadn't been collared?"

He shrugged. "I'd have felt it. I'd have known."

Whether it were that strange idea or the cold, something lodged in my chest and my breath were gasping round it.

"Let's get you home." He stood and looked out over the lake. "If you're ready to come back."

The thought of who else waited back at the camp pushed into my head, and I rubbed my knuckles. "Why would John kiss me, Rob?" It just jumped out of my mouth. I looked at him.

He crossed his arms. "Aren't you two—" He closed his mouth sharp. "The other night, you were sleeping together."

I blushed hot. "It weren't like that. I were shaking, and he were trying to warm me up." I felt his eyes on me, but I didn't want to look at him. I didn't think he believed me. He saw how black my soul were—why wouldn't he think my virtue were easy as they come?

"He likes you, Scar. You shouldn't toy with him." The words were awful sharp, and I looked up.

"I'm not toying!" I snapped back. "And just 'cause he wants me don't mean I want him."

Rob's eyebrows went skyward. "You don't?"

I wrapped my arms around my stomach. "Not sure." There were so much more to the thought that I wanted to tell him, but I just swallowed. "I'm not the sort of girl that goes with a lad."

Rob smiled. "So what, you'll swear off men forever?"

"It's worked so far."

Rob looked surprised, but before I could ask why, he said, "Well, what about babies? You looked awfully thrilled with Mary's son."

"You think I have any right to bring a baby into my life? I'm a thief and an outlaw and a poor example of a girl. You think I could be any sort of mother?"

He looked away at that, and I felt it again, that ax of hurt in my belly. I didn't much like saying it out loud, but it were worse that he agreed.

"If you want a man, Scar, for marrying or not, John's the best you can come by."

I know it sounded nice, but to me it were a pretty insult. Like it or not, I would never deserve a man like Rob, and John were the best I could do. I knew it were true, but hearing him say it like that, so careful, made me feel hollowed out like a dying tree. I didn't want him to see, so I smiled big and gave a little laugh. "That's not fair true. John's a charmer."

Rob shrugged. "Well, if he charms you, that's enough, isn't it?"

I shot him a look and didn't say nothing.

"As to babies, don't fool yourself, Scar."

Shame filled my face and I looked down. I weren't the sort to fool myself, to be sure.

"You'd be an uncommonly good mother," he said.

I looked up, blood filling up my cheeks 'stead of shame. He looked fast away from me, and I stood, wanting this chat to be over. "Let's go."

When we came to the cave, the lads were around a small fire under the rock overhang, and they both stood up. I crossed my arms, feeling like I ought to apologize for something, but I weren't 'bout to. Much laughed with surprise and ran over to hug me, and I gave him a little smile and hugged back.

When he let go, John were standing behind him, and he looked at me with a smile. "So, you're back."

I laughed. "Not for you, John Little."

He looked like I slapped him.

"Just because you kissed me don't mean I'm your girl none," I told him.

I heard Much chuckle, and John stepped closer to me. "Maybe I wasn't asking you to be my girl."

"I'm nobody's bit of fun either," I told him, right serious 'bout that. I went toward the fire, and John threw up his arms.

"What does that mean, Scar?" he asked me.

"I guess we'll have to see."

Rob and Much both laughed at this, and John glared at them. "Will one of you talk to her?"

Rob shook his head. "I don't get on the wrong side of a lady thief."

"Well, how am I supposed to get on the right side of her?"

I leaned back in front of the fire. "Try harder, Little John." Much laughed and John grumbled and sighed, and I looked across the fire to Rob, hiking my chin higher. Never would I have a man saying what or who were best for me, and that were all there were to it.

—⁂—

The next morning we all took some bread and hoofed it to Nottingham; the sheriff had been bandying 'bout that he had an announcement to make, and though I figured it were 'bout Ravenna, we still all wanted to hear.

We got to the town center, where market would often be, and instead of shops, there were a raised dais and a scaffold. Three nooses hung empty, swinging in the wind like the bodies that would swing later. The guards were keeping people off the two structures, but the sheriff weren't there yet, and neither were Ravenna.

People were crowded into the town square, and it weren't hard for us to blend in. The trumpets began to sound, and a procession from the castle began.

The sheriff were flanked by many men in black and silver, but he were on foot, not horseback, which were fair surprising. He never liked to mix with the common folk. Gisbourne were on one side of him, and at the sight of him I stepped back.

Robin caught my arm. "Scar?" he said, soft in my ear.

"Fine," I said, shaking him off, blushing, and tucking my hat down.

Ravenna were on his other side, and she looked beautiful. Undeniable, she were the prize of the shire. She had long black hair curling down all around her, and she were wearing a white dress with gold bits on it. Her family walked behind them, and they were fair beaming. Even Godfrey looked happy.

The sheriff reached the dais, and he helped Ravenna to her seat. That were when the prisoners were marched out, and I felt like my gut had been sliced: it were Lena and Mark Tanner and Thom Walker. I grabbed Robin's arm. His eyes hit mine and I looked to the side. He nodded.

"Spread out. Scar, take John. Much, come with me." To me he whispered, "Take any chance you have to get them down, Scar."

I nodded, tugging John's arm and sliding through the crowd.

"Good people of Nottingham!" the sheriff called, and everyone hushed, looking from Ravenna to the scaffolds. "Today, we have great cause for celebration. I am thrilled to announce a truly blessed event not only for me personally but for the whole shire. In one month's time, I will take a wife, and rather than marrying a noblewoman from a far-off land, I have chosen a bride from our fair shire. One of your own to show you my love and devotion." He gestured to Ravenna, and she took his hand and stood, smiling at him. People gasped, whispered, and murmured.

I circled round to behind the scaffolds. Lena's hands were tied, bloody and raw. They hadn't just arrested her that morning—they must have arrested her bare after I left. My hands itched. I wanted to hold my knives, but with the guards scanning the crowd, I didn't want to give myself up till the last minute, and I weren't in the best position yet.

"Welcome the future Lady of Nottingham, Miss Ravenna Mason."

The crowd began cheering and I darted forward, moving into position to let a knife fly. I raised my hand to throw it, but I got jostled and had to pull back.

The sheriff quieted the crowd, and I swore, losing my cover.

"Now, you have not shown to me the love I show to you. These three refuse to pay back what they borrowed from Nottingham's coffers. For that, I have ordered their establishments burned and their lives forfeit." Gasps and cries went up, and I raised my knife. "But the love of my future wife has reminded me that sometimes I must forgive you for being less kind, and less loving, than I am myself. My only hope is that in the future, you will remember my devotion and forgiveness. All I do, my fair people, is for your sakes, and yours alone."

I spat to show what I thought of his words. He were a blowhard, talking 'bout love and devotion when he honestly meant monies and death.

"To illustrate that, I will let these people go free."

Someone nudged me, and I fell straight back into John, more off balance than I ever were from the sheriff's words. He were letting them go?

Sure enough, the executioner peeled back his hood, slid the ropes off their necks one by one, and helped them down into the crowd. The townspeople began to cry and proclaim their love, saying it were a miracle. The sheriff just nodded and walked back into the castle. Gisbourne never turned his back to the crowd as they walked, sweeping his eyes like a restless cat's tail.

Keeping my head tucked low, I ran to Lena, and I told her how glad I were she were safe. She were crying, big tears running down her face, and shaking something fierce. She said Death brushed her hand and passed her by.

I didn't feel like that. The sheriff weren't no man of the people. He weren't like Rob in the least bit. The sheriff doing something kind felt like Death wrapped his fingers round my throat and were starting to squeeze.

CHAPTER
TEN

The crowd started to break, and we all walked back to Edwinstowe. Lena came with us, Mark Tanner and Thom Walker following behind. Tanner were from Edwinstowe, but Thom Walker were a merchant in Nottingham. I knew their homes were gone, but I weren't sure why they were coming with us. Sure, Rob walked like a leader, and it weren't surprising that people followed behind him, but still. I weren't sure about it.

"What happened?" I asked Lena, walking beside her. "After we left, how did you get pinched?"

She rubbed her wrists. "When the guards came to, I gave them the money, but it wasn't what they wanted, as you can tell. They shackled me and burned the inn." She hung her head.

My pipes felt thick. "I should have stayed."

She shook her head. "They would have pinched you too, and then where would Robin be?"

"He'd be right as rain, I think."

She chuckled. "You don't see how much he cares about you, but he does. Ran into that fire last night like a fair angel, he did."

"He'd do the same for one of his men, or any of his people. Don't make me special in his eyes." It were shameful, but there were a fair amount of bitter in my voice.

She leaned her head close to mine so the others wouldn't hear her. "Ah, he has many men, but he only has one woman."

I just shook my head. It were fair obvious I weren't his woman.

She put her arm around my shoulders, which felt awful wrong. It weren't like it had been me at the gallows. "You and that Robin are almost too fine a pair. Both of you can't see your own virtues."

I winced. "I hate to tell you, Lena, but I ain't been so virtued. I steal things. And I lie a fair amount."

She laughed. "Exactly what I mean, love."

Were she gone mad?

"You know, the only thing I saw when they put the noose around my neck was my husband's face. I wasn't even that fond of the mongrel when we were married—he was yelling and carrying on more often than not—but there were moments, little tiny ones, where it was nice to have someone with me."

"I'm not the type to have someone." Why were I saying this so much these days? I looked at Robin, John, and Much up ahead. They were someones, to be sure, but that didn't mean they were for me. They were *with* me, maybe, but not *for* me.

"More people care about you than you know, Scarlet. No matter how you got your scars."

I covered my cheek, looking at her.

"Not just those scars. The ones that make you think you're unlovable."

She linked her arm through my arm and we walked. We didn't say nothing after that. Weren't much to say, neither.

—⦿—

When we got to Tuck's, half the shire were breaking down his door to yap about the goings-on in Nottingham. Tuck saw John walk in and grabbed him, roping him and Malcolm into hauling some extra tables and benches outdoors and setting up 'neath the sky. It weren't dark yet, and the day were strange warm for fall. It would get colder when the sun set, but by that time the drink would be keeping most warm.

Tankards and mugs were passed through the crowd and people copped places on the benches. We stayed together, near the corner, but people knew Robin and started asking for his story of the whole tale, and Much helped him tell it.

"Oh, John," Ellie said, draping herself over John's back. Her skirts swished around, hitting me where I sat beside him. I smiled, watching them. "Missed you, lad."

He patted her hand. "Ellie, my love," he greeted. "Pretty as ever."

She twined herself around and sat in his lap. "Didn't you miss me?"

"'Course I did," he said. He looked at me. "Only, I'm having a drink with the lads here, you know." He took a swig to make it more obvious.

She rubbed my leg with her foot, and I winked at her. "We'll get Will a girl too. I know he's shy, but we all hear how skilled he is."

John spat out his mouthful. "Him? Couldn't find his way around a girl with a looking glass and a map."

I chuckled at that.

"See? Doesn't even deny it. Besides, after last week I would have thought you'd been talking 'bout my skills."

"Won't you remind me of them?"

"Maybe later, love. You've got too many thirsty people here. You're needed."

She gave him a quick peck. "Just don't tell me 'later' and run off with Bess or Mariel."

"Promise." He pushed her rump as he hefted her off his lap, and she giggled and sashayed away from us. John looked at me square. "I'd be more gratified if you looked jealous instead of gleeful," he said quiet.

I grinned. Couldn't help it. "Jealous? Oh, John, don't give up swiving on my account."

He smiled. "I'm irresistible, Scar, and one of these days I'll win you over."

I shook my head, but I were smiling too. "So what made you decide you liked me after all this?"

He chuckled to himself, and it looked fair like he were

blushing. He slapped the brim of my hat. "You keep me on my toes, Scar."

I wrinkled my nose. "Like fighting? Is that a good thing?"

He nodded. "Sometimes I don't know what you're about at all. Girls"—he ducked his head down—"girls don't surprise me much. That's generally why I like them. But you, I'm always trying to catch up with you." He looked at me. "And it's better than with the other girls."

"Why would you like people not surprising you?" I asked. "I'm always trying to figure out some thing or the other."

He shrugged, and his mug went different, like all the charm went out of him. "For a while now, I felt like I've had enough surprises."

Under the table, I pushed my knee against his. I knew he were talking 'bout his family, and I wanted to show him I knew. He swallowed, making his throat bulge out. I wanted to say something, but I didn't know how to yap with John about this sort of thing.

"Did she die?" he asked me.

"Who?"

"That friend of yours. The one you never want to talk about."

Lead settled in the pit of my stomach. "Yeah, John. She died." I looked at him. "It were so quick. Not her dying—that weren't quick—but the way the world slips upside down. I thought I were free, and then the worst things happened."

He nodded. "Like, for a moment of happiness, you'll be paying your whole life."

His hand twisted and grabbed my hand under the table. I pulled back, surprised. "Uh—" I said quick.

"Never mind," he said.

I looked at my drink and took the mug and went to fill it. When I came back Ellie were beside him, and I went to go sit with Rob and Lena on the other side of the table.

—⁓—

We were all fair full of drink a few hours after sundown, which made it all the more terrible. We didn't hear the hoofbeats over our own laughter till it were too late, and twelve black horses came to the tavern.

Everyone jumped up and pushed forward, but the horses stopped, and we stopped too. We all went quiet, and Lena's cold hand gripped mine. Tuck walked out, his stomach rolling along in front of him, Malcolm thundering behind.

The front man lowered his black hood, and Gisbourne were there, shaking the dark hair back from his face. I noticed with some pride the stitched-up scar on his cheek, same place as mine lay, but my gut wrenched and my heart started hammering. A hand touched my lower back, almost my waist, but I didn't know who it were. I could see John pushed farther ahead, so it weren't him.

"Are you Tuck?" Gisbourne asked.

"Aye," Tuck answered.

"We've had a report that the Hood is here among your customers tonight."

Tuck looked horrified. "The Hood, sir?" His eyes swept the

crowd. "Search for him, my lords! Don't let the vagrant get away!"

"Two men on these in front, two flank the back, the rest with me inside. We don't want him running."

The hand moved around my waist. "Scar, get out of here now," Rob whispered.

"No." I were trembling, but I weren't a coward. "I'm staying here."

"John, get her out of here," Rob ordered, and John turned back to us, looking at me with new alarm. Rob's arm left my waist only to have John's arm replace it, his other arm trapping both of mine against my chest.

"Put me down, John—I'm not fooling!" I snapped, twisting violent against him.

He crouched low, dragging me so the crowd hid us.

"Hush," John hissed. "Let me get you out quick so I can come back and help Rob. No one's risking you to Gisbourne, all right?"

"Second you put me down, you big lout, I'm heading straight back to Rob and Much."

"We all agreed to keep you from Gisbourne!" John growled. "Don't you dare risk the rest of us to play the hero."

I scowled at this logic, but I knew he weren't wrong. "Get Lena too—she's scared stiff."

"I'll do what I can, Scar, but I'm with Rob."

I elbowed him hard. "I'll stay to the side only as long as you're all safe. And that includes Lena."

He held my arms tighter and straightened as we made it to

the trees. "If I get Lena out, you give me another kiss. A proper one."

He let me go and I cracked him one 'cross the face. "You're a dirty dealer, John!"

He laughed. "Is that a yes?"

We both jerked, hearing someone scream, "No! Don't!"

I pushed him. "Fine, deal, go!"

I hid behind a tree, keeping my knives in hand, ready to help where I could. It weren't Lena they were interested in. I watched as Gisbourne grabbed a boy I didn't recognize, not much older than me, and held him high on his horse for everyone to see.

"Where's the Hood?" he asked.

"He ain't here," called one man.

He slit the boy's throat and dropped him to the ground before I had an inkling it would happen. I fell back against a tree, vomit rising in my throat.

I saw Rob push forward, ready to own up to being the Hood, but it were Malcolm who pushed him back.

"How many more do I have to kill?" Gisbourne demanded. My eyes shot to Rob; I knew if Malcolm and the others didn't keep him back, he would step forward in the beat of a heart to take an innocent's place.

"He's not here!" a woman shrieked. It weren't Lena, but it made me jump. "What must we do?"

"I don't believe you. You all hide him and harbor him like a hero, but you must see him for what he really is: the man who brings slaughter to your people."

He motioned for another to be brought. This one struggled, and the whole crowd began to struggle with him. Gisbourne's men surrounded the people, kicking them into one another and pushing the group. I couldn't see any of the lads until Gisbourne dragged another up in front of him.

It were Much.

I inched away from the tree. I saw Rob struggling against the townspeople. No one wanted him to move forward, but it would be bare breaths before Gisbourne caught sight of it, and I didn't wait.

One hand were on Much's chin, pulling him upward, stretching his neck for the knife in Gisbourne's other hand. I knew it were awful close to Much's face. I had to trust my aim.

I gripped the knife tip between my fingers and threw it.

It sank into Gisbourne's forearm and he dropped Much, who hit the horse's neck and sort of barrel-rolled to the ground. He scampered out quick, though, and Gisbourne yelled, "Follow me! The Hood's in the woods!"

Yells erupted, but I heard clear Rob roar out through it all, "SCARLET!"

My heart chopped hard at my muslin-wrapped chest. The horses started to thunder at me and I grabbed the nearest branch, swinging up and dashing through the trees.

"The tree!" Gisbourne called, bringing his horse to heel around it. "They're in the tree!"

I scrambled higher.

"Bring it down," he ordered.

My blood ran to ice as I heard the order. That were all right. Cold makes me think better.

I got up high as I could and flipped into the next tree, almost missing the branch in the dark. I did it again, but this time I startled an owl off its perch, and the men heard the flutter.

"He's over there!" Gisbourne roared.

I swore and froze. They couldn't see me—it were too dark—but they knew within a tree or two which I were on. I leaned my head against the bark, trying to shake off the picture of the young boy with his throat slit and my knife still in my hand. I could hear Gisbourne scrambling, some of his men still hacking at the trees, some of them trying to climb and failing.

They drew bows and started shooting at random. Arrows rained into the trees around me, scaring the night birds. An arrow whizzed past my mug and another grazed my hand before one lodged into my shoulder. I whipped my head against the tree not to cry out. I snapped the arrow off and threw it down, the tip still stuck deep.

"He's gone, my lord," one of the men said, dropping the ax he'd been hacking with.

"They say the Hood is part fey, a spirit of the trees. They'll never betray him."

"Damn right," I muttered.

—∞—

All the same, it were almost an hour before Gisbourne called it off, and even then, I'd started to swing slow 'cross the trees to move farther away. I had been watching—there weren't much else for me to do up there—and the boys had left Tuck's 'long with the rest of the crowd. I hopped down from the trees some mile or more from Tuck's and ran the rest of the way to the cave.

"Scarlet!" Much called, and before I knew it, Rob caught me off my feet in a hard hug, crushing my bones to my blood. I didn't care none when my shoulder burned with pain. I pushed my face against the cords in his neck, squeezing him just as hard.

He put me down, clutching my sides like I would fall apart in his hands.

"Scar," John said, and I turned sharp, almost knocking into him. He tilted his head to mine like he were going to kiss me, pulling me out of Rob's arms, but I pushed forward, hugging him instead.

He chuckled. "Not so easy, Scar. You promised me a kiss."

"You're bleeding," Rob said, taking my arm. "Much, get the kit." John let me go.

Much went into the cave, and Rob tried to roll up my sleeve, but it wouldn't go so far. His fingers went to the neck of my shirt, and my eyes leapt to his. The tips of his fingers felt like burning steel on my skin. Looking at me, he tugged it over, but it still wouldn't clear the wound.

He touched the laces of my shirt that kept it together, and my heart started fluttering in my pipes. I weren't even breathing.

"Hold it up a bit so I can open it without showing anything," he told me gentle.

Heat pounded through my face. His fingers hovered by the laces for a second, then touched the bones by my neck the littlest bit. Something jolted through me, and I could have sworn that Much were lighting off powder again.

"I wouldn't mind catching a glimpse of her," John said, and Rob let go of me to whip around. He pressed his hand over John's neck.

"Don't *ever* talk to a woman like that, John Little," Rob growled. John sneered and shoved him but Rob pushed him back.

I held my shirt tight round my neck. Seeing Much come out from the cave, I fair ran to him, then sat on a rock and undid the top of the laces. I let the shirt fall off my shoulder and clutched the rest tight. I knew I had my muslin on, but still. I were a girl, and they were boys, and I never felt more sure of that than when Rob were touching my skin like I were gold.

Much looked to Robin, standing a few paces off now, and I looked at him for a bare second. "Will you do it, Much?"

"If you want, Scar. But I'm not very good."

"Sure you are."

"I have to dig out the tip, Scar."

I nodded, and a hand filled mine. Rob sat beside me, flipped around so that our faces were looking at each other and his back were sheltering me from John. A fluttering breath filled my chest.

"Do it, Much," Rob said, squeezing my hand.

He raised his knife and I looked away, gripping Rob's hand.

I felt the first lance of the knife and swallowed down a scream, ramming my head into Rob's shoulder and crushing his hand. He crushed back, putting his arm on my back and keeping me on his shoulder. Rob's cheek pressed to my cheek as the knife dug deeper.

I didn't yell or holler. That boy died because I didn't trust what I knew already 'bout Gisbourne, and if this were my punishment, so much the better.

When Much were done I fair collapsed against Rob, and he picked me up like a baby and brought me deep into the cave, wrapping me in furs and blankets. "You need to sleep now," he told me.

"Lena and the others?"

"Boarding with villagers in Edwinstowe." He brushed the hair back from my forehead, pushing off the cap.

"The boy died."

Rob nodded. "Thank God he didn't get you too, Scar. We underestimated him before."

I nodded, feeling weak and sleepy.

"Scar." He squeezed my hand. "If John gets out of line with you, Scar, I'll handle it for you."

I fisted my hand in his shirt, fair passing out without another word.

When I woke, it were light out, and Rob were at my feet, leaning against a trunk and hunched over his bent-up knees. I grunted as I rolled onto my shoulder, not remembering it were injured. Rob straightened as I sat up.

"Morning," I said soft. I looked back; the other two were still sleeping.

"Morning. How's your shoulder?"

"I'll live, I reckon."

"You scared me yesterday, Scar."

"I couldn't not help. You were going to turn yourself in." I shrank my knees up, feeling smaller.

"He slit the throat of a boy he didn't know from Adam. What's he going to do to you?"

I looked down.

"You need to tell me how you know him, Scar."

"He gave me the scar," I told him. I didn't look up. My bones shivered like they lost something; I held on to that one secret for so long, it felt fair strange to let it go so easy.

He didn't say anything. I ventured a glance, and he were just looking at me, waiting.

"This scar," I told him, covering my cheek.

"He was trying to catch you?"

"Something like that."

"Scar, tell me."

I looked at Robin and opened my mouth, and just like that it were 'bout to come pouring out. But then John sat up, yawning and calling to us, and I stood and went out of the cave.

Robin followed me. "Promise me you'll tell me later. I need to know what kind of threat he is to you."

I looked back at John, coming out of the cave as well, and nodded. I felt cold to my bones, but I nodded. Honestly, if there were ever a time for God and praying and such, I were praying hard that Rob didn't turn me out of the camp after he knew.

"All right, lads," Rob called, and we all came to the burned-out fire. "Taxes will be called on the farmers in less than a fortnight, and the townspeople need money, so we need to get it for them. We're going to be on the road collecting a tax of our own, and when we're not collecting, we need to be training. Gisbourne got the drop on us last night; we need to be prepared."

We all nodded.

"Scar, I want you up in the trees, spotting us but staying out of it until your shoulder heals up."

I nodded. That were fair.

"And from now on, I'm switching the pairs. John, you're going with Much, and Scar goes with me."

John chuckled, cracking his knuckles. "Come on, Rob. Don't tell me you're jealous."

I felt my mug heat up, and I looked to Rob.

"Jealous?" Rob repeated, crossing his arms.

"Scar and I are gettin' friendly, and you're jealous."

I looked down.

"You may have kissed her, John, but since then she seems damn uncomfortable around you, and more important, despite the fact that you're so interested in her, you couldn't be bothered to protect her from Gisbourne last night."

John jumped up. His face were flat as sheet rock. "I got her out of there. I protected her."

"After I told you to."

"I can protect my—" I tried.

John's jaw went bumpy with muscles. "Just because you thought of it a hair before I did don't mean—"

"Actually, that's precisely what it means. Gisbourne won't hesitate, and so if I think quicker than you, I'm with Scar and you're with Much. Figure out how friendly you are when no one's at risk."

"Both of you shove off!" I snapped, crossing my arms. "John Little, just because you kissed *me* don't mean we're getting friendly. I *might* kiss you again, but only if I damn well feel like it. Stop pushing and charmin'—I don't like it." I heard Rob chuckle, and I whipped round to him. "And as for you, Robin of Locksley, on your big noble horse, I don't remember you helping none neither. I got myself out of there, I got Much away from Gisbourne, and I am part of this band much as you. Stop talking 'bout me like I'm some lily-fingered lady!"

Everyone stared at me.

I shook my head. "Honestly."

"If the problem is how to split into pairs, perhaps you and me should stay together for now?" Much said.

"Perfect," I agreed.

Rob and John shot daggers at each other. With their eyes, leastways. I'm the only one who shoots real daggers.

"Fine," Rob agreed.

John nodded.

"Let's get to work," I said, and Much shouldered John on ahead.

I fell in behind them to walk to the road, and Rob held back to walk with me a moment.

"Figure this out, Scarlet. Figure if you're with John or not, because while you toy with him, you're toying with my band, and that means you're toying with the people of Nottinghamshire."

Horribly, I felt tears pushing my eyeballs. "I thought you said you'd handle him for me."

He shook his head. "You're toying with me too, Scar. I'll help you if you need it, you know that. You make me watch you like a hawk, and I don't want to. Be with John or don't."

He pushed ahead of me on the trail.

CHAPTER
ELEVEN

~o~

I sat in the elbow of a tree, leaning on one knee and flipping a knife in my hand. I watched over the lads, whistling to them as needed and just thinking. I looked at John. It were strange. Talking to him alone, I felt like we were fair kindred, but then put him with the lads and his blustering bits came out. I didn't like him much when he were like that—well, I did, but as a bandmate and not as a fellow—but when it were the two of us, it were . . . nice.

I looked to Rob. It weren't like I wanted him. Or that I could have him, which were the same thing, right?

He felt me watching and glanced up, meeting my eyes. His eyes scrunched together like he were worried, and I shook my head and turned away.

The roads were busy, and for once it felt like we weren't fighting back such a mountain of trouble. A pair of noblemen offered up hefty purses, and a small convoy of knights gave us some nice weapons, including four huge broadswords that would fetch a fortune in one of the larger market cities.

Seeing movement down the road, I whistled to them and leaned forward.

Four knights came in the front, guarding a carriage. I rolled my eyes. Christ's bones, it were a lady. I hated this.

Four knights came behind. It were a high-ranking lady, too. My mother had traveled with no less than eight, often more. Part of that had been my mother's deserving rank, but part had been her own silly pride. The right things weren't never important to my mother.

Rob were running lead on this one. I liked his style for it. Me, I like to talk, but Rob gets right to the point.

"Stop, in the name of the people of Sherwood!" Rob called.

All eight knights charged ahead of the carriage, and I watched as John jumped into the carriage, grabbed the fair lady, and hauled her out of there. She sparkled like the sunny ocean with all her jewels.

"My lady!" the guards called, wheeling around.

Rob walked through them. The guards all froze when there were a lady in trouble. I crossed my arms.

It weren't that I were resentful. I liked bowing and scraping and such fair enough if it got the job done. Ladies were prey just like any other far as I were concerned. Rob, 'course, were a bit of a different matter. And it weren't like I had any right to be resentful of him bowing and scraping. I gave up that life. I gave up being the sort that he'd notice and bow to and such.

Strange, but none of such thoughts soothed the burning in my belly.

"My dear lady," Rob said, bowing over like the lord he were and kissing her hand. "Where are you headed?"

John let go of her, but she were still breathing hard enough to faint. "Northumberland," she peeped.

"To what purpose?"

She flushed. "Marriage to his lordship."

He nodded. "Ah, the duke. He's a nice fellow. Very rich," he told her. "Rich enough that he should buy you a whole new chest of jewels, don't you think?"

"Step away from her ladyship, ruffian!" one of the guards bellowed. They didn't move. Couldn't risk her ladyship, and my boys were closer, with weapons.

She were clutching her heavy necklace. "Why do you want them?"

"He's a thief, my lady!" her guard roared.

"The sheriff of Nottingham starves his people, my lady, and taxes them into submission."

Her mouth opened a little. "And my jewels would help?"

He nodded grave, like she were saving the world. She pulled the rings off her fingers, the jeweled comb from her hair, the bracelets from her wrists, and the bobs from her ears. Last she pulled off the huge necklace, and Rob bent his head to let her put it on him. She kissed his cheek.

Oh, she could be a lady and still grant her favors round? Fine bit that were.

"Then save your people, Hood."

Rob smiled like he swallowed a mouthful of diamonds. "You knew me?"

"Women talk, my lord, and everyone loves a legend. I am happy to sacrifice my jewels to your cause."

He kissed her hand again. "Then be on your way, my lady. And give my regards to your intended."

She curtsied. "Guards, let these gentlemen go freely."

"What?" her lead guard called.

Rob helped her back into her carriage, and she waved her fingers at her guards. "You heard me, sirs."

———

Rob were still strutting 'bout it when we brought all her jewels back to the cave. We had loot now that we had to fence, and the jewelry didn't even need to be snapped apart to sell because the lady wouldn't be looking for it. Rob were holding and twisting her ring with a big dumb grin on his face.

I glared at him through the lot of it, hating the lady, hating the ring, hating him.

"You treat them different, you know," I told him.

He looked over. "Who different?"

"Ladies. You treat them different than common folk."

I were sitting against a tree, holding my long coat wrapped tight round me. He were at the mouth of the cave and he smiled, crossing his arms. "Do I?"

"You know you do."

"Then why are you telling me?"

"Why do you treat 'em different? What's wrong with common women?"

"I treat everyone with respect, Scarlet," he told me, and the way he said it sounded fair insulted.

"Yeah, but there's no bowing and kissing hands, and you even talk different. You think rich folk don't understand plain speaking?"

He chuckled. "Of course they do. But they also understand speaking in a gentler fashion."

"And you think common folk can't speak gentle?"

He laughed outright. "You're sort of proving my point, Scar."

I glared. "Would you then assume, because I can speak in a light and lofty manner, that I was born of noble blood?" I asked, aping his "lady." More than that, aping the life I didn't have no more—and it tasted like a mouthful of salt. "Talking this way or that don't make you no better. And you act like it do."

His eyes squinted like he could see straight through me. "You act like I'm doing an unkindness."

"Ain't you? To common folk? You think you're some outlaw, Robin Hood, but you were born noble and you won't change that none."

"I am who I am, Scarlet. It's no secret I was born noble, and that's part of the reason people look to me as a leader. It's my birthright to protect them."

I tugged my shoulders, pulling my knees under to stand up. "True enough. Still don't mean noble folk are any better."

"Never said they were. I'm doing all this for the common folk, Scar, not the nobles. And when did you become the moral compass of the band?" he asked.

That stung. It weren't meant to, but it did. I took the bag of jewels he'd left. "John, want to come with me to Nottingham to sell these off?"

"We can wait till tomorrow," Rob said.

"Don't want to," I said. "John?"

"Sure," John said, running over. "I'll even carry the bag, m'lady." He gave me a big, lord-like bow.

"I'm courteous to common women too, Scar," Rob yelled as I walked with John.

I waved a hand, not looking round. Rob weren't neither. But he didn't want to cop to that, and I didn't want to fess that I were a little jealous. He weren't all "courteous" to me. *You make me watch you like a hawk, and I don't want to.* He wouldn't never say that to a gentle lady.

"You're frowning," John told me.

"Rob's so high and mighty," I said. "Rubs me wrong."

"He's an earl, Scar. We can't forget that."

"He won't let us."

"Come on, now, you follow him for the same reason I do. He's a good leader and he's that despite hard injustices. He came home from the Crusades and found he had no home. That's hard enough."

"It's stupid. Men think they are their title, and women can't even hold one till they squeeze onto their husband's."

"I thought all this was arguing against noblewomen. Change of heart?"

"No. I don't like that Rob thinks he's better than us, and I don't like how women get nothing for their own selves."

"Rob *is* better than us, Scar. Better than me, for sure."

I pushed him. "Don't say that. Why, because he's noble? You're just as good as he is."

He gave a little when I pushed him, and he rocked back and then forward. "You saying you wouldn't take the chance to be a noble?" he asked. "All silver spoons and 'yes, milady's?'"

My cheeks flushed dark. "No. I wouldn't. And what do that have to do with being better or worse?"

He shrugged. "Everyone wants to be wealthy, and landed, and titled. That's why they're better—because they have what everyone wants."

Before I could stop myself, I stamped my foot like a child. "It ain't better, being wealthy, landed, *titled*. If I had a choice, I'd choose to be just as I am. Over and over again!" I shouted. Only, that didn't quite strike true in my chest. Seeing that lady, seeing Rob's smiles, it all made me wonder. If he had known me back then, before the thieving and the scars and before my soul turned so black, would I have earned his smiles?

Would that have made that whole awful life worth it?

"No, I'd take it in a heartbeat," John kept on. "Chests of jewels to shower on all the ladies in the kingdom. Bribe one of them to marry me."

I rolled my eyes. "Come off it, John. You needn't bribe any girl, and you're a fine enough man as it is."

He caught me, pulling his arm round my waist. "Now, who could resist you when you say something like that?"

He pushed me up against a tree and tilted his head like he were going to kiss me. I tried not to laugh as I put a hand over his mouth. "John," I stopped him.

He opened his eyes. "What?" he asked, my hand still on his mouth.

"Do you know how many girls I've heard you say that to?"

He grinned. "Don't mean it's not true." He kissed my hand and I pulled it back. "Can I kiss you, or not?"

I put my arms round his neck. " 'Spose you can, but I don't reckon you want to."

"I don't?"

"You just like to shine on someone, John."

"Yeah, and I'm looking to shine on you for a while," he told me, mushing his nose against mine.

I shrugged. "But not forever. I'm not that sort, John. 'Sides, I think I like you better without all the courting."

He laughed. "Really?"

I nodded, craning up to kiss his cheek and pulling out of his arms. "Let's go, you big lug."

—⟋⟍—

We managed to fence most of the jewelry before dark and got out of the market before the gates closed in Nottingham. I wedged the purse into the back of my vest, along with some bread and dried meat wrapped in muslin that I'd swiped.

"How much did you end up getting?" John asked.

"For the jewels? You were right there!"

"I meant, how much did you steal?"

I blushed a little. "You saw me stealing?"

He chuckled. "No. But that doesn't mean you weren't doing it. Every now and again I'd see you someplace I didn't expect."

"What does that mean?"

"That you were thieving, I reckon."

I shrugged. "Some bread. Some meat. Coin besides. Let's stop by Edwinstowe and give it to Lena and the others. Do you know where they're staying?"

He nodded, stepping closer, his shoulder rubbing mine. "So, what about your story?"

"My story?"

"You know about my family. What's your story?"

"I don't, you know. Much whispered it to me once, that they died in a fire. I don't know the whole story."

He looked down. "My father was a blacksmith. I was born down in Locksley, you know. I knew Rob as a boy. Well, I met him, really. But we moved a lot, wherever the trade was best. We came to Nottinghamshire not long after the sheriff took over the Huntingdon lands. The sheriff ordered a hundred swords from my father and then wouldn't pay the price for them.

"My father wouldn't give them over when he wouldn't pay, and he sent me to market to fetch a price for them. It wasn't like we could sell them in Nottingham, so I went up to Newark at the Trent. I had to stay there the night." He shook his head. "I tumbled my first girl that night."

I stayed quiet.

"I'd spent every day of my life with my family, Scar. I could look at my little sister and guess her thoughts in a blink. With that kind of closeness, I thought I would have felt it, had some sense that they were in trouble. That they had passed. But I didn't feel anything. My little sister and baby brother died, crying for . . ." He trailed off, and I weren't sure if they cried for him, for help, for their lives, or for what, but it felt terrible. He swallowed, and it looked like he were choking down his own heart. "And I was with a girl."

I weren't the sort for much touching, but I couldn't help it. I put my fingertips on the inside bit of his hand. It didn't feel so strange, so I slipped them down more. His fingers curled on mine, and without meaning to, I were holding his hand.

He stopped, tugging my hand so I were pulled against him. I looked up. He held our hands between us like a dressed duck. "I don't tell girls that story, Scar."

"I won't tell."

"I know. But Bess and Ellie and them—I don't tell them, all right?"

I bit my teeth into my cheek a little. Were that meant to be a good thing? I didn't like holding secrets. I had enough to hold on to. "All right."

He tugged my hand again, and we started walking. I pulled my hand out. He didn't need it no more, and if you weren't careful with things like that, it could go on and on, never letting go of the hands. "So, what about your story?"

I shrugged. "Got lots of stories."

"How'd you start thieving?"

Shrugged again. "Same way most do, I figure. Needed something I couldn't pay for."

"What was the first thing you stole?"

The answer to that were only a single question away from Joanna. "I don't remember."

"Sure you do."

"I thought you said I wouldn't have to answer no questions with you."

"You never have to. I was just curious."

"It were medicine," I told him. "From the monks, for a cough."

He chuckled. "You don't go halfway, do you? Awfully brassy of you to steal first from a monastery."

I smiled, but it were less for him naming me brassy and most because he didn't ask who were coughing.

—❦—

Lena were at the Morgans', a farming family in Edwinstowe, and they welcomed us in as soon as they saw us darken their door.

"John Little," Matilda Morgan greeted, wrapping him in a hug. "My dear boy, how are you?"

"Very well, Mistress Morgan. And you look lovely tonight."

She blushed. "Little charmer." She let him go and saw me, and her mouth went flat like a toad's. "Will."

I tipped my hat to her. "Hullo, Mistress Morgan."

She looked behind her, and I saw the three curly-headed ninnies she liked to call daughters. "Keep to yourself, Will," she told me.

I ducked my head, but I felt anger twist in me. John were the swiver, not me. Just because her daughters liked who they thought I were didn't make it my fault. And I knew for a fact that John ain't always been a gentleman with Aggie Morgan, her red-haired oldest.

He smiled at her, and she giggled.

I tugged my hat down and went to the hearth, where I saw Lena. I thought she were sitting with Mr. Morgan, but it were Mark Tanner.

"Will Scarlet," Lena greeted, jumping up. She hugged me and pulled me down next to her.

Mark shook my hand. "Will," he said.

"Mark," I said. "Didn't know you were staying here too."

"Oh, I just came to call on Lena."

My mouth opened, but just then John came over, trailing the girls behind him. I pulled a little closer to Lena, but they crowded around us.

"Did you give it to them yet?" John asked.

I flushed, but I reached round behind me to pull out the food. I passed the meat to Lena and started to hand out the rolls, but Matilda pushed past her daughter. She grabbed the meat and threw it back in my lap. "No," she snapped.

"Mother!" one of the girls cried.

I blinked. "What?"

"I know what you are, Will Scarlet, and how you come by your 'gifts.' We are a good, Christian family. God, and not a thief, will provide for us."

I knew my cheeks were red as my name, and I couldn't think of a word to say. "But—" I tried.

She cuffed me on my ear. "You heard me. Shame on you, and shame on Robin for letting you do it."

I shrank back, holding my head in shock.

"Steady on!" John said, jumping in front and pushing between me and her. Lena's arm came around me. "Will's only trying to help."

"We don't need help," she said. "Certainly not from the likes of him."

"Will isn't *like* nobody," John said. "And he works harder to save our people than anyone else."

"It's noble of you, John, but I think he should go. Now."

I weren't waiting around for her to kick me out. I were already on my feet and past Mark Tanner, running out the back door and not waiting for John.

I bundled up the food and left it for George and Mary and little baby Robin, and I went back to the cave. Rob and Much were there, so I climbed the trees, going up over the cave without talking. I don't think they even saw me.

"Rob!" John called, crashing through the forest. "Much, have you seen Scar?"

"No, why?" Rob called, standing straight, his bow in hand.

"Mistress Morgan tossed her out for stealing."

Rob's face went flat and hard, and I felt sick. "She stole from the Morgans?"

John scowled. "Of course not. She brought them food for caring for Lena, and they practically tossed it in her face."

Rob sighed. "Because she stole it."

I pushed my cheek against the tree.

"She's probably just run off for a while," Much said. "She does that."

"I know, Much. But she can't run off every time someone says or does something." Rob shook his head. "Or she can, but if she wants to do that, we can't count on her as part of this band."

I opened my mouth to tell them I were there and hadn't run nowhere, but it didn't come out.

"We can always count on Scar," Much defended.

"I'll admit, I've called her a coward in the past," John said.

I hugged my knees.

"But we can count on her," he continued. "She's allowed to be hurt."

"She's not a coward," Rob said. "I have never and will never accuse her of that. She's as brave as they come—but her first instinct is to hide from us. To hide from me."

"Why shouldn't I hide?" I called. "When with every odd breath you tell me how fast you want me out of this band."

I hopped lower in the trees, standing, staring defiant at him. Water were in my eyes but I didn't much care.

"Christ, Scar, you've been here the whole time?" Rob asked.

My face went wobbly. I had to ask it, and I couldn't shake or shiver none. "Do you want me to go, Robin Hood?"

His jaw moved like he were chewing it over. He heaved a sigh and threw his bow across his back, climbing up the tree. He came up beside me and I didn't dare blink. Tears would have gone every which way, and I weren't never going to cry in front of Rob. "Go up," he told me.

I climbed, blinking and wiping my mug on my sleeve. I climbed faster than Rob, even though my shoulder set to an awful aching. I waited for him on the branch that were highest I could sit on.

He came and sat beside me.

"Yes, I want you to go," he said, and I thought I heard wrong. I looked at him, and more tears jumped out. "I want you to go, Scar, if you can't trust me. If you can't let me in, then you have to go."

"I trust you, Rob. I always have. I don't even want to, but you're just . . . you. It's terrible. Do you have to know the whole awful story for you to trust me?"

"No. Sometimes I worry that I don't know you at all, though."

"You don't trust *me*."

He sighed. "I want to. But we both know you lie to me."

I hung my head. "I can't lie to you, I don't think. I try not to talk 'bout things, though."

"I know. Why is that?"

"Telling secrets ain't done me no favors in the past."

"Who was she?"

"Who?"

"The girl in London. The one you don't want to tell me about."

I swallowed, but her name bubbled up in my throat. "Joanna," I said. "My sister."

He closed his eyes. "She protected you."

I nodded, tears tripping down my nose.

"And you stole food for her." He sighed. "What happened to her?"

"She caught sick. She kept coughing," I said. I hugged my arms over my stomach. "I stole food, and medicine, milk and water, and some Scottish whisky—and nothing worked. She coughed blood everywhere."

"Consumption?" he asked soft.

I curled up a shoulder. "Don't know. Never had a name for it."

"She died."

I nodded. "The day after, I met you, and I let you catch me."

He pulled back. "Let me catch you? You didn't let me."

I pushed water off my face, not looking.

"But that's foolish. Why would you ever let me catch you?" He stopped moving, and I didn't look, but I could feel his sorry stare. "Because the punishment for stealing is death, and you thought I was a high lord. You thought if you just stole from me, you would die. And you'd be with her. And you're so pious, you'd never take your own life."

I sniffed back tears. "Don't think I count as pious, quite."

"But that's it, isn't it?"

I nodded. "You didn't do what you ought," I told him. "Prison were a bit of a different matter than dying. I never want to die the way she did, diseased and slow, even if it would get me back to her."

"Christ," he murmured.

"I just left her in the room we rented," I told him. It were like the dam had cracked and a geyser were shooting out, and for once all I wanted were to talk about Joanna. "She were like stone in the bed, and with blood all around. Her hair didn't even look like hers, where it were still on her head. I didn't—I didn't know what to do." Tears kept falling. "I left her there. There weren't nowhere for her to be buried. I wrote her name in a book and left it on her bed so they might find our kin, but I never checked. I just left."

"You lost everything you had, Scarlet. No one could judge you no matter how you reacted."

"It were worse than letting her die. I left her alone."

"Where did you go?"

I wiped my eyes. "Church. I sat there and cried and all the saints were fair glaring at me and it were raining something awful. A candle knocked over and a bit of the wall caught fire. I put it out, but I ran. I couldn't do nothing but run. I figured it were a sign from God that I weren't welcome nowhere on earth. So when I saw you, it seemed like another sign." I shook my head, and more water ran out. "But then you didn't let me die. You made me come with you, and you made me watch how many other people were hurting, and you make me fail every day when I can't fix it."

He were quiet for a long stretch. "Do you still want to die, Scar?"

I shut my eyes. "Don't know," I whispered. "Sometimes I don't see much worth living for. Sometimes I think I'm a curse on everyone because I live so contrary, and give the Church stolen money, and break most of the Lord's laws. But as long as the Lord's giving me a chance to 'tone for what I done, I'll take it." I sniffed, rubbing my face on my sleeve. "You know 'bout me going to church?"

He nodded. "I saw you there."

I looked at him. "Thought you didn't go to Mass."

"I don't." He shifted round, and his voice got quiet. "I wish I could. I followed you there once, hoping maybe if you were there I could go in. As much as I desperately want forgiveness, God's not offering it at the moment." He swallowed, and it pushed the bulge in his throat out. "Why do you wear a dress?"

"Can't lie to God."

"You're not lying, Scar. You are who you are. God knows you in skirts or breeks." He shook his head. "The good and the bad, unfortunately."

I shrugged. "Always feels wrong."

He leaned forward a little, shifting on the branch, to rub his thumb under my eyes and pull off the tears. "When did Gisbourne give you the scar?"

"Years ago. He caught me and Joanna running from our

home and he pushed a knife in my face. I said he'd never use it on me, so he did."

"Bastard. To cut a girl, and you must have been just a little one at that."

"Thirteen," I countered. "Two days before fourteen. I weren't so little."

"It's strange. It sounds so young, but most noblewomen are betrothed at fourteen. Some even wed, though traditionally they wait till fifteen."

I swallowed a hard lump. "Heard that." I raised my eyes to him, my strange eyes, and for the first time, I wished that I would blaze in his mind. Truth were, I'd met Rob. Before Gisbourne cut me and before Joanna and I ran to London, I'd met Rob—just once, not for long. When I saw him in the marketplace that awful day after Joanna died, knowing he were a lord, it felt like a gift. I'd known him straight off—but in all the time then and since, he'd never remembered my long-ago self.

"So you know, Scar, I don't want you going anywhere. And I'm sorry about the Morgans. That was cruel."

"I don't mean to run," I said, ducking my head down. "Just sometimes I feel like everything will come out, like a bleeding slice, and . . ." I shrugged.

"I know. But no matter how you bleed, we'll patch you up. Just trust us."

I nodded.

"Will you come down with me?"

"I'll just stay up here. Hurt my shoulder enough to get up; I'll let it rest a bit."

He took my arm. "Christ, I forgot about that. Come on, get on my back. I'll carry you down."

It did hurt a fair bit, and with all the waterworks I felt tired and weak. Still, I shook my head. I think I'd rather tumble my way to the ground than scrabble on his back like a monkey— or worse, like some tot of a child.

He frowned but didn't force it, and he climbed 'longside me down the tree. When we touched ground, John called me to sit by him. I gave Rob a bare glance and went, sitting near John. He passed me some soup and moved closer to do it, putting his arm round me. Part of me squirmed a bit, like it weren't quite right, but most of me were just glad for a warm arm and warm side and warm soup.

"The soup should go down pretty easy," John told me soft. I nodded, and he squeezed my hand a bit. "Sorry about the Morgans."

Taking a sip of the soup, I felt like pushing his arm off, felt like climbing back into the tree and pulling Rob up there with me, staying there and graining into the wood.

I caught Rob looking at us, but soon as I looked up, he went to Much without looking at me again.

CHAPTER
TWELVE

~o~

The days started drawing on faster. We spent them training and working the road, collecting as much as we could in coin. It were coming in quick enough. During the nights, we hunted the king's forest and we gave out the meat, but in almost two weeks, six people got nabbed, and we knew it would be worse come tax day.

Gisbourne weren't killing them, which were good and bad at the same time. Good that they weren't dead, but bad that they were all in the prison still. I knew he had the castle trussed up like a fortress; even during the day, people couldn't come and go anymore. If we were going to break them out, it would have to be all at once, and we wanted to wait till hanging day. Or hanging night, I suppose, because hanging morning wouldn't do anyone much good.

My shoulder healed up; it only hurt if I hit it. Which were

good—when my shoulder hurt, it made climbing tough, and these days I found myself up in the trees more. Gisbourne couldn't go where I went, and it were the only thing made me feel safer.

—⁂—

I swung down from the archway onto the road. The travelers had passed, and John tossed me the large bag of coin he lifted from one of the lords. "Awful heavy, Scar. Good spot."

Shaking them, I listened to the rattle like soft rain. "Sweetest sound there is." I tossed it to Much as Rob and I started picking up the jewels and weapons. Rob and I grabbed for the same sword and our eyes crossed looks.

I pulled back, letting him have at it.

John grabbed at one of the swords, pointing it toward me. "Come on, Scar, feel like a fight?" he asked. Then he saw a dagger and we both jumped for it.

His hand nicked it a hair before mine and John lifted it high above his head. "You want this, Scar?" He swung the dagger back and forth.

I jumped for it and he grinned, catching me and holding me off the ground so our noses were level.

I stared straight at him, not afraid of him none. "Not what I were jumping after, John."

"You sure?" he asked, his eyes fixing on my mouth.

He leaned toward me a tiny bit and I kicked his shins before he might do some fool thing like kiss me.

John dropped me with a groan and I snatched the knife from him, catching Rob's eyes and seeing the dead scowl on his face.

Even Much were frowning at me, and I turned away, feeling my belly twist. It weren't fair. Rob wouldn't never be the sort to get his belly in a twist for me, but if me and John got any bit of friendly, he acted like I were wrenching the band apart.

—⚒—

We had a decent haul on the road that morning, all told, and Rob and I headed to Trent to sell the more expensive bits.

"I think it's been too long," I told him.

He looked at me, curious. "What?"

"Too long. Since we were in a tussle or something. Something feels wrong today."

"Maybe it's because John isn't with you." He smiled, but his teeth looked sharp. "World not right without him?"

I glared. "It ain't that way. Needn't be mean about it."

"That wasn't mean."

"Well, don't tell me you're just starting in on me."

His smile got a little soft. "No."

"Honestly, though. I have an awful sick feeling."

He looked at me. "About going to Trent? Or selling the jewels?"

I rolled over the two ideas. "Trent, I think."

He nodded. "We have to be double-sharp, then."

I smiled. I liked that about Rob. He teased me a bit, he scowled at me more, but he trusted me.

"So what 'bout you?" I asked. I felt my mug heat up for asking the question.

"Me?"

"And girls. Ladies. You don't ... I mean, John's always in love with someone, but you never seem much interested."

"Is that what you think you are to John? The affair of a moment?"

I kicked a stone. "Weren't my question."

"I was like John, before I left. Every girl was a new adventure. But then came the Crusades, and then came this mess, and now I'm a noble without a title." He shook his head. "To marry a commoner would dishonor my family's lineage, but I have nothing to offer a noblewoman."

"It's not like Bess or Ellie would want you to marry them none."

He pulled up his shoulders. "I'll leave the tumbling to John." He looked sharp to me. "I don't mean to say he's been unfaithful to you, Scar."

I shook my head. "I hope he ain't faithful to me."

"What?"

"I told you before, I'm none sure 'bout him. I'm hardly sure he even likes me and isn't just after nabbing a tumble."

Rob rubbed his head. "He seems pretty sure about you."

I chuckled. "I reckon Bess or Ellie would tell you the same." I pulled my long coat tighter; the wind were creeping through the rubbed-down elbows. "'Sides, I told you I won't marry."

He smiled. "So you refuse to be sure about him so you won't have to marry him."

"Something like that." I looked at his feet. "Don't it get lonely, though?"

"Is that why you're with John?"

"I'm not *with* him. But if I ever were, I reckon that'd be the cause. It's fair nice, you know. Someone holding on to you makes you feel like you're really there."

He nodded. "I know. Nice isn't for me right now, though. I need to focus on protecting the people so they can feel that comfort, not selfishly take it for myself."

"Maybe you just think you don't deserve it." I felt like that, mostways.

"Maybe I don't."

I nodded, walking on beside him. Me and Rob could be fair kindred sometimes.

―⁓―

When we got to Trent, it were midday and no better time to do the selling. We put our hoods up, set deep so our faces hid back. Knives were better cover than a bow in a crowded sort of place, so I split off from Rob and watched him, ready to throw a blade if needed.

While he circled round the place, I cast an eye over the weapons on offer in the market. I had only seen the like of the blade I wanted to fetch for Much but once, and I didn't expect to find it here, but it were always worth looking. Maybe John could make it for him once things got a bit quieter.

I settled in and watched the jeweler. His eyes were darting

about, and he ain't even looked at Rob yet. There were no reason for him to be so nervous. I whistled twice, two short tweets,
and Rob halted, veering from the jeweler's stall and looking at
the tanner's goods. I stayed close to the shop, following the
squirrel looks of the jeweler. Gisbourne's men, in their black
with crimson trim, were in the market.

My blood set to rush like river water and I gave three short
whistles this time. Rob turned away sharp and started moving
through the crowd.

A hand clamped on my head, grabbing the hood and my hat
and ripping backward. I jerked and twisted, and all my secret
hair flew round like streamers from my head.

It were one of Gisbourne's men, and he were staring at the
hood like I were staring at him.

"Help!" I shrieked in the highest voice I could muster.
"Help, please!"

Men seem to like helping ladies that need it, so when I turned
to run through the crowd, men saw my long hair and smooth
chin without noting the breeches and all, and they stopped
Gisbourne's men long enough for me to clear the market.

I ran past Rob, who were waiting for me, fisting his shirt
and jerking it along while he gawped at me. "Christ's blood,
Rob, come on!" I yelled.

He ran with me then, and we both bolted into the trees like
a crash of thunder. When Rob slowed down, I tried to keep
running, looking back over my shoulder.

"Scar, it's fine. They didn't mark where we went," he told me.

I stopped running and took a deep gulp of air. Then I spat out every foul curse word I'd ever learned, even knowing I'd have to confess them all on Sunday.

Rob looked a little shocked. "Don't you look at me like that," I snapped at him. "Just because I can't trim a beard don't mean I can't swear."

"Like a sailor," he added. "I've never heard so many curses in my whole life. All combined."

I glared and uttered another one for good measure. Then I spat on the ground. If there were ever something to draw evil near, it must have been curse words.

"Should I ask what has you so upset?"

"Gisbourne's man knows I'm a girl now, Rob!"

Muscled bits of his jaw rolled into bunches. "That's not good."

"No, it's bloody not!" I shook my head. "He'll come straight for me now. God knows all you lads are good and tough, but he puts a blade to a girl's throat and you'll give it all up. And while he's doing that, he'll get a long look at my face and—" Words dried up, and my bones started quaking. God, if there were ever a time for hiding, it were right now. I should run. I had to run. After the lads went to sleep, I could walk at least as far as York before they caught up, maybe even to Scotland. Maybe I should head for Dover and catch a ship to France.

"*Scarlet*," Rob said, like he'd said it a few times already. Had he? His big hands clamped on my shoulders. I looked to him.

My eyes felt like they'd jump out of my skull. He met my eyes and his head tilted a little. "You're fine. You're going to *be* fine. We won't let Gisbourne get near you."

"You won't have much of a choice when you're breathing through a slice in your neck," I snapped. I pulled away.

He let me go, then caught my face, his hands on my cheeks, his eyes on mine like the sun-warmed sea rushing round me. My breath and my wild mind froze. "You don't think I'm a match for Gisbourne?"

I didn't say—don't think I could have, him holding my face like that, no words would have come—and his eyes got this dark, cold glint.

"You really haven't seen what I'm capable of, Scar. He's the one who should be very much afraid."

I blinked.

His thumb ran over my scar, and it jangled through me like I were tangled up in rope. "He has a lot to answer for already. If he comes for you, he's a dead man."

I felt my mouth hang open but I couldn't do much about it. I couldn't do much of anything with him touching me like that. His thumbs kept rubbing, sliding my mind clear away. My cheeks felt hot and red under his fingers, and he smiled, his eyes heavy like the weight of the ocean.

"All right?"

I drove my teeth into my bottom lip, nodding a little.

He let go of my face, but his fingers caught in my hair a bit. "You have nice hair, you know."

My pipes felt tight and I couldn't much breathe. "Thanks," I managed. "Um, you too."

His hand dropped and he chuckled. "Thanks, Scar." He moved on.

What in all of Heaven and Hell were that? I screamed. Well, I didn't scream none, but I wanted to. *Why do you put your hands on me like that? You can't touch me and make my skin squirm when we both know you ain't in love with me.*

The very thought made my anger die like a leaf on a branch, and I followed behind him. It were fair torture when he put his hands on me, and looked at me, and stood with me, but Robin were a lord, and his heart would never turn to a thief.

—⁂—

"Well, maybe they were just in the marketplace," Much offered. "Maybe they weren't watching the jeweler. After all, they grabbed for Scar, not you, Rob."

"I never got close. She was closer than I was." Rob shook his head. "I think they were watching the jeweler."

"He were all shifty," I said. "He were why I warned you off. The man must have spotted my hood and figured me for the Hood."

"Then maybe Gisbourne's man didn't know you for one of mine after all."

"Know her?" John's face ran white. "You mean *he's* how you lost your hat? Gisbourne knows you're a girl now?"

My hair were braided back, but I grabbed at it anyway. I nodded.

"Oh, Christ," Much moaned.

"It's not the worst news we've ever gotten," Rob said.

John rubbed his head. "It's bad."

"Hey," Rob said, scowling. "Don't any of you, including yourself, Scar, forget exactly how deadly Scar is. He comes after her and he'll have a bit of her mind carved into his hide."

I smiled.

"And then the rest of us will kill him."

I grinned at him.

"Regardless, we don't have time to fret over it." We all looked to Rob. "Tax day is the day after tomorrow, and we need to fence these jewels immediately. Meanwhile, we can't leave the cave unprotected."

"No one knows where it is," John countered.

"Can't risk it. Not when we have tax money for almost everyone in Edwinstowe, Worksop, and Nottingham in there."

"Why haven't we been parceling it out?" Much asked.

I sighed. "People are poor, Much. They'll spend it on something else before taxes, and then they'll be strung up or worse."

"What's worse?" John asked.

"Ask the boy at Tuck's," I muttered.

"Anyway, we're going to have to split up even more than usual. Scar, I want you to head to Leicester. John, you go to Derby. Much, you're going to head up to Lincoln. I'll stay and protect the treasure we've got."

"We're heading off alone?" Much asked.

Rob rubbed his head. "No. Can't endorse that. I'm going to

send Mark Tanner with John, Thom Walker with Scar, and, Much, go with Lena. She'll charm you straight out of trouble if you need it. Better than a strong arm. They aren't the best choices, but they're the only ones not killing themselves to bring in harvest."

"Are they even good with weapons?" I asked. "Lena ain't."

"No, they aren't there to fight. They are there to spot you and keep an extra set of eyes—and run, when needed."

I crossed my arms. I weren't fond of Thom Walker. I didn't trust him in the least bit, but then I didn't know him neither, and he hadn't done much to ever earn a trust.

"Look, it's for one day. We need this done."

We nodded.

"All right, pair off and let's practice weapons. Then we're tucking in early tonight. We all need to be up before the sun."

—∞—

John gave me his cloak the next morning, with a big heavy wool hood attached to it. I could fit my shortbow 'cross my back under it with no one the wiser, so I took it. I pushed some twigs into my hair—I used to do it with fine combs, so I knew how to keep it all pinned back, but I wanted a new cap. Maybe I could swipe one in Leicester.

I picked Walker up like some kind of foundling in Edwinstowe, just nodding at him and starting off down the road.

"So," he tried. "Leicester, right? That's what the earl said."

Didn't say nothing. Didn't like that people called Rob "the earl" neither.

He chuckled. "You're the thief, aren't you? Can't reckon you lot like the sunshine much."

I rolled my eyes. Honestly, I weren't some demon.

"Not in the mood for a bit of a chin wag?"

I just walked faster. God knows I ain't comparing myself to no Son of God, but at the moment I might have taken the scourging and thorny crown 'stead of listening to Thom Walker chatter for hours as we walked to Leicester. Just as long as I didn't have to die at the end. Less I were going to rise again—that puts death in perspective a bit. I reckon even Christ would have been right happy with death if he knew it weren't such a sticking situation.

We hopped a cart after about two hours of walking, and I shut my eyes for a while, never sleeping in true. I didn't like someone new so close. Walker didn't move much, just shifted around. And he stopped chattering.

We rode the cart for a while and then hopped off when the road forked. It were still morning, and the road were fair full, so we faded in. I did, leastways. Walker were big—not so big as John—but none too aware of his own size, and he stuck out like the thumb from your palm.

When we got close to Leicester, I told him to keep away from me, so we could both keep an eye on the other. I told him 'bout hanging back from a fight, and to whistle if something were wrong. He smiled like it were some fun, and not people's lives, that we were trading for.

The market were packed. Fair taxes and decent landlords made for hardy trade, and the market showed it. There were such wares as I ain't never seen, clothing and pies and big cuts of meat, knives and swords and all sorts of weapons. I got far too eager at the stall of one seller. Caught by the dark glint of some cheap-made Saracen metal, I went closer, and I saw what I'd been looking for, the weapon that would be perfect for Much and none other.

My fingers twined toward it of their own accord, and the man, a brawny blacksmith with shoulders like a tree trunk stretched across, smiled. "A *kattari*," he said. "From the East—a very rare and unique weapon."

I picked it up. The bottom bit were like an *H*, with a crossbar to hold on to and a shield for your knuckles. Just above the crossbar the blade started, wide as a man's palm and near as long as his forearm, tapering quick to a blade almost like a triangle. Without a moment's thought, I pulled out my two Saracen knives.

"A trade," I offered.

He scoffed. "Cheap imitations are nothing compared to a *kattari*."

"They're real. With rubies."

"Paste," he insisted.

I withdrew my arm. "Fine, then. I'll sell them elsewhere."

He jerked forward, dislodging some blades on his table and letting them clatter. "An even trade, then."

I smiled and nodded. It weren't quite even, but I didn't mind for Much, and he wrapped the *kattari* in burlap and made the trade.

Once away, I tucked the covered blade into my vest and went looking next for a new hat. There were some caps, and I swiped a felted wool one that were cheap and funny shaped. I didn't leave money behind; after all, I were a thief and it weren't like these sort were hurting like they were in Nottinghamshire. I tucked it in my vest too and sought out the jewelers.

Leicester had three jewelers: one who dealt with metals, one for precious jewels, and one who, it seemed, worked only for nobility. All the same, the three men were buying, and it weren't hard to get a good price like that. I just went back and forth, working till I got a good high price, three times what we were bartering for in Newark.

When I were getting paid at last, I saw the shadow inching to the side of the door, waiting for me to come out. I looked sharp; where were Walker? I didn't see him straight off, but I had to get out of there before I could find him.

It were the jeweler who worked for nobles that I happened to be at, and so, a touch shameless, I lowered my hood so the jeweler could see my mug and the twist of my hair. "Please," I whispered. "Please help me."

His eyes went big. "Holy Mary, you're a lass," he said.

I lifted my chin. "A *lady*," I insisted. "Please, you must help.

There are men outside, trying to take me back to my lord husband. He'll kill me," I told him. My eyes even went a bit watery.

"Yer husband? I don't cross a nobleman, not even for a ladyship."

"He'll kill me," I said again. I put my hand on his arm. "You must have a back way out? Just pretend I ran past you, let me go, and you needn't cross anyone. Please." I met his eyes, showing him the full oddity of my eyes. "I've had to sell my jewels; don't trade them for my life."

He sighed, and he jerked his thumb over his shoulder. I took the pouch of money, pulled up my hood, and bolted.

His workshop led to a small bellows room and heating pit, and there were a big back door from there that led to a small space with a horse in it. I gave the horse a look, tempted.

I climbed up the roof 'stead. Leaning on the crossbeams, I looked down.

Swallowing swears, I spotted three men and maybe a fourth trolling the market. How had Gisbourne's men found us again? He must be following me somehow. I were the only person at both places. 'Less the others had been followed too.

Walker were still in the market, staring after sweetbreads, full blind to the danger. Some lookabout he were. I hopped over a few roofs and dropped into the market, grabbing his arm and pushing him out.

Running, I slid through the crowd. I were fair good at slipping away, but Thom weren't. He kept stopping and starting and bumping people, saying excuses to them too loud.

"Damn it!" I growled, flipping a knife at him and turning, meeting his eyes head on. He halted. "Shut your yap, follow me, and run, or I'm going to leave you here, and *you* can fend off Gisbourne."

He swallowed. "I'm coming."

I nodded, holstering my knife and running.

CHAPTER

THIRTEEN

~o~

We ran to Edwinstowe, and once I got Thom Walker safe and looked after, I ran to the cave with my loot, taking a long loop round Thoresby Lake so no one followed me. Couldn't risk it. There were some way they were tracking us, that were damn sure, but now we had bare hours left before the sheriff's men came collecting in the morning, and lots of money to parcel out before then.

I got to the cave and only John weren't there yet.

"Oy!" I called. Much and Rob turned. "Were you followed?"

"No," Much said. " 'Course not."

I cursed. "Gisbourne were in Leicester. He must be tracking me, Rob."

His mouth twitched up. "I doubt he's following you, Scar. You're too suspicious by half."

"Then what, a damn good guess? He has to be marking us somehow."

"If the thief taker has it out for you, and he's got tabs on you, wouldn't he have roughed you up by now?" Much asked.

I ran my knuckles over my scar. It weren't a bad point.

"We don't have time to worry about it, Scar. There's no way he can be tracking you, or he'd have made his move on you, us, or the cave already. We need to focus and start splitting up the coin."

I nodded. I weren't too sure of it, but he were right— other things needed time more. "How are we going to do it?"

"Let's count what you've got, we'll count John's when he gets back, and then I think we'll split up again tonight. We have to get all these people money."

I rolled my shoulders, a creep sliding down my neck. "I don't think we should be alone, Rob. We've got time enough to give out the coin before sunrise."

"I definitely don't want anyone in one town alone—it won't allow enough time to parcel out the coin. Same partners as today."

I shook my head. "I don't trust Thom Walker, Rob. He were more like a ball round my leg anyway. Slowed me down terrible."

He chewed this over.

"Even if we pull the same partners as today, someone needs to be alone. I'd rather go alone than with Walker."

"Alone's not a good idea. Not with Gisbourne and the sheriff in full force tonight. Besides, we need all the hands we can get."

"What's this?" John called, slinging a sack down that clinked with coin. "What about hands?"

"We're talking about tonight," Much said quick, looking down. "We need more people, but Scar don't want to go with Thom Walker."

"I'll go with Scar," he said quick.

"I just said, we need more people, not fewer."

"Well, we'll take Edwinstowe, and Much can go with Lena in Worksop, and you, Thom, and Mark Tanner can take Nottingham. That will work out."

"Not really," Much said. "Really it should be me and Tanner in Worksop, and you, Lena, and Walker in Nottingham, then Rob with Scar in Edwinstowe, to balance out fast and strong. Different sort of thing than selling jewels."

Rob sighed. "Fine. Let's just get this counted and parceled and be on our way."

I nodded, but still I couldn't shake the bad feeling. Something were wrong, and I knew it. I just hoped I had enough knives when it came to bear.

To that end, I pulled Much away while Rob and John kept counting, and I shuffled the blade from my vest. I held the burlap package out.

"What's this?" he asked.

"I think it might be your weapon," I told him.

He pulled the burlap off and, using his good arm, hooked the belt that the sheath were lashed to over his shoulders so it lay high on his hip. He slipped his hand between the long metal braces to grip the crossbar.

Much pulled it out, and the metal looked richer in the dark

forest, dappling green earth and silver sky. Much smiled, slicing through the air. It were like his fingertips had welded tight
and become a wicked blade.

"This," he said, "is much better than a knife!"

I let my smiling teeth show my pride. "The 'Much' part is
more important than being 'better,'" I told him.

He chuckled. "Now I've just got to figure out how to use it."

"You're smarter'n all of us, Much. You'll get it."

Holding the blade away, he stepped forward and hugged
me with his bad arm. It were tighter than I thought he might
hug, but he pushed me away after a minute. "Get your knives
out, Scar. Let's fight!"

—⁊⁊⁊—

It were after dusk when we all went to Edwinstowe, and Lena,
Mark, and Thom were all in front of the Morgans' house. I
hung back from there. I knew I weren't any more welcome
than Saladin in that house.

"Right," Rob said. "Mark, will you head off with Much?"

He nodded.

"Lena and Thom, you two are with John."

Thom looked over to me, and I felt it again, the creep on
my neck.

"I'm not going with Scarlet?"

I narrowed my eyes. "Call me Will."

He chuckled. "Why? I know you ain't a boy."

It felt like hot lead slipped down my pipes.

"And how would you know that?" Rob asked. Were more like a growl. John stepped in front of me.

"Was it a secret? I could tell."

"She's coming with me tonight," Rob said.

"Yeah, and you leave Scar to me," John said.

"Oh," Walker said, like he just understood something new. "You're her fellow, then."

"No."

"Yes."

Me and John spoke at the same time, and I crossed my arms. "I ain't your girl, John," I hissed at him.

He winked at me. "I'm getting there."

I shook my head, and we all broke up. Much and Mark headed off, and John came over to me and rubbed my arms.

"So why aren't I your fellow yet?" he asked me.

I shut my eyes so that I didn't look after Rob. "Come on, John, you ain't serious about me. It wouldn't end well if you were my fellow and I saw you charming Bess, or Agatha Morgan."

His arms went round my waist. He had a big grin, full of teeth like stars. "You saying you're the jealous sort, Scar?"

"I'm saying that some girls slap, but I have knives."

"For me or for Agatha?"

"Both." He pulled me tighter, but my arms were still crossed so my elbows pushed into him.

"What if I kept all my smiles to you?"

I chuckled, shaking my head. "You ain't that sort, John. Why go changing for me?"

"Because. You're worth changing for."

That gave me some sort of flutter inside, but I put my hands on his big chest to push away. He let my waist go. "We've got work to do, John."

He sighed. "All right. Let's be quick, and I'll buy you a drink at Tuck's after."

"Deal."

The others left, and me and Rob split the bag in two and started at opposite ends of Edwinstowe. It were two long rows of houses, with a big well in the middle and a church by the well, and more houses clustered there. There weren't no village gates, just a big barn where they all kept their livestock. I started at the far end, and Rob started at Tuck's end. This weren't the type of delivery that I could just drop off, so I knocked quiet at every door, passed a handful of coin, enough for taxes and some food besides. Most were fair grateful, but some were more gruff 'bout it, and that were fine. I got that sometimes pride got in the way of things.

I got through maybe ten houses, which weren't much— there were about thirty-and-five houses to go—when I heard a *whish*.

I turned in time to watch a branch slam my side, knocking me to the ground beside a house. The air ran from my chest and I couldn't take none in. My nails clawed at the ground, but someone flipped me over, ripping back my hood.

"Thom?" I gasped. Pain shot through my chest, and I couldn't breathe in. He grabbed my hair, dragging me back over the ground.

My eyes ran as I tried to breathe in, huffing Rob's name

and twisting against Thom's hold. He dragged me behind the house by the woods, rocks cutting and scraping as I went. I managed a little breath, enough to fuel my rage and swing a kick to his knee. He crashed down, falling on top of me and knocking the air out again.

"Have it your way, then," he said. "Gisbourne said I only had to stall for a few minutes, and this is as good a way as any." His fingers dug in my hair, and his legs were pinning my legs down, one of his arms trapping mine.

"*Bastard*," I hissed, snapping my forehead up to slam his.

He roared in pain and slugged me 'cross the mug. I punched him one back, grabbing for a knife, but he took my wrist and wrenched my arm up, holding both my arms above my head. I flopped angry like a caught fish, my hair flying out everywhere.

"How could you?" I asked. "Gisbourne?"

His free hand fisted in my shirt and jerked, tearing the fabric down the front. "He pays well! But there are certainly some benefits to the position."

His hand grabbed my bits over the muslin, and I spat at him. I jerked up, headbutting him again. If he thought I were going to be some helpless lass, he were dead wrong. His eyes closed in pain, and I snapped my head against his nose once more.

"Rob!" I shrieked.

Thom twisted and yelled in pain, enough to free my leg to knee his male bits. He wrenched up and I drove my little fist through his jaw. Then the damn fool collapsed, pressing all his weight straight on top of me. I tried to move him, but he were out cold.

"Rob!" I shrieked again. "Hurry!"

I angled to lever my leg out, and I heard crunching in the lane. I pushed him off me, standing to meet Rob.

But it weren't Rob's shape I saw. It were Gisbourne up near the road, casting his shadow on me from between the houses. He chuckled, and I froze.

"I knew as soon as Thom mentioned your eyes. Before that, I didn't dare hope," he said, his smile gleaming like a wolf's. "But when he said you had eyes like moonstones, I knew I'd found my wayward girl at long last. So they call you Scarlet now, do they? How ironic that you ran so far from your old life and named yourself for your expensive ribbons." He walked closer. "What, no sweet words for your fiancé?"

My back were pounding with pain and I steadied myself on the house. A shadow were moving closer to me from behind the house, and I could only pray it were Rob and not Gisbourne's men. I spat on the ground, showing Gisbourne my teeth like some wild animal.

"Wonderful," he said. "My dear girl has become a heathen. Well, I'm sure it will be entertaining to break you of your bad habits." He tilted his head. "I see your last punishment healed nicely. Hopefully it will make you think better of leaving me again."

"You're a monster," I snarled. "And I will never stay with you."

"You *made* me a monster!" he roared. "You think I have nothing better to do than roam around London at the last mention
of you? To scour the country for you? You haunt me, you little
she-devil, and I won't tolerate being left. So I'll be a monster
until you're mine, in marriage or in death." His eyes blazed.
"Maybe both."

Rob came from behind the house before Gisbourne could
come closer, grabbing my hand and yanking hard. My legs moved
without never being told, running with him. "Rob, the gold!"
I cried, seeing it spilled on the ground and pulling back on his
hand.

He didn't even mark me, just plowed on, dragging my hand
like a tether and running into the dark woods as Gisbourne
called his men to follow us. I heard Gisbourne laughing as we
ran, and the sound rattled around in my mind.

Rob ran like he'd never tire, like demons were chasing him,
with his hand clamped on mine like an iron shackle. His jaw
were tense and hard, his eyes set forward like a hawk's. My legs
and strength were crumbling beneath me, but I kept moving if
only to keep my hand in Rob's as he wove a wild track through
Sherwood. I couldn't tell if we lost Gisbourne or if he never
followed us to start with.

When we got to the cave, he let me go, and I found I were
shaking hard. My shirt were all shredded in back and torn in
front, and there were a sticky heat on my back that my tangled
hair were sticking to. I clutched the shirt to me and it fell apart
in my hands.

I sank to the ground and curled over my knees. My back
skin stretched and I yelped with the pain.

"Here." Rob handed me a cloak. "Hold it to your front;
your back's a mess."

He trotted into the cave, getting the kit. Our supplies were
fair dwindling; I'd have to steal more soon. He sat behind me,
and his fingertips touched the muslin. My back bunched up
against him and he let go, pushing my hair over my shoulder. I
could see pieces of fabric shiny black with blood.

The first pull of the cloth from my ripped skin were like
fire. I clutched the cloak tighter, shuddering. He plucked out
bits of dirt and rock, and every touch seared. Water were leak-
ing from my eyes. I didn't make a sound, though. I just heard
Gisbourne laughing over and over in my head like a sick ballad.

"Try to stop shaking, Scar," he said. He didn't sound gentle,
like usual, but tight and hard.

I curled tighter, and my back hurt worse.

He finished plucking things and started rubbing salve into
my back, and I buried my face in the cloak as tears poured out.
It hurt; it felt like pain on top of pain.

"Here," he said, and I hadn't even realized he had stopped
rubbing until I saw him in front of me. He stripped off his
shirt and bunched it in one hand, pressing it to me. I looked
up at him with my wet face, and his jaw muscles rippled. I took
the shirt with a shaking hand, pulled it over me gingerly, and
then handed him the cloak. His look were more like a glare. "No.
Put it on."

I obeyed, chewing my lip. "Rob, I'm sorry 'bout the coin—"

"Stop."

I stopped.

"Don't you say anything."

I blinked.

"I don't think I can listen to anything right now. Not after that. Not after seeing you, your shirt all torn like Thom—" His mouth tightened like a drawstring. "And then hearing Gisbourne say *fiancé*."

I were trembling so hard I felt like my belly were rattling loose. "Rob—"

"Not. A. Word." He shook his head, and his eyes went shut. "I just don't know which one is making me feel like this, like I'm going to vomit up my organs. Did Thom hurt you?"

I shook my head, too scared to speak.

He pointed a finger at me. He weren't facing me but standing sideways, his arm stretched straight out and his chest bare. "And you're Lady Marian Fitzwalter, aren't you? Lord Leaford's younger daughter. Gisbourne's intended."

I clutched the cloak tight, frozen inside and out.

"Answer me!" he snapped.

I nodded. He looked away from me and my eyes stung like they'd been whipped, but truth were, I were crying. Crying like the stupid girl I were. My whole body were beating with pain, and it felt like someone were pressing their thumbs into my eyes.

He nodded, going into the cave and finding a tunic that

looked foolish without a shirt. "Don't move," he ordered as he walked back out and headed toward the woods.

"Where are you going?" I asked, a hiccup escaping. I pushed my face into my hands. I didn't want to look at him.

"To warn the others. If Thom's a traitor, Gisbourne will be on them soon. Stay here." He took a step. "No, go to Tuck's. Have him *hide you*. If I see you sitting in the tavern, I swear I'll murder you myself."

I ran all the way, letting the wind pull my tears away. Tuck put me in a small room at the inn, and I curled in a corner, taking the blanket from the bed and wrapping it around me. I twisted up over my knees and sobbed. It felt like losing Joanna all over again, like the only thing that loved me in the world were dead and gone.

—⁓—

An awful long time went by before someone knocked on the door. I jumped.

"Scar?" he called. I didn't say nothing and he just opened the door. It were John, and the tears started again. I didn't want it to be John. I wanted it to be Rob, saying everything were just fine and I hadn't failed everyone and everything. "Aw, love," he said, and came over, sat beside me, and pulled me into his lap, letting me curl around him. I started to cry harder, and he rubbed my back.

I wailed, pulling away. He made soft noises, pulling me closer again, careful of my back. "Hush," he whispered, like

I were a child. "I'm just glad you're all right. Girls downstairs are awful worried about you. Well, they don't know it's you that Tuck put up here, but they said someone was crying."

I gripped his shirt. My tears were making me shake again, and I just wanted it all to stop.

"I'm here, Scar. I'm not going anywhere." His hands pushed back the tears on my cheek and his thumb stroked the side of my head. I looked at his eyes. "I'm not going anywhere, Scar, because I love you."

He pulled my head closer and pushed his lips against mine, and I kissed him back. I knew it were a damn fool thing to do, but I couldn't help it. He rubbed my neck and kept me close to his face.

It didn't help any. Honestly, it made it worse than ever. I were hollowed out and twisted up, sick in all kinds of ways. I felt like nothing would ever be good again, and I pulled my lips back. His hand kept me right there. "John," I said soft. "I'm—"

"Don't stop on my account."

I jerked to look at Rob, standing in the doorway, his fist white-knuckling the door handle.

"Guess you've recovered, then."

"Did you find Thom?" John asked.

"Not yet."

"Robin," Tuck said, appearing in the hall. "You lot need to come see this."

Rob glared at me again, and I stood up. John started to help me, but I were on my feet. Everything hurt. My side ached where the branch hit me, my cheek were pulsing, and my back were throwing off heat like a fire and making the rest of me feel shivery. My head felt like someone were banging a pot against it, and the kiss didn't help any of it none.

Rob stopped me at the door, blocking my way. He wouldn't look at me. "Cloak," he said. The word sounded like a curse. John put the cloak over my shoulders, pulling up the hood, and Rob let us both pass.

Much weren't in the tavern, which I thought were odd. There weren't anyone there. Tuck went outside and we followed.

I stopped dead in my tracks. Everyone were quiet, standing in a circle. We pushed through, and vomit, pain, and blood all started fighting each other in my body.

I'm not proud of it. It were fair shameful. I took one look at the body and drew about four desperate breaths before the pain won and I fainted. Thom Walker were on the ground, his body staked out with knives, his shirt hanging off in tatters. His mouth were sewn shut with black blood-soaked thread, the mark of a traitor. Blood were dried all over his face, and on his chest, through a thick cover of blackening blood, Gisbourne carved the words GIVE ME MARIAN.

CHAPTER
FOURTEEN

~o~

I'm to die today.

I woke up back in the room at Tuck's, and this time I were in the bed, the cloak off and the blankets round me. I felt like a rock. I moved, and my whole body were sore. My eyes were like wood dust and my side were hot and swollen. I were bruised and bloody, inside and out.

I stayed for a long time on the bed, not moving, just blinking. That's all I could think, over and over. *I'm to die today.* Because I knew that as soon as I started moving, I had to turn myself in to Gisbourne. I couldn't let anyone else get hurt.

The lads wouldn't like it. I'd have to sneak off. I wouldn't have the chance to say good-bye neither. And then, when Gisbourne got ahold of me, he'd kill me. God knows I'd done enough to deserve it, and since my father signed the marriage contract all those years ago, he had the right.

"I can tell you're awake, you know."

I turned over to my other side, biting my lip as I rolled onto my bruises and back. I sat up and dizziness rocked me over.

It were Rob, sitting with his back against the door. He were rumpled and soft looking but for his eyes. They were hard, staring at the floor.

"How long were I asleep?"

"You mean passed out? You fainted, Scar."

The memory of the body ran over me like ice. "Right."

"You've been out through the night. You never moved."

"Why are you in here?"

"Because I know you. And I knew that as soon as you woke up, you were going to run off and turn yourself in to Gisbourne." He smiled a little bit. "Or run away. Either way, I'm not letting you go."

My mug went hot, but it sounded more like a threat. "Coulda sworn you hated me yesternight."

"That has little to do with whether I'm turning you over to Gisbourne or not."

"It ain't lawful, you know. Keeping me from him."

"Last time I called accounts, I was an outlaw, so it's moot. Why do you speak like that?"

I looked down, picking at the threads of the blanket. "When I were young, I used to do it to set my mother hopping. I figured they could tell me what to do but they couldn't force me to speak right. I'd mimic everyone I could to make her angry. But then we ran off and Joanna, being oldest, did most of the talking, and

we got in hot water awful fast. So I started aping the common-
ers, and the rougher the better. It were so easy. And the more I
spoke that way, the more I thought like that, and the more
I thought like it, the farther I felt from Leaford and my parents.
The rougher I spoke the freer I were. Was."

He shook his head. "I should have known. When you were
so angry about me treating noblewomen differently, and you
spoke like that . . . I think I knew."

I scoffed. "You didn't know, Rob."

He sighed. "No, I didn't, but I should have. I saw you steal
the ribbon from Gisbourne's things, I knew when you spoke,
I had all these inklings that I didn't want to put together." He
swallowed. "I met you once. You probably don't remember. You
were just a little girl. I passed through your land when I left for
the Crusades." He touched his chest. "You and your sister
made me a garland of some little flowers for luck."

"I weren't so little," I told him. Even knowing how angry
he were with me, the notion that he did notice me all those
years past sent my cheeks blushing. "Or I didn't think I were.
It were a fair bit more than a year before the business with
Gisbourne, though, so I reckon I were little."

"I should have known, Scar, when I saw your eyes. I didn't
want to know."

"I didn't want you to know, either."

"Why did you and your sister run away from home?" he
asked.

I sniffed. "Joanna were the only person who meant anything

to me. And I to her. My parents had signed my contract to Gisbourne, and it were expected that an offer for her from a Scottish lord would arrive any day. They had so much land and no money to keep it, but they couldn't sell it because it were our dowries. Gisbourne and this other lord came courting with coin, and my parents jumped at the chance." I shook my head. "We would be so far apart, and," I whispered, screwing my eyes tight against the notion, "I were so scared of him. My parents introduced us and he were allowed to take me walking in the garden. Going with him, my body felt like ice all over. Couldn't explain it, but he gave me such an awful feeling. I sent my maids to talk to his servants, and the stories I heard from them put chills in my blood. When I told my parents I wouldn't marry him, they said I were a headstrong girl and didn't know best. So we ran." My teeth bit hard into my lip, twisting it 'bout till it felt like a worm in my mouth. "She would have stayed. She would have married her Scottish lord. It were me."

"Who made her leave?"

My eyes hooked into the floor and didn't let go none.

"She made her own decision, Scar. She was older than you."

"Didn't matter. If I hadn't been a coward, she would have stayed. And if she stayed, she wouldn't be dead."

The words fell soft between us, and they settled and grew till all I could think of were the quiet. Then Rob sighed. "Why couldn't you trust me with this? Why couldn't you tell me?" he asked.

I looked up and his eyes were on me, bleak and open and reaching toward me. "Because you're honorable, Rob, and by your honor, you should give me back to him."

He shook his head. "You aren't a horse. Gisbourne doesn't own you, and I won't return you to him against your will. And as for my honor, it's of two minds about the situation."

I squirmed. "Is either of them good for me?"

He smiled, but it weren't a real smile. "Gisbourne's a monster. I told you I would protect you with my life, and I would spend my whole life keeping girls like you from men like him."

"But my father made the promise," I said. I knew he were going to say it.

"No," he said. His voice made me look at his eyes again. "No. You're *engaged*, Scar. All the rest, I should have known, but that—" I've seen the ocean but a few times in my life, and one of them were during this rough storm. The sky were black and pierced with angry veins of light, and the water roiled like it were boiling in a pot. It were all I could think of, looking at Rob's eyes. "Letting me think you were unattached? That's the worst damn lie you ever told."

The pain were gone, and my heart beat against my chest. My mouth went dry, like my whole body didn't want me to ask what I were 'bout to. "Why?"

He shook his head, and lightning cracked 'cross the storm of his face. "Don't ask me that, Scar. Marian. Whatever your name is."

I stood. "Why can't I ask?"

He stood too, coming over to me. He were taller, tall enough to look down and make me feel small. His gaze most often made me feel bigger than I were. His thumb ran back 'long my jaw, slotting in front of my ear, the rest of his hand around the back of my neck. My breath flew away. "Because you're engaged, and because even if you weren't, you're with John."

"I'm not," I said.

His hand pushed me away, and he sounded angry but his eyes just looked like I'd stabbed him. "Well, then that makes you a whore."

My eyes set to burning at that awful word. "You would say that!" I snapped. "Gisbourne is a monster, so I can't belong to him, but John's a nice sort, so he's all right to own me, ain't he? He says he loves me so it don't matter how I feel, do it? He didn't care none and neither do you."

He grabbed my arms. "Scar, you kiss him, you sleep with him, you're alone with him—what the hell do you want me to think?"

"Why are you thinking 'bout me at all?"

"I'm not." He looked at me, straight in the eye, and pushed me off. "I *won't*."

I stepped back. God in Heaven, how could he do that— make me feel hurt and small and alone with one stupid word? "By the Holy Rood, Robin of Locksley, I hate you," I spat at him. I pushed him aside, snatched my cloak, and opened the door. He grabbed my wrist, and I jerked away.

John were in the hall and he caught me round the waist. "Hey, love," he said.

Pain shot through my back and I pushed him. "I'm not your love, John!" He looked so slack-jawed, and I felt hot tears rush to my eyes. I stopped and put my hand on his cheek. I could feel Robin standing right behind me. "I love you, John, but I don't want to be kissed by you none. And you only want to kiss me because you saw my bits in a dress."

He rubbed his rough cheek into my hand like a cat. "That's not true. And you *do* want to be kissed by me. Don't lie."

My hand fell and my face ran hot. "I don't, John!"

His eyes narrowed on me, fair worried. I shook my head but Rob scoffed. Then John's eyes went to Robin and John laughed, but it weren't a happy sort of laugh. "Oh. I see what this is about."

Shame rushed over me again, feeling Rob's awful stare on my back, and my face crumpled. John tensed.

"Something you and I should be discussing, Rob?" John asked.

"No," he said. I pushed past John with water on my cheeks and Rob said sharp, "Where are you going, Scar?"

"You know where," I said.

"Where?" John asked.

I kept going, but Rob kept after, saying, "If nothing else, you need to undo what you've done. The sheriff got twenty-seven people for not paying tax. Thirteen of the twenty-seven are children, Scar. You don't get to just walk away from this."

"I'm not!"

"And you'd have them see you die? You'd have all those children watch you be killed and know it was their fault?" he roared. "You'd put that on their shoulders, on their souls?"

I went boneless against the wall. I didn't turn to look at him; I didn't much dare. He were furious, but I wondered—wished—if he were saying *he* didn't want to watch me die. Rob had that way, sometimes, of talking 'bout something other than what he meant.

"It's not her fault," Much said, coming up the stairs.

"The hell it isn't," Rob said, and I winced like he'd hit me with the words, dashing my wishes on rocks. "I'm not going to let her turn herself in, but yes, right at this moment, I think it's her fault."

"Rob!" Much said. "We're all angry. Some for different reasons, but this isn't the time to blame others for it."

My eyes burned. "It's right fair to blame me, Much."

"You didn't do this," he insisted. "Besides, what can you do without us?"

"It's easy," I said soft. "Gisbourne will do just about anything to get me. I can trade for the townspeople."

"What are you talking about?" John asked, stepping closer.

Much sighed. "Are you Marian, then?"

I nodded.

"Scar, you can't go. He barely knew Thom. What's he going to do to you?"

"It doesn't matter. My life can purchase twenty-seven others, Much. What would you have me do?"

Much stepped up a stair, closer to me. "Fight."

I looked at him.

"Fight, Scar, because God knows I can't fight the way I want to."

I never thought 'bout Much's arm if I could help it, the scarred, black stump where his hand were cut off by the sheriff's men. He kept it away, in a pocket or under a cloak. He put it between us now. I put my hand on it. If I could ever heal anything, I wished it could be that.

"I'll help, then I'm leaving," I told him. "For good." Much looked to Rob, but I pushed past him. The front door of the tavern looked awful tempting, but I went instead to the kitchen, taking some broth. Relief were washing through me in pulses with the pain, and so were a toppling, crushing, mind-cracking amount of fear.

—∞—

Tuck let me stay in the room for the next few days. I needed to heal up a bit, and it were better done warm and fed. I think the lads agreed to it because Tuck and his wife kept a closer eye on me than they did. It felt strange to be so far from the lads. Felt strange to be far from Rob, but I didn't want to think about that none.

I didn't want to go into the town. I were sure they'd stone me or something fair awful. I needed to come up with a plan, but nothing were coming. Any minute Rob were going to walk through and tell me the townspeople were set to die the next day, and I wouldn't have a plan.

The lads came together while I were mopping the floor. Ethel, Tuck's wife, thought that there were no reason I shouldn't be put to some light work since I weren't paying none. I stopped, straightening up. "When is it?" I asked.

"Five days," John said.

"Five?" I asked. "But isn't that Ravenna's wedding?"

"The sheriff's, you mean?" Rob said. "Four days. They're hanging everyone the day after the wedding. Because the sheriff is disappointed that the locals don't love him as they should."

I looked at him. He looked worn, like an old doll.

"There's more," John said. His voice sounded heavier than a ship anchor. "They've moved the prison. All our townspeople are being held in a place where we've never been and don't know how to break out of."

The mop fell from my hands. "How do you know?" I asked. This were all kinds of bad.

John looked to Rob, and Rob leaned forward, wary of the other bodies in the place. "Ravenna."

I craned forward, sure I heard him wrong. "What?"

"Ravenna. She passed us the information, and she's going to try and get a map of the prison."

I double-stepped forward, pushing at Rob's big shoulders. "You stupid blighter, you're going to get her killed!" I hissed.

John pulled me back. "Easy, Scar. Godfrey gave it to us. We didn't go asking for it."

"Well, you shouldn't take the map! They'll figure it out. Gisbourne's smarter than all you lot and he will know, and he'll tell the sheriff and the sheriff will *kill her.* I may be responsible for the rest, but you're to blame for her, Robin!" I snarled. It weren't true, and I knew so, but I felt sick and angry and awful hateful toward him.

Rob pushed John off and shoved me. I stumbled, more out of shock than pain. It were the least gentleman-like thing he'd ever done. "They are *all* my responsibility, Marian," he said, spitting out my given name like a curse. "Every death and every pain that they bear gets charged on my soul—do you understand that?"

Fury and shame caught like kindling inside me. "You don't get to do that!" I bellowed. Well, as much a bellow as I could muster, leastways. I caught his shoulders and kneed him in the bits, making him double over as John and Much each gave a moan for him. I heaved him onto the ground. "You do *not* get to be some goddamn martyr, you hear me? You are a pigheaded, stubborn, stupid boy and you are not going to put more people in danger. We will figure out the lay of this prison like we done the last. We will get them out and get them free without her help. And don't you ever, *ever* call me Marian."

I picked up the mop and started washing again as Rob struggled to his feet, red faced. John laughed, and Much covered a smile.

"You lot think this is funny?" I asked. "I'll unman you too, if you wish it."

They jumped back, and Rob grunted, "You haven't *unmanned* me, and I resent the implication of it."

"It were a warning blow," I told him, shoving the mop 'cross the floor. "Next time I'll try harder."

Rob covered himself. "No next time, Scar."

I could lie and say that I didn't even notice him calling me Scar, but I did, and it thrilled me.

"Look," I said, continuing to mop, "I might have a plan."

Rob crossed his arms, but the others looked fair interested.

"Gisbourne's mucked with everything in the castle, but there's one sort can still get through."

"Rats?" John asked with a chuckle.

"I don't think she means animals, John," Much said soft.

"A holy sort," I told them, and I looked to Rob.

Robin's eyebrows shot skyward. "You want us to impersonate the *clergy*?"

—⚏—

"He knows your secret," Rob muttered to me, rearranging his monk's robes as we walked behind Brother Benedict.

"Can't lie to God."

He jammed a hand in Benedict's direction. "He's not God."

"He's a monk, Rob."

"So you never told me because I'm not holy enough?"

"Just hush. When this is done, we won't never have to talk 'bout it again, and never see each other neither."

"You're really going to leave?"

"I told you I would."

"You told John you would before too, and that didn't happen."

"I don't tell you lies, Rob. I never talked about my past, but I never lied to you none, and I'm not lying now. Once the townspeople are safe, I'm gone."

"Fine."

"You're the one who's always telling me to go, ain't you?" I snapped.

"I said *fine*."

I glared at him, but I were hidden in the monk's hood, so it went unnoticed. Dark were falling on us as we came to the castle, and the guard looked us over.

"Too many, Brother!"

"I was told you have a great many to tend to."

The guard looked to the portcullis. "God's truth. Go in," he said, waving to the other guards to open the gate.

Honestly, this were what I liked best about being a thief— even a dirty one at that. Sometimes, if you just had a bit of ichor in your blood, you could walk where no one else could and do things that no one else dared. Like walk into Nottingham Castle with an escort that didn't mean to lock you up.

We walked through the levels of the castle, past the old prison on the middle bailey and on up to the uppermost bailey.

The guard led us to the side of the residences where, almost a full month past, I'd seen all the builders and guards going to and fro. Fool that I were! Why didn't I look in on it? We would have known this all ages ago, and I would have had time for a proper plan.

There were a set of stairs carved into the ground, and we started going down into the rock that Nottingham Castle were built on. The staircase were narrow and bottomed out into a wide bailey with several guards, which meant that the entrance may as well have been Death's own scythe; we'd never sneak in through that way alive.

The guards let us into a big U-shape of cells, thirty in all. Light were coming from lamps, but the air were thick and close, crawling over my skin. There weren't no fresh air coming down, and that meant no vents, no way for me to sneak in nor out. There were a staircase leading lower in the far corner, and my mind went to it first.

I heard a whip crack from that way, and I guessed what lay on the next floor down. I hit Rob's wrist, and while he and the others began to move to the prisoners and pray with them, I darted off to the side, going down the stairs.

I stayed close to the wall, not sure whether playing the monk or the darting thief would help me with whatever stood at the bottom of the stairs. I walked down slow, seeing the rough, carved-out wall. It were wet with water. I crouched low, looking into the room, then pulling back. There were a big fire and blood. Blood everywhere. The prison were bare weeks old, and it already looked soaked into the ground, draining into a grate in the center of the room. There were manacles and chains and a wall of torture devices that made my knees weak. Some were stuck in the fire to make them hot and ready. By the fire there were a block with a groove chipped into it, washed over with blood till it set and stained. I knew what that were for: cutting off hands like they done to Much.

I swallowed back the sick taste in my mouth and went down the stairs. A big man with hair furred over his chest were there. He only had pants on and his skin were the color of bronze, but I didn't know if it were from firelight, blood and sweat, or his own strange coloring. Whichever way, he were half again as big as John, and I felt fear creeping up.

"Who the hell are you?"

"Brother Francis," I said. "Come to pray with the prisoner."

He spat on the floor into the river of blood and nodded, going up to give me time alone with him.

The man sagged in his manacles, his ripped back seeping blood. His chains twisted and he wheeled around slow. It were Hugh Morgan, fool Mistress Morgan's husband. "Brother," he groaned, lowering his head. I could hear water running and the fire roaring, but he were gasping low, rasping out breath, and with it came spittle and drool.

"My child," I said, my voice rough. "Why are they treating you like this?"

"They think I know where the Hood stays."

"And you will not tell them?"

"They've taken everything from me. My wife and my daughters are upstairs—have you seen them?"

"Not yet. I'll look."

He nodded. "Tell them I love them."

"You aren't dying, Hugh."

"You know my name?"

Damn. "Eh," I said. "I'm a man of God, Hugh." It were a weak lie.

"I won't give them anything when they've taken everything else, Brother."

I laid my hand on his chest, hoping he were too much in pain to see that it were small and smooth, with no furry knuckles. "Salvation will come, Hugh." I leaned closer. "On the fourth day. Hold on, Hugh. Please, hold on."

"Will the Christ come for me?" he groaned.

"No," I said, tipping up my hood enough so he could see my eyes. "I will."

I saw it then, in his eyes. Hope. The whole reason we did any of this, the whole reason I weren't sure I could ever leave Rob—it were all hope.

"Stay strong, Hugh. And pray. It helps."

"Look after my family."

I nodded as the torturer came down the stairs. I went to him. "This man has confessed his soul to me, and he swears no knowledge of the Hood's hole. I cannot fathom he would risk his immortal soul to protect a rapscallion."

The man heaved a grunt, looking at him. "Done with his

lot anyway. If the Hood has a haunt, these people don't know of it."

I started up the stairs, then paused. "If you want to confess yourself, God and his Son both wait to lighten your soul," I told him.

He thought it over a moment. I didn't know if he had a ripe secret to confess, and I were sure I'd have to confess it myself on Sunday, but it were worth the chance. "No, Brother."

I nodded, going up the stairs. The others were with the prisoners, speaking to them, praying with them. I walked through and saw Mistress Morgan and her girls huddled together and sobbing. I slipped bread in through the bars, not meeting her eyes as she took it. She caught my wrist and squeezed it, not a cruel thing but a kind one, and I nodded. It weren't the time for pride.

I parceled out the rest of the food that I snuck in, and I didn't speak. Hugh would spread the word more quiet than me.

It were a terrible feeling to leave. I thought of Ravenna, and Joanna, and all the times I left someone behind and near killed myself for it later. It wouldn't be the same with them. I could get them out.

We three left, and we never spoke till we gathered at Tuck's after returning Benedict and the robes. Once there, we went down to the cellar, and Tuck brought us ale to drink.

"It's not far from the tunnel," I said. "Much closer than the last."

"Yes, but we'll have to have a monumental distraction.

Something to draw all those guards out of the prison, because the only way in and out is the front entrance."

I nodded, thinking of the grate in the floor below. I'd have to see where that led before I piped up, though.

"I think I can create a distraction," Much said. "With the powder from the cave."

"An explosion?" Robin asked.

Much shook his head. "I haven't found enough for an explosion. Close to it, but not enough."

"But what can we light that they'll care about?" I asked. "The residences are too close. It won't give us near enough time."

"The noble residences," Rob said, draining his cup. "But I reckon all the guards have families in the shacks. And we want the guards defecting, don't we?"

"Without hurting anyone," I added.

Much nodded. "That I can manage. With John."

John looked to me, and I felt his eyes on me. "You'd have to really protect her, Rob."

"I'll protect her with my life and bones, John, you know that."

His words were fierce and he meant them, and I found myself staring. He flicked his eyes over my side and back.

"Got to keep you in shape enough to walk away from us, Scar," he told me.

"We all protect each other. No one is getting hurt, pinched, or nothing," I said.

"We have two days to get everything we need. We'll go the night before the wedding," Rob said.

"Why not the next night?" Much asked. "We've a lot to prepare."

"We can't risk it," Robin said. "If anything goes wrong, if they anticipate us, we need the extra night to ensure that everyone gets out of there alive."

CHAPTER

FIFTEEN

~o~

Two days passed in a rush. I had checked the stream by the castle, but there weren't so much as a drop of blood in it. If the prison grate led out, it weren't to here. Sticking to our plan, we stood in the cave together, dressing for battle. I covered every bit of me with knives, and Rob had his big sword from the Crusades, knives, and a longbow besides. Much had his *kattari* and John his quarterstaff and sword. The boys had bits of armor we'd lifted, but nothing fit me right, so I were girded in heavy leathers. The mother cat were making rings round my ankles, and I told myself it were luck, like she were patterning me with old Celt magic.

John took my wrist and drew me outside, out of view of the others. He kissed me, a quick little one. I scowled and he said, "For luck" before I could holler. "And this is for luck too."

He pushed cold metal into my hand, and I looked down.

My favorite knife, the one that guard had broken, were reformed and perfect, down to the small red garnet in the handle. He'd tied my ribbon to the hilt like I liked.

"You have to stay safe, Scar. Maybe it's your bits in a dress and maybe it's just you, but I'm awful fond of something in there. So don't get killed."

I jumped a little to wrap my arms round his shoulders, and he held on, hugging me off the ground. "You too," I told him. "And keep Much alive. I'm pretty fond of all you lads."

He let me down. "No special fondness for me?"

"Don't think it's the kind you want, John."

"Come on, Scar, we both know you like me." He grinned at me, but I looked away. Much and Rob had appeared at the edge of the cave, and my eyes went sharp to Rob's form.

John's face folded into a scowl. "You do like me. But I disappear as soon as the noble Earl Huntingdon is around, isn't that right?"

My eyes came back to him. "John—" I tried, but he shook his head, walking away from me.

I slid the knife to its rightful spot in my vest with a sigh. I hugged Much and then went to Rob, standing before him for what seemed like a whole life. "We'll get them out, Rob. I swear it."

"I know," he told me. "You're the only person I'd trust with this, woman or not."

My heart swelled up. "You're the only person I trust, Rob."

His face jerked, like I'd slapped him. "I don't want to hear that you trust me. You don't trust me. You lied to me about everything."

"I didn't lie 'bout everything, Rob."

"No? What's something you told me the truth about? Your name? Your family? Your intended?"

I scowled. "I gave you more than anyone. Ever. No one knows 'bout Joanna. I've never told no one the things I've told you. I know you're cross with me, and you've a right to be. But you said it yourself—you saw me, and you knew me, when I didn't want anyone even taking a peek."

He shook his head sharp. "And that's the worst part, Scar! I thought I knew you better than anyone. I thought it meant something, that I could tell you these things shackled around my heart and trust you with them. That you could do the same with me. I was a *fool* to think—" He stopped short and shook his head again. "But I was wrong. You know me because I gave you me. But you were not your own to give, were you?"

"Rob," I pleaded.

He put out a hand to stop me. "Don't. We might die today, and of all the times that we've teetered on the edge of death, this is the first time it feels like there isn't any kind of hope to come back to. So let's just get the townspeople out and it will be done. Everything will be done."

Rob's thunderstorm eyes met mine and I felt water pull up in my eyes. His jaw worked, but he just stared at me till I nodded, and then he turned away.

—ɷ—

We split off early, Rob and I first going to the tunnel and setting ropes for the people to climb down. Then we scaled the wall, jumping over in a gap in the guards and climbing down to the ground. I went and opened the door to the tunnel, then came back to him. We waited in the dark by the prison, shoulder to shoulder, my heart hammering a steady beat.

We heard the crackle of the fire being set, then the cries, and people started moving to the wall to see what were the matter. Then voices pitched higher and more people came out. It took a while for the guards to come up since they were underground, but when they did, and saw the fire, they didn't hesitate. They took off at a run, heading for the main gate, one, two, three, four.

That meant one were still down there. Rob went to the entrance first, drawing his bow and charging down the stairs fast. He let loose one arrow and moved forward. I followed behind him, seeing the guard go down with an arrow clean through his throat. I heard him gurgle his last breath and I cringed. Someone dying made it a bad night, especially so early in.

We shot forward, Rob grabbing the dead guard's keys as I set to picking locks. This were the worst bit; we hushed everyone, but we knew no matter how long it took, it would be too long. Every breath ratcheted up the danger.

People started coming out, families lumped together, and I counted as we sent them to the front.

"Rob," I called.

"Yeah?" he whispered.

"Twenty-six."

He nodded. "One must be downstairs."

"He'll have company."

"I can handle it. Get these people into the tunnel and I'll meet you; we're running out of time."

I nodded, racing up to the front.

"Follow me as close as you can!" I told them, going up the steps and peeking out. Nobles were flooding out of the residences now, giving us some small bit of cover for the next part, true, but every pair of eyes that were looking the other way could just as quick look at us and raise the alarm.

"*Run*," I ordered, and I shot up, going to the door and pushing people into it. The fire sent smoke pluming in the air, and everyone in the courtyard were watching it.

Thirteen people had rushed past when I saw Ravenna. She came out of the residences 'cross the courtyard, the sheriff a step behind. She looked at the people and spun sharp away, taking the sheriff's arm and leading him toward the arrow slots in the wall. When they moved I saw Gisbourne there, standing by the wall, looking out.

Sixteen went, then eighteen, then twenty, then Gisbourne turned. He saw me, and his chin lowered and his eyes turned evil and hateful.

"Run!" I shrieked, lacing knives through my fingers like cord till steel pointed out between every knuckle. He yelled for the guards. The rest of the townspeople flew up out of the prison, and I hid them, standing in front of them and blocking the way to the tunnel as guards began to charge me.

I began spitting knives, going for killing blows. There were too many people here, too many that could turn on me and start to fight against me. I needed more time, and I needed Robin.

"That one is mine!" Gisbourne roared, jogging up and drawing his sword, a huge Claymore with a black hilt. He crashed the first arc down and I twisted away, throwing two knives into the necks of two guards as they headed for the tunnel door. Gisbourne grunted and lunged forward, but I stepped close and managed to stab his sword arm. I ducked away but he grabbed my hood, ripping backward.

He had the coil of my hair inside my hood, and he chuckled, jerking me backward till I fell.

"Got you," he laughed.

My blood fair boiled as he tugged again, dragging me. "You think I give a damn about my hair?" I spat. I twisted quick, ducking my head and slicing off the hood and my hair with it so I could wriggle away and jump up to stand against him. "And you never had me, not for a second."

With that I flicked a knife at him that landed in the soft outer bit of his shoulder. He dropped his sword like deadweight, falling onto a knee with the heft of it.

An arm grabbed me round the waist and I stepped on the guard's foot, then slammed my elbow to his face, knocking him out. At least that were one I didn't have to kill. Another guard were opening the door to the tunnel, and I vaulted past Gisbourne. Clutching my last two knives, I flipped till I stood on my closed fists, the knives sticking out like wagon wheel spokes, and came up in time to spin my sharpest into his neck. He fell just short of the door, and twin threads of horror and victory spun through me at the sight.

Rob crested the stairs with a man covered in blood, bare walking on his own, leaning heavy on Rob. Gisbourne jumped to his feet, a black thrill in his eyes as he moved toward Robin. For a full breath I were frozen, staring. Gisbourne fixed on Rob, but Rob never so much as raised his eyes to Gisbourne. Rob were only concerned for getting the man safe.

Rob were a hero, through and through.

And I were none. But then, disreputable, angry, once-noblewomen had their place too, and whether Rob wanted it or not, I would always stand between him and Gisbourne. A thief could die to let the hero live.

It took me three steps, pushing off the dusty ground fast as I could, to get to Gisbourne. He were raising his sword at Rob, a twisted smile on his face, as Rob tried to pull the man away and weren't fast enough. With a banshee scream I dove forward, darting at Gisbourne and tackling him round the waist, heaving him away from Rob. Gisbourne's sword came clumsy down over my shoulder, and I shrieked as the blade split my skin in two, biting deep.

He grabbed my throat, flipping me over and heaving himself on top of me. He squeezed my throat, and water popped out my eyes. "That's all I want, you little tramp," he spat, spat in true, all over my face. "I want to see you die. I want to see the light tamp out of those devil's eyes. You humiliated me and taunted me for all these years, and now I want to feel it as you die."

I scrambled for breath, scratching at his face and twisting my legs 'bout. I punched his face but he just laughed, like he were possessed by some demon. I pressed my thumbs into his eyeballs and he swatted me away like a bug.

Fireworks were going off inside my own eyeballs, zigging strips of lightning that dazzled. I could feel my body flipping around without my say-so, panicking for air.

"Get the hell off her!" Rob yelled, and I saw his sword appear at Gisbourne's neck, ready to stroke through his throat.

Gisbourne let me go and rolled away to block. Robin charged him. Between the smoke in the air and the lightning in my eyes, he looked like some angel, all holy fury and righteous fire. Their swords hit and sliced through the smoke, Robin battling him back fast. "Get to the tunnel, Scar!" he roared. "A guard made it in, I don't know how far!"

I were still sputtering for breath, and a guard came at me, but I kicked him in the chest and sliced his face, sending him to the ground. "I won't go without you!" I snapped.

"How sweet," Gisbourne said, hacking at Rob. "So you're the little drab's new lover? Don't believe her if she says she'll marry you," he taunted, lunging at Rob again.

"Get the guard or the people are *dead*, Scar! I'm behind you!"

"Guards, don't let her get away!" Gisbourne called.

I fought off another guard, hesitating. "Rob, come now!"

Gisbourne backed him up against the wall, and Rob hacked him to the side.

"He's a little busy, Marian!" Gisbourne said. He had blood on his face and it made his smile look like it were slashed with demon blood, wicked and mad.

"Robin!" I shrieked, letting the guards push me back.

"Dammit, Scar, get that guard now!" Rob ordered.

Every bit of me screamed, but I dispatched two more guards and made for the tunnel. I slammed the door behind me and started running, listening for the sound of the door opening again or for the heavy chain-mail steps of a guard ahead of me. It were pitch-black, but I listened, hearing the people's voices far ahead, and a labored breath close by.

"Robin?" someone asked.

I touched a body, and it were wet with blood. "You're hurt," I said. "Where is he? Did he get far ahead?"

"Who?" he asked.

"The guard!"

He heaved out a breath. "I was hurt in the prison," he said. "Where's Robin?"

It were the man Rob brought out. I turned back, realizing what he'd done as my belly pushed up into my pipes and the world went off-kilter round my ears. I could hear guards now, entering the tunnel.

Rob had sent me running off without him, knowing he

wouldn't be behind. Knowing Gisbourne would kill him. He'd lied 'bout the guard, knowing it were the only way I'd leave him.

And he'd done it to save my life.

I dropped to a knee. My muscles couldn't hold me none, and my eyes went wet. My head felt fair twisted, because half my heart squeezed with fear for him, with awful guilt, for his life were worth thousands of mine. Then, worse, the other half of my heart flew with the thought that maybe he trusted me after all. Maybe things weren't as broken as I thought.

It were a terrible thought, for Rob might have been dying for me just then.

My mouth twisted to a frown. That damn hero needed a few lumps to the head if he thought I were just going to let him do it.

The heavy sound of chain mail rattled through the tunnel.

"Come on," I told the injured man, struggling to my legs like a new foal and pulling his arm 'cross my shoulders. "We have to run now so I can get back to Robin."

He hobbled and I ran, seeing bleak moonlight at the end of the tunnel, hearing the heavy steps come closer. John stood at the end of the tunnel, and he took the man from me. I turned to go back and he grabbed me. "Scar, can't you hear them? The guards are coming!"

"Rob's back there!" I wailed, fighting him. "Rob's back there—I have to help!"

"You can't take on the army yourself!"

"Get your damn hands off me!" I shrieked. "I have to help Robin!"

John didn't let me go, climbing down and cutting the rope with me fighting him tooth and nail. Every inch farther he forced me sank and broke my heart. We were almost to the bottom when the guards appeared, watching us and the injured man climb down to Much and the rest of the villagers. John pulled me into the cover of the trees. "Christ, Scar, you're bleeding everywhere."

I couldn't feel it. I felt sick and numb, my heart racing and slamming without any emotion behind it. I felt tears—or maybe blood—on my face and I ground my palms into my eyes.

"Scar?" Much said.

I ignored him.

"Scar, I doubt the sheriff will kill him. He'll want someone to hang, and the Hood is a pretty damn good catch. Come on. We'll fix you up and come back; no one's leaving Rob to die."

The only thing I could hear were running water. Running water and my heartbeat, beating my insides up. Wait— *running water.*

I looked up, searching the rocky cliff. There it were, tucked far to the side, not so much a tunnel as a spout, a river of water draining out from the castle. From the *prison.*

"Scar!" John yelled.

Before anyone could stop me, I scaled the rocks and slid into the spout. Water splashed down my front and I yelped, but I fit. I fit, and no one else would. I pushed forward against the water, crawling deep into Castle Rock.

He damn well better be alive.

—∽—

The tunnel ran at a sharp incline and I had to claw my way up, freezing water running over the worn rocks. It ran over me, too, like it didn't know that I weren't no rock, quick and cold through my wound so I didn't feel it none. I weren't sure if it were still bleeding or if it would kill me, but I didn't much care.

My feet slipped now and again, sending me sprawling against the rock or, worse, sliding back down till I caught my feet again. My shoulders burned and trembled and shook, but the longer it went on, the less I noticed it. It didn't matter none. I were going onward and upward till I couldn't fit no more or till I found Rob.

After a long while the tunnel started getting tighter, scraping my sides round. The water didn't have nowhere to go, so it ran over my front and back and shoulders and face and thighs. I spat it out of my mouth, trying not to think of the blood and ash and sweat and waste that were in it.

A rock tore at my shoulder and I stopped for a moment. I pushed my head to the side, tears welling up about the stupid fix I were in. He were more than like dead, and I would die in this tunnel, and then the sheriff would burn the whole shire trying to get a drop of tax out of the people.

I stayed there too long, leaning into the rock, the water pulling over me, pulling tiny little pieces of me down the tunnel and away. There were no light in there, no day, only the sound of the water, never stopping.

I may as well have been dead already. If there were a Hell, this were it, hung in limbo between the living and the dead.

"Gisbourne says we can muck you up a bit, as long as you're alive to hang," I heard. My head twisted; it were the torture master. Were I closer than I thought?

"You can kill me all you like. Have at it."

My blood lit up like a torch. It were Rob. Rob, sounding cavalier and confident and, more than anything, very much alive. I scrabbled along the rock. The water didn't matter no more, nor did my flesh or the rock against it. I saw a thread of light twisting through the water, and I went for it like a hound.

I didn't hear any cries, any whip cracks or none, which didn't sit well. The tunnel opened up a bit beneath the prison, and I pushed above the water, hugging to the side to avoid a thick trail of blood sliming down. I could see firelight and the shadow of the torturer.

"A little more?" he grunted.

I heard Rob heave a breath and spit, and I dodged to avoid that as well. I gripped the grating, trying to move it. It were welded and strapped into the stone with heavy iron spikes.

There were a deep groan, and a few moments later there were more blood drooling down. Stupid, helpless tears burned at my eyes. It were Rob's blood. Rob were bleeding a fair lot. I took out my knife and started stabbing at the rock around the iron pins.

"I'll let that set till morning, and we'll see what you can take then."

I heard the footsteps go, and I began working the grate

hard. With no one to hear, Rob's groans got heavier and more labored.

"Christ, Rob, I'm coming," I called to him. The knife were slipping off the rock, not finding any space or purchase.

"God, haven't I been tortured enough?" he moaned.

I stopped, pain sinking into my belly. "Rob . . . ," I tried.

"Don't turn my own heart against me, please," he said. It sounded pitiful. I heard something shuffle and then a rattle of metal and heavy chains.

"Rob?" I wailed.

No answer came.

"Rob!" I shrieked. "Rob, answer me! Rob, I'm so sorry, please! Please!" Tears started, fierce and hot from my eyes. I slammed my knife at the grate, cutting my hand. "Rob, please, I'm sorry I got you into all of this. I'm sorry I brought Gisbourne down on you. Please, just be alive."

No answer came. My knife snapped, and so did my will. I stayed, calling his name till my pipes gave out. When I couldn't yell anymore, I dropped my knife and let the water carry me down.

What had taken so long to mount took nothing to go down, and I were dumped off the ledge and into the main fall of the river. I let it carry me down, away, rinsing me clean and sending me back to Sherwood and the lads.

CHAPTER

SIXTEEN

—o—

My feet were dragging over the roots and rocks as I stumbled back to the cave. I didn't make it all the way, falling against a tree. My body felt encased in lead; a deep breath didn't move my chest none. I whistled, and closed my eyes.

It weren't long before I heard crashing through the woods. I opened my eyes. John were there, hauling me up by my arms. "Can you walk?" John asked.

"Of course she can't walk," Much said. "Look at her." John started to pick me up, but Much yelled, "Careful of her back! It looks like her shoulder's bleeding pretty bad."

John slung me over his shoulder, and he began taking big-legged steps through the forest, his bones jammed deep into my belly. I let my arms dangle and drop, laying limp.

It weren't long before John's footsteps got closer and slower, and he pulled me off him. He laid me down on one of our sleeping pallets. I rolled on my stomach, and Much pushed my shirt off to get to my wound. I balled it up in front and closed my eyes.

"It's deep, Scar."

I nodded.

He began to brush the dirt out of it, and it were sore and hot. "Scar, we have to stitch this shut."

"No," I said, sitting up, clutching the shirt to me. "Don't." I'd had cuts stitched before, and it were the kind of painful where you passed out for a day and had to drink heavy besides.

"Scar," John said, his voice warning me.

"Don't," I repeated. "Rob's in Nottingham, and they've been torturing him all night." My back caved over and I felt sick, saying it loud like that. "I'm not sure he's alive," I said soft.

John sat down, and Much sat back on his heels. "Christ," Much whispered.

"You got in? Through that tunnel?"

I nodded. "To right beneath the prison, but the grate is welded into bedrock. It won't move none."

"And you saw Rob?"

"I talked to him. I didn't see him."

I remembered the clinking chains and silence, and I shuddered. "Just patch me up, Much. We have to get back there."

"You aren't going back there, Scar," John said.

I looked sharp to him, then rolled onto my back. "Just bandage it, Much, please."

"You're turning loose," John said. "You just ran off last

night, cut up and half dead, and we didn't know what was going on."

"Rob were in there, John," I said, wincing as Much bandaged my shoulder. "I weren't turning loose. We're a band and Rob would have never left none of us in there. He saved my life, and I'm not leaving him. And we're going to go back and break him out."

"Except Rob kicked you out of the band," John said, crossing his big arms over.

I looked to him. "What?"

"Might as well have. You told him you were leaving, and he took that as word. Robin doesn't want you coming after him, Scar. He wants you gone."

Stupid tears pushed up at my eyes. "What?" I said again.

"It isn't like that," Much said, quiet.

"You think I'm wrong?" John said.

I looked to Much, and he shook his head. "No, you're not wrong. But you're making it sound bad."

"It doesn't matter how it sounds, Much."

"Yes, but you're acting like the reason he wants her gone is because he doesn't want her around, and that's not it."

"*Much*," John snapped.

Much looked at me. "He loves you, Scar. He always has. And he wouldn't want you to get hurt. He risked his life to get you out. So don't make his sacrifice for nothing."

I bent my head and tears slid down my nose. I thought of Rob, standing in the inn and calling me a whore, walking in the forest and saying he wished he never saw me. Worst, I saw him fighting back Gisbourne and sending me on, and the tears squeezed faster, fair leaping out of me in jumps and starts. "He doesn't love me, Much." Pain shuddered through me and I curled over myself. My whole chest hurt.

Christ Almighty, were this what a broken heart felt like? I hiccuped, and John put his hand on my neck, rubbing a little.

I pulled away, jumping up and stumbling away from them. They looked at me with their mournful eyes and I slumped on a tree. This were why I never wanted none of them. Not their looks or their stupid pity for the scarred girl who hung her heart on a hero.

Humiliation broke over me like a wave, and my eyes screwed shut. I wiped the tears, still shaking a little. "I owe him my life. I'll make this right, Much. I'll make sure he won't sacrifice a thing."

"We won't let you go back there."

I shivered. "I don't need you two to do this. But it might be easier to get Rob out if you're there. You'd be going for him, not me. And then you won't never have to see me again. Promise."

"We don't want you to leave, Scar," Much told me. "We never did."

I shrugged. "You're right, though. Rob wants me out of the band. So I'm out, and I'll get him back to you so we're square."

"What's your plan, then?" John asked. "Turn yourself in? Gisbourne will *kill* you."

"No. This all started because I forgot who I were. It's not

like a noblewoman can live like this, and I were stupid to think otherwise. I wanted to forget." I shook my head. "Gisbourne will trade anything for me. For me to go to him willingly, yes. He'd trade anything. Even Rob."

They looked at me, and I glared back.

"Do you want Robin back, or don't you?"

"Of course we want Robin back, but neither of us are willing to trade your life to Gisbourne to get him out. Robin will never forgive us," Much said.

A tremor rumbled down my back. "If he's even alive," I reminded.

"It's a stupid plan, Scar! Aside from you being little better than an idiot, the sheriff will just come after us twice as hard. They'll follow Rob right out and let us all swing," John said.

"We had a plan for Ravenna's wedding gift all along, remember?" I asked. "Much, have you searched the other caves?"

He shook his head. "Haven't had the chance."

"Then we'll search tonight. We'll find enough, and we'll tumble the castle. Or part of it, at least." I nodded. "That's what we'll do. Between the wedding and offering to trade me for Robin, the guards will be distracted enough. You'll be able to tumble the castle, we'll get Rob out, and the people of Nottinghamshire will have a bit of time while the sheriff rebuilds."

"I don't like this plan, Scar," John said. "We look out for each other, and this is the pure other end of that. Gisbourne could kill you in a heartbeat."

I gave him a little smile. "I'm sure he will. But if I'm out of the band, what does it matter?" They lurched forward, and I stepped back. "I'll do this with or without you, lads. Let's at least take Robin and the castle wall for me."

There were a long quiet where they just stared at me, and I looked back, trying not to think of how much I loved them. Losing the band, I were losing brothers—like I had already lost a sister. Meeting my fate with Gisbourne would be almost a relief.

"I think it's brave as hell, Scar," Much told me. "I think Rob was right. You're the bravest woman I've ever known."

I looked down. "This were the eventual end anyway, lads. I just managed to put it off a bit. Now at least some good can come out of it. Just get Robin out of there as soon as you can."

A few moments passed and I didn't look at neither; we just stayed there, quiet.

"I'll need some help finding more of the powder, then," Much said.

I nodded. "Tell us what to do."

—⁂—

Not much time passed before we had to come right back to Nottingham. Ravenna's wedding had nobles and peasants flooding into the castle, as the sheriff hosted the entire town for the wedding feast. The wedding would take place in the Great Hall. Though every guard were on post, the castle were at its most vulnerable, and we were going to swim right through like silvery trout.

We crowded in, pushing through bodies to get into the

hall. Girls had flowers in their hair, and the clothing round the
place were bright with color. My hood were down, my lopped-
off hair out, and I weren't hiding from anyone today. I had
scrapes all over my face, and my chin were fair red raw, but it
didn't matter. I were marked and scarred and bloody and
filthy, but today I weren't going to hide my face.

The hall were awful hot, so many bodies rubbing together
like sticks for kindling. As we got closer, I saw Ravenna, looking like a noble lady in a blue velvet gown shot through with
gold threads, her face covered over with a veil like most noble
women wore. I never fancied the veils. They were nice that
no one could see where your eyes were wandering for, but they
weren't near so soft as they looked.

Her family weren't up there with her, which I thought
were fair odd. My eyes set to casting about, and that were when
I saw him.

Hanging above the dais where Ravenna stood swung a heavy
gibbet, an iron cage twisting on a beam. Robin were inside it, far
off the ground, standing stiff and proud. The cage hung from
heavy chains, not rope that I could saw through, and guards
stood round the wheel that held the cage in place.

I felt my stomach twist and hollow as the priest climbed
the stairs to the dais. The sheriff and Gisbourne came with him.
Gisbourne looked up at Rob with a smug smile; I could kill
him for that if nothing else.

The whole place fell quiet and the priest began to speak the
wedding Mass. I started to sneak round the side. Much and
John were busy elsewhere in the castle for now.

I didn't listen to the priest speak. I'd heard wedding masses before, a few, and they general made me think of things I didn't like to think none about, like Gisbourne and how I near had to marry him. I heard Ravenna say that she'd honor the sheriff and obey him, and I fair wondered if that were anything he'd ever do for her.

Before I got to the guarded wheel the Mass were finished, and the priest stepped down as the sheriff kissed Ravenna, pulling off her veil to do it. She looked scared, but she took his kiss, and she left her face unmasked.

I saw Gisbourne signaling guards to surround the dais before I knew what happened. The sheriff were holding Ravenna still, but then her shoulders drew up like she were trying to push him off. I saw his dagger flash over her neck, like lightning slicing through the sky. Her head jerked and a short, stunted scream came out from her lips.

"No!" Rob cried.

"Ravenna!" roared Godfrey.

The whole hall broke open, and women started screaming and crying and men started to roar.

The sheriff yelled over it all, "Silence!"

The people quieted but didn't quit moving, fighting against the guards as Ravenna twisted, showing her throat slashed bloody and wide. She fell to the ground like so much trash, blood making her blue velvet black and shining with wet. Her body lay in a heap, and her big skirts took a while to lie flat. I looked back to the sheriff, frozen, my breath gone.

She were dead. He had killed her, with no reason, no defense, nothing. He killed her because he could, because she were a bird that he could crush.

"Good people, I try to show you my love, and this is how you repay me! You deny me my rightful taxes, you flee your punishments, and you send one of your own to beguile my heart and betray me. Ravenna Mason was helping the Hood from mine own hearth!"

"No!" Godfrey hollered. "No, no!" He broke through the guards and Gisbourne tackled him, pushing him to the ground and holding him there as Godfrey fought and strained, trying to get to his fallen sister. His arm whipped out from Gisbourne, but not to fight him. It stretched 'cross the space to Ravenna, trying to get to her, trying to touch her before her soul flew out.

"I've dealt with my unfaithful wife, and now I will deal with your last bastion of insurrection—that outlaw they call the Hood."

I jerked into motion as the cage began to lower. Rob, with his heaving chest and angry eyes, looked every bit the caged lion, like they called King Richard. I scrabbled over people, using nails and elbows and fists to punch my way through. I pushed and pushed, getting closer body by body, standing a few feet away from the guarded dais.

I looked toward the entrance. They needed more time to set the explosion, and I needed some sort of miracle to get Rob free. My eyes skittered round the room; there were guards *everywhere*. There were windows high up, with big iron chandeliers filled with candles hanging down from the rafters. The part of me that weren't happy to die today looked after them with longing, imagining scrabbling up to them and swinging—pitching knives this way and that like an avenging angel.

But that weren't to be today.

I looked at Gisbourne and felt my stomach twist and my whole chest squeeze, like someone put me to the rack.

The gibbet landed with a heavy clang. Rob sagged against the side with the jolt of the cage, and the whole place were dead quiet, shocked silent by the sheriff's cruelty, by this strange day where a wedding meant death instead of new life. Guards had taken Godfrey in hand, keeping him on his knees at the side of the dais. He just stared at Ravenna's body, dead and lifeless and abandoned. Gisbourne were now free to draw his sword and go to the cage.

"No!" I screamed, my voice mixing with hundreds. I went forward but the crowd wouldn't part, keeping me hard back, holding on to me. Gisbourne's sword didn't go farther, and he waited till the cries subsided.

"On your knees," he ground out. "You'll die a common criminal, worse than your traitorous father."

Rob's head were unbowed. He looked around the gibbet. "I'd love to oblige, Gisbourne, but there doesn't seem to be enough room to kneel."

"Open the cage," Gisbourne ordered. The sheriff didn't protest. A guard came forward with the key, and the door opened. I saw how heavy Rob leaned on the side of the cage. He were exhausted, and weak, and in a fair bit of pain. He turned to Gisbourne and I saw his back. The cloth were punched through hundreds of times in perfect little rows, and my whole body burned.

They had put him on a Judas board. It were a big board punched through with spikes, filthy and covered with blood and flesh, and they had put Rob on it till his skin broke and the spikes pushed into him.

Whether or not it were today, I'd kill Gisbourne for that as well. If he didn't kill me first.

"On your knees, Hood."

"Wait!" I shrieked. This time my voice were above the crowd, and everyone looked at me. The crowd let me through now, and my shaking legs brought me forward to the guards. "Let me through!" I demanded.

Gisbourne chuckled. "Do it. Let the little thief come."

Maybe Gisbourne already knew my plan, 'cause he looked like he just swallowed a canary whole and it were singing out his throat.

They parted and I climbed the dais, meeting Rob's eyes. He didn't look angry now. He looked lost. I felt lost. I stared at him and my heart broke fresh again. Loving him felt like drowning in his ocean eyes, like a tide I couldn't hold back, crashing on me again, filling me up with hurt and shame and despair. Standing so close to him, all I could think were the hundred things I should have told him long ago. A hundred moments I'd lost because I were scared and weak and shameful.

It were fair twisted, but maybe doing this, maybe this sacrifice would make me, for one breath, the person he could love.

"Please tell me you aren't really here," he murmured, hanging his head. "Please tell me I didn't save your life for nothing."

"Needn't make it so hard, Rob," I told him. "I'm getting you out of here."

His head jerked up, and it weren't anger in his eyes. "The hell you are. Not with him, Scar, please."

Gisbourne's eyebrow twitched at this, but he just crossed his arms, all patient-like now that he were getting what he wanted. I looked back to Rob, all my inner bits crowded into my pipes, and I weren't sure of a single thing. "Do *not* ask me to watch you die," I hissed at him.

Rob's eyes shifted, shimmery blue and wet like rain-slick rocks. "You think you're going to fare any better?" he whispered. I looked over and saw Ravenna's blood, and Gisbourne's sword, dry and thirsty. I shook my head.

"Are you fixing to join him, or did you have another reason for annoying me?" Gisbourne snapped.

"A deal," I said quick, standing in front of him, standing between him and Rob one more time.

His eyes scraped over me. "What could I possibly want from you?"

"The one thing you couldn't ever get, not by force or my father," I told him, and his eyes flared bright. "Two words, Guy."

The sheriff chuckled. "I believe the lad wants you to marry him, Gisbourne."

"Another reason you need a thief taker, Nottingham, is that your men should have realized long ago that Will Scarlet is merely a girl." Gasps ripped through the hall, and Gisbourne laughed. "Christ, no one knew? Not only that, she's a noblewoman in clever disguise. None other than my delinquent betrothed, Lady Marian Fitzwalter of Leaford."

Everyone were staring at me now, but I just raised my chin. "Well?"

"What are your terms?" he asked.

"Release Robin and Godfrey. Both of them unharmed."

He grinned, looking at Robin. "Well, I've already harmed him a little."

"Do you agree or not?"

"And why shouldn't I just kill him now, and then force you to marry me?"

"Like I said, Guy, you can't force me to say the words. And we ain't married till the words are said. If you want me, this is your only chance."

He stepped forward, squeezing my chin between his thumb and forefinger. He smiled, but he looked more like a dog baring its teeth. "I will make it a living hell for you, Marian. That is, if you last longer than your friend," he said, looking to Ravenna. Rob jerked forward, but I stayed still. "Are you willing to submit to me for his life?"

"Robin the Hood, Robin of Locksley, Earl of Huntingdon— whatever you wish to call him—is the prince of the people, Guy. He is worth more than my whole life."

"Little that's worth," he spat, pushing my chin away. "Call the priest back," he ordered.

"Scarlet," Rob whispered behind me.

My pulse set to drumming. "Rob has to be away before I'll say the words," I told Gisbourne.

"How do I know you'll actually say them?"

"You have my word."

"I had your word before."

"You had my father's word. Now you have mine; I'll marry you today, once Robin's free and clear."

He grimaced. "Fine. If not, at least I'll get to kill you."

"This is hardly your decision to make, Guy," the sheriff said, wiping his blood-wet dagger on his arm.

Guy's lip curled back, his big head whipping round to glare at the sheriff. "I caught him."

"I *hired* you to catch him."

"And I'll catch him again. But this," he said, swinging to look at me again, "can't wait."

"You let him go, and I won't pay you a farthing until he's dead."

Gisbourne chuckled, staring at me, and his teeth shone white. "I don't do it for the money."

The sheriff's mouth twisted into a sneer, but he shut his yap and didn't stop Gisbourne none.

Gisbourne leaned closer. "If this is a ruse, Marian, you will know the full extent of the pain I can inflict."

"Two women dying on their wedding day sounds lucky," the sheriff mused.

"Trust me, I'd take a lot longer than just a day to kill her," Gisbourne said, speaking to the sheriff but keeping his evil eyes on me alone.

I glared at both in turn. "I ain't as easy to kill."

Gisbourne looked pleased by this. "I like a challenge." The priest appeared, and the sheriff nodded. Gisbourne sighed. "Very well, let the Hood go."

I turned, whipping my arms round Rob before I could think or stop. He hugged me tight. "I'm so sorry, Rob," I whispered, my voice breaking.

He gripped tighter. "Don't do it, please. Please, let's run."

"You can't run." I shook my head.

His hands came on either side of my face, holding me up to him. Waves were crashing in his eyes, sure and strong and sweeping. "You are my whole heart, Scarlet. And this is breaking it."

My heart cracked open and clear dropped out of me. My mouth opened, and I looked round me and stamped my foot. "Does this look like a good time to tell me that, you damn stupid boy?" I meant to sound mean but my voice wobbled. "Now?"

He gave a little smile. "My foul-mouthed warrior."

"Marian," Gisbourne said, and it felt like a slap.

Shaking, I leaned up and kissed Rob's cheek, blinking back watery eyes. Hell would rise up to Heaven before I cried in front of Gisbourne, even for Rob. "This isn't over, Robin. You have an awful lot you need to explain."

He squeezed me tight. "Stay alive, Scar, so I can have that chance."

"Go."

He slipped away from me and struggled down to the people. Their murmurs rose like water to catch him, and several stepped up to support him, carrying him like the prince he were meant to be. Guards brought Godfrey forward and let them both go from the hall free. It were a strange thing to see, outlaws walking away without so much as a skirmish. Rob didn't look back at me, and I felt Gisbourne's hand close over mine sure as if it were closing over my throat.

"I haven't a ring for you, but I hope you'll forgive the oversight."

"Nonsense," the sheriff cried, pulling the silver band from his finger and passing it to Gisbourne. He knelt over Ravenna's body, pried the band from her still finger, and handed it to Gisbourne too. "Someone might as well use them."

My stomach disagreed as Gisbourne took it and handed me the man's ring, still warm from Nottingham's hand.

"Sh-shall we begin?" the priest asked. His hands on the Bible shook.

"Yes," Gisbourne snapped.

The priest's voice wobbled as he said the ill-fated words for the second time that day. He turned to Gisbourne first, asking, "Guy of Gisbourne, will thou have this woman to thy wedded wife, will thou love her and honor her, keep her and guard her, in health and in sickness, as a husband should a wife, forsaking all others on account of her, so long as ye both shall live?"

"I will," he growled, clawing his short nails at my hand.

"And Marian Fitzwalter of Leaford, will thou have this lord to thy wedded husband, will thou love him and honor him, keep him and obey him, in health and in sickness, as a wife should a husband, forsaking all others on account of him, so long as ye both shall live?"

I waited three breaths, and I felt them rush through my lungs like the last gulps of air before drowning. "I will," I said. I felt dizzy. All this time, all this fighting it, and I had married him.

"You have the rings?"

Gisbourne nodded, taking my hand and pushing Ravenna's pretty ring on my finger. "I take you, Guy, as my wedded husband," I said, my voice shaking. "And thereto I plight my troth." Sickness washed over me. I trembled as I put my ring on Gisbourne, and he smiled, big and smug.

"I take you, Marian, as my wedded wife," he told me, pulling me closer. "And thereto I plight my troth."

"Receive the Holy Spirit," the priest told him, kissing Gisbourne's cheek. Gisbourne turned to me, grabbing my chin in one big paw and pushing my mouth to his. It were hard, so hard my teeth bit my lip, and he pushed his tongue at my mouth but I kept my lips closed tight. He pinched my side vengeful-like, but I didn't open.

He let me go.

"You are now married in the eyes of God," the priest said. He sounded mournful.

I didn't wait longer.

I pulled away from Gisbourne, turning to the gibbet, but he grabbed my shirt and threw me back. He stamped his foot on my chest. "Running so soon, my dear?"

I drew a knife and snarled, trying to drive it into the tendon at the back of his heel, but he jumped free of me. I whipped up, wincing at the pain in my back, and the sheriff caught me, bringing his knife to my throat.

His beard rubbed my cheek and he laughed. "Gotcha."

"Let go of my *wife*, Nottingham," Gisbourne growled.

I didn't think Gisbourne could surprise me, but that fair did it. The sheriff too, far as I could tell, because he loosed enough for me to wrench his arm back and slam my head into the bridge of his lowborn nose.

Gisbourne slashed his sword at my stomach and I jumped back, hissing as it nicked a light slice. "If anyone's going to kill you, it's damn well going to be me!" he bellowed.

He had to yell for me to hear him. The townspeople were taking the guards and working them over, trying to get to the dais. The bright colors were running blood black, the wedding shattering into violence.

Maybe there were too much going on. Maybe the fierce pain, like a flame coming from my sliced shoulder, were addling my brain. Maybe the cursed ring on my finger meant I weren't so interested in staying alive anymore. Whatever the reason, I weren't as quick as I should've been. I backed up again and tripped over Ravenna's body, and Gisbourne stepped forward and grabbed my throat.

He dragged me closer to him, and I tried to regain my feet, but I kept slipping in her blood. He squeezed hard enough to hold me up, hard enough to kill.

I tried to yell, but the sound came out a raw gurgle.

He tossed his sword up and snatched it from the air by the blade, his hand protected by his thick leather gloves. I started flailing, kicking, and hitting, but I couldn't get him. And where I could, it didn't seem to matter—he didn't notice, couldn't feel it. "It seems you need a reminder of just what kind of a man I am, Marian," he said.

He twisted my head so my left cheek were up, and I drew in a thin little wisp of a breath and tried harder to kick, to stab, to claw.

He pushed the tip of the sword into my cheek, biting deep and drawing a new gash where the old scar had lain.

My eyes went starry dark, and without any sound on my lips, I moved them in prayer.

Whether they meant it or not, my band (and I'm fair sure God, too) were still watching my back, because it were just that minute that the whole place rocked with the force of an explosion.

He dropped me. My head slammed against the floor and the cut on my shoulder from the day before screamed. A cough grabbed my chest as I sucked in a breath, scrambling to my feet.

It were chaos. The townspeople had charged the dais, and someone were fighting Gisbourne.

I took a deep breath, wiping the water and blood from my

eyes and scrabbling on top of the gibbet. I gritted my teeth as I started to climb up the chain, pain lancing through every bit of me and blood running down my cheek.

"Marian!" he bellowed, so loud his voice shook the chain. "You are my goddamn wife!"

"I said I'd marry you—I never promised I'd stay with you, Guy!" I spat back.

He felled the farmer he were fighting, and I halted on the chain, watching the man fall. My hands were slipping and I held tighter, not sure whether to go down and help or run.

"Scarlet!"

I slipped a bit as I swung to the voice, seeing John thunder through the swinging swords with nothing but his fists. "John!"

"Get the hell out of here, Scarlet!" He met Gisbourne and smiled. "I've got this under control."

I watched John strike a blow that knocked Gisbourne's sword away, and I shook my head. My husband were a fool. John would trounce him in a moment's time. Relieved and hurting both, I took my time climbing toward the rafters.

"Honor, obey?" Gisbourne shouted, grappling with John. "This is what you call being a good wife?"

I stopped. "I never said I'd be a *good* wife, Guy. Just that I'd marry you."

"Guards!" he roared. "Guards! Someone will burn alive for this, Marian!"

But the guards were all fair busy at that point, and no one paid him a bit of mind. I kept climbing.

"You traitorous bitch!" he yelled. "You goddamn liar!"

I laughed. "You knew I were a bitch and a liar when you married me, Guy. It's your own damn fault for agreeing to it."

I made it to the rafters with muscles burning, and I clung to the wood for a long moment, trying to breathe, trying to force down the beating pain in my shoulder, my cheek, my whole body. I searched for John as I hung there, and it took me precious seconds to find him.

I saw John's head pressed tight against Gisbourne's, the two of them twisting as one, whipping each other round. John got an inch of space and fired a ham-fisted punch to Gisbourne's cruel mug.

Gisbourne sprawled out at John's feet. John dropped to his knee to grab Gisbourne's sword and rose with flashing steel in his hand, ready to make me a widow.

But he didn't. John's face jerked up, and when he saw me on the crossbeam he just froze.

Panic rushed through me. "JOHN! DO SOMETHING!" I shrieked, but he couldn't hear me.

The sheriff broke from the crowd behind John and came at him, his sword raised and an awful snarl on his face, like a wolf in a fight.

I screamed to the high heavens and pointed, but John still couldn't hear me. He saw me point, and his face folded like he were fair confused as the sheriff made it a step closer to him.

My feet ran on the rafter before I knew what I were 'bout, but there were no way I'd get to him. This weren't a battle I had a place in, and I were set to watch my friend die for it.

The sheriff's foot struck the ground, coming to my eyes

unnatural slow, like it were staged so that I could see every move, every turn. His sword came down at John's neck as John just bare started to turn. I screamed again, and screamed and screamed.

The blade never cut. The steel flashed and flew in the air as the sheriff were swept sideways. Men poured over him like a tide, and I could see James Mason in the fore, pinning the sheriff down. Someone dragged the sheriff's chin back, and Mason didn't hold but for a moment before he made the sheriff's neck bloom like red roses, drawing the same line over his throat that been done drawn over Ravenna's. The blood poured down over the side of his neck and dripped down, and from the rafters it all looked like one big puddle, Ravenna's blood and the sheriff's mixing together, married in gruesome truth as they died side by side.

James Mason had avenged his daughter, even if it were his awful fixings that got her into the marriage to start. It weren't as if our problems were over, but on this day the villagers, and not just Rob and my mates, stood up and fought back the flood.

Even if the wave of evil and pain and injustice would break over us again, just this once it were pressed back. And that were more a start than anything we'd done.

Gisbourne got on his feet again, and John fought back against him, moving like lightning so none could interfere. They circled and fought, and I hung on the rafter. Part of me thought I should be fighting 'longside John, but part of me thought damned little of that plan, and so I hung there, not moving.

I heard a sound like thunder outside, and breath snaked
away from me as the rafters shook; one broke off, snapping
from the side and falling to the ground. The whole structure
began to wobble and I moved like I were sparked. The roof
were made of thick layers of thatch, and I clung to a beam and
kicked my way through it, running along the edge of the roof
to the castle wall. My whole body hurt and ached and burned,
but I weren't stopping till I saw Robin again.

Making it to the outer wall of the castle, I scrambled up,
huffing hard with breath. I slid off the wall and ran into the
forest, my heart pounding louder than I'd ever heard. I didn't
know which way they'd take to the cave, and it were a long
time before I heard footsteps crunching over leaves. I ran
faster, feeling tears streak out of my eyes and my heartbeat
break into a fluttering.

I saw the shapes ahead, small and slight for Much, tall and
thin for Godfrey, and the last shape, the one that meant everything, leaning a little on Godfrey.

"Robin!" I shrieked.

He turned, standing away from Godfrey as I came at him,
slamming into him and tumbling him to the ground. I gripped
him tight, sobbing into his chest. I felt hot blood from his
back on my hands, but I let it wash my skin, pulling his weight
on top of me so his back weren't in the dirt. I didn't care none,
even knowing how much we both were hurting.

I heard a ragged sound, and I felt water on my neck. "Tell
me you didn't marry him, Scar," he whispered.

"I had to," I mewled. "I gave him my word."

"But you're here."

I nodded. "And married or not, I ain't never leaving you, Rob."

His nose rubbed at my neck, then along my right cheek. "You're married, Scar."

New tears squeezed out my eyes. "I know."

"To him."

I nodded, hiccuping.

He rested his face against mine, blood and all. "Let me heal up a bit, and we'll see if we can make his part of 'so long as ye both shall live' a little shorter."

I gave a short, watery laugh, and I sat up, dragging him with me. I pressed my hand over his heart, and he covered mine.

"Those eyes," he murmured, stroking hair back from my face, careful to avoid the new slice on my cheek.

"Come on, Robin Hood. I'll heal you up fast as I can," I told him, taking his hands and pulling us both to our feet.

"As soon as we stitch you up, Scar," Much reminded.

Robin leaned heavy on me, and I looked to Much and Godfrey. I'd forgotten 'bout them. They just stared at us, and I felt my cheeks go red. Under the blood, leastways.

"I felt the blast. How much tumbled?"

Much smiled. "Wasn't even that hard. With everything going on, they never noticed us or the rope fuse. I'll tell you, the fuse took longer than I thought it would. I thought they must have found it or cut it, but then I felt the blast and saw Robin."

"What did it do?" Rob asked.

"Toppled most of the middle bailey," Much told him. "What happened in the hall?"

"John's still fighting: he told me to go on," I said. "The sheriff's dead."

"Dead?" Much asked, his face forlorn. "Christ. Christ, we'll just get a new one, won't we? Worse, probably!"

Robin's mouth worked before he spoke. "The position can never be vacant, and it's true, we have no way of knowing who Prince John will next appoint, but it's still something. We needed time. For the moment, the people—their homes and their children and their very lives—are safe." He closed his eyes and sagged against me. "For now, it's more than enough."

Much stepped forward, his eyes full of worrying. "Let's get you two back to the cave."

Rob nodded, and we started to walk, but Godfrey hesitated.

"I don't . . . I can't go back to my father. Not after he agreed to this, and let her die." He closed his eyes, like just saying it hurt him. "I don't know what I can offer you lot, and I know you won't trust me after all I've done, but—" He stopped short, like someone cut his tongue off.

I slid slow away from Rob, making sure he could stand on his own. I walked to Godfrey, and I touched his hand. "It were your father what killed the sheriff," I told him. His face twisted up like he were bare keeping something in behind it. "We trust you, Godfrey. You're one of us now, and you'll always be."

"She told me how you tried to get her out," Godfrey said soft, his voice snapping like a twig. "And she—she wanted to stay."

I nodded.

"Christ, I'm so sorry I hit you."

"I know. Come on, you need to rest. We all need a bit of fixing up." I went back to Rob, slipping under his arm again, and he kissed the bit of my forehead on the side. It made warm heat shoot through my head, run over my body, and slide around my wounded shoulder like it were healing it.

—m—

"I'll patch you up first, Scar," Much said to me as we got to the cave. "Your shoulder must be awful and your cheek doesn't look so good either."

I shied away, hugging tight to Robin. "Not a chance. I ain't the one been tortured."

"I'll fix her, Much," Rob told him. Close to my ear and quiet he said, "From now on, no one but me sees you with your shirt off, Scar."

I rolled my eyes, but fair true, I didn't want no one but him doing the same. "Come on," I said, leading him into the cave. "Let's get your shirt nixed for starting."

He chuckled, but he were leaning heavy on me, and it scared me deep.

"John!" Much yelled.

We turned to see John jogging into the camp, blood and lumps and a big idiot grin on his face. Robin curled forward a little, swaying on his feet.

"What happened?" I asked.

John pushed his thumb over his busted lip. "Gisbourne ran," he said. "But I either broke his arm or rolled his shoulder. Either way, he won't be holding a sword for a while. Most of the hall fell after a minute, and we got the people out." Robin's face twisted, and John looked to him, losing the grin. "You all right, Rob?"

I hugged him tighter. "He will be."

John nodded, looking at me, but I pulled away from his eyes and took Rob into the cave, helping him sit. "Don't move none," I said. "I'll get the supplies."

I went back out and John were standing there, right at the mouth, with his arms crossed. Much and Godfrey were wandering farther, going to get the little food we had stored. John raised his eyebrows.

"What happened with Gisbourne, John?"

"Told you. He ran."

"Before that."

John full looked at me, staring at my face. "I got distracted."

"Don't look at me for your distractions. I didn't do nothing for it."

His face twisted in a funny way, sad and confused. "You did. I went to kill him, and I just thought, if he dies, you're with Rob. You're with Rob forever, and I haven't got a chance. I didn't mean to think it. It was just there. And it stopped me cold."

My breath died in my chest and my skin roared with blood. "What?"

John swallowed. "And then the sheriff was there, and the

chance was gone." John's eyes fixed on the ground. "I'm sorry, Scar." He lifted off from the mouth of the cave and went over to Much and Godfrey, leaving me staring after him.

It were anger rushing through me more than anything as I thought over his fool words and gathered the supplies. I weren't even sure what it meant, him not killing Gisbourne, but hearing him say it like that—like he wanted to keep me and Rob from the other? I could have killed him for it.

Least until I went into the cave again and saw Rob there, bent and hurt. Then every other thought vanished from my mind, and my heart set to a strange sort of beating and the anger left me. John's words didn't matter none, and the awful band on my finger didn't neither. Walking into that cave, it crashed over me again: I loved Rob.

I loved Rob, and there were so many things he damn well better explain.

"Come on, Godfrey, let's show you more of Sherwood," I heard John say. "Get the lay of the forest. Much, come along with us."

I blushed a bit, but I were happy for the chance to be alone with Rob after all that had happened.

In the cave were cooler than outside, and it felt like everything had peeled back like the skin of an orange and I were left with this, the heart of it all.

I came quiet behind Rob, touching his side and picking up the edge of the shirt. He nodded and raised his arms, letting me pull his blood-black shirt off him. Hundreds of holes punched his back, bleeding and red and oozing. Some looked sick and poisoned already. "Christ, Rob. I can clean it now, but I'll have to go to the friars for a poultice."

He nodded, his body easing out, muscles loosening. I set to work, taking some of our water and the last of our muslin bandages to rinse the blood away and draw out the dirt and grime of the prison. I started a fire and set some water by it to warm, and by the time I rinsed him once, the water were warm and my hands were shaking a touch. I soaked bandages and laid them in strips 'cross the mass of wounds, trying to pull out anything sick and deep in there. I stayed lip shut, letting my heart lay down its drummer's sticks and feeling doubt slide into my ribs.

I stroked my fingers light along the strips, pressing them gentle as I stared at the back of his head.

"Time for the reckoning, Rob," I said soft. "What did you mean back there?" The muscles in his shoulders rolled, like he were trying to move or turn, but I touched his back to keep him still. Maybe also to keep it so his face weren't to me as I said it; I weren't sure. "I know . . . I know you thought I'd die in there. Thought you failed, thought all kinds of wrong things. I ain't going to be murderous if you didn't mean it all." Lie. If he hadn't meant it . . . I weren't sure what I'd do. Maybe go back to Gisbourne and let him finish the job for me.

"If you're not going to let me move, you damn well better come where I can see you, Scar," he said, and his voice were awful rough.

Careful and slow, I went round front of him, my back to the fire so its full dancing light shone bright on his face. He took my hand, tugging my fingers out from a fist and twining his through. He gripped it tight. "Christ's bones, Scar." He heaved a sigh, and his hand squeezed mine. "You changed everything. Everything. That day in the market in London, you don't know what my life was like before that, when I came home and found everything just gone. I had nothing. I hadn't a soul. And then you appeared with your magic eyes, and you just changed everything."

Every pain flew from my bones and I stood still as a pillory. "But . . . you hate me."

He sighed, and his eyes flicked up to mine. The storms were gone, the seas the kind of calm that comes after waves have wrecked a ship. "I hate myself. I wish I didn't feel anything. I wish I could protect these people—*you*—like I want to, but I can't. I don't. In the Crusades, in my whole life . . ." He trailed off, his eyes and hand left mine, and his throat worked, the sound fair loud. "There's so much I have to atone for, so much I've done wrong. If I were a better man, I would have sent you far from here long ago, but I haven't, and I can't. I wish I could stop thinking about you, Scar, stop caring about you. Most days I wish I never met you, because it is torture." A dry cough came that half sounded like a laugh. "More than, you know, just bodily torture."

I quieted for a moment, chewing my lip. "You called me a whore, Rob. You said awful things."

"Ah," he said, and his hand took mine again, tight. "Hurting you is the best way I know to punish myself. And, despite that I'm not much proud of it, I can't truly control myself when I see you even looking at John." He chuckled. "Or Jenny Percy."

"Christ, you're a stupid boy," I said, shaking my head.

"And you still haven't said what I want to hear."

I met his eyes. "What do you want to hear?"

"If I'm a fool to even think about you." He looked down. "If you're with John."

I smiled a little. "Are you a fool? Of course. I ain't the sort of girl you ought to have. The sort you deserve." I pressed my mouth to his knuckles, then looked up to his ocean eyes. "But tucked inside of you is the only place my heart's ever been at home." A grin took over my mouth. "And I weren't never with John."

His fingers loosed mine, and before I could cry their loss, his trembly hand slid over my cheek. "I'll keep your heart, Scar," he whispered. "If you keep mine."

I nodded. Fair shy, I touched his face, running over a bruise on his cheek. He let me, closing his eyes and dropping his hands from my face as I touched his skin.

"Gisbourne won't stop looking for me, even with the Sheriff gone."

His hand gripped my knee. "You can't ever go back to him—you know that, yes?"

"Yes."

He nodded. "He won't have such an easy time of it now. The new sheriff won't be named for a while, and until then, the land reverts to King Richard—and Prince John's care while he's away. Gisbourne lacks authority here now. And when a new sheriff is appointed, they'll have to start with rebuilding the keep. We've got time."

He groaned, and my lip twisted. "Do you want to rest?" I asked.

Rob nodded, and I helped him lie on his side, lowering him down to his pallet by the fire. Moving closer to him, I hung there, unsure and leaning over him. I were fair shy to do it, but I kissed his cheek.

He caught my hand and tugged me closer before I moved away. "Stay here," he said. "Please."

"I wouldn't go nowhere," I told him.

He tugged again. "Stay *here*," he said, and kept tugging till I were against him. He pulled my hips against his, my back to his front, and held on tight to me. His breath huffed into my hair and shivers broke like fire sparks all over my body.

I squeezed his hand. "We'll keep fighting. For the people, and for you and me."

"One day, we'll all be free."

I sighed, looking at the glowing tongues of the fire. "Or we'll be dead. But then, I suppose that's a kind of freedom too."

He twisted our fingers together again. It seemed to be how he best liked my hand, like we could tie us together as easy as braiding fingers. "Let's try not to be quite that free, Scar." He were quiet for a moment, and his nose nudged my head. "Should I be calling you Marian now?"

I sighed. "Not sure. I never wanted to be Marian, but it's not as easy as just saying I never were. Or that all I am is Scarlet."

"Maybe I'll call you Lady Gisbourne."

"You can try. See how long you live."

He pulled me closer, and I took a breath, letting my shoulders roll back against him. His breath went slow and even, and it settled in my chest till I breathed the same. I were cut and clobbered, but holding his hand, deep in Sherwood, even as a married woman, I never felt so safe, and I never felt so free.

AUTHOR'S NOTE

Why did I want to retell the story of Robin Hood when there are already so many different versions and interpretations of the Robin Hood legend? Between the numerous books, TV shows, and movies, there's obviously already a lot of material readily available. Yet it's a story that gets continually retold in almost every generation.

I felt compelled to write *Scarlet* because I really love Robin Hood. I have always been fascinated with him—the pain he must have endured, and how tough and strong he was—but especially because he was tough *for* the people he loved and strong *because* of their love. That was the best part. My Robin is a little younger and perhaps a little moodier than most Robin Hoods, but I couldn't change much else about him—because I have loved every juicy detail I could collect about the classic Robin Hood legend.

Little about Robin is known for sure. Some historians believe that Robin Hood must have been an outlaw in the twelfth century; others insist it was a name given to many outlaws in early medieval times. Most legends place Robin in Sherwood Forest, but there are historical references to many different parts of England. There is no one person historians can agree was the real Robin Hood. If he did really exist, historians believe that he could have lived at any time during a roughly two-hundred-year stretch from the twelfth to the fourteenth centuries. His title, history, and personal ethos all vary dramatically, but the one thing that remains the same through all Robin Hood stories is that he robs the rich to give to the poor.

Whether or not Robin participated in the Crusades, the story is typically set during the time of King Richard I, when England had a heroic king who was never at home, and King Richard's jealous brother Prince John was left to manage the country. This fits so well because Prince John did in fact heavily tax the people of England to pay for King Richard's ransom at the end of the Crusades (he was captured by an Austrian duke who, frankly, was kind of kicking him when he was down, but that's another story)—even though John didn't really want his brother to come back to England. I've thought a lot about the kind of ruler John must have been to allow for an environment where Robin Hood had to exist. He may not be directly involved in Scarlet's story, but he is the driving force behind the deterioration of Nottinghamshire's situation.

Within the last hundred years, most Robin Hood stories have featured Robin as an outlaw, typically a former noble, who resides in Sherwood Forest. There's a little wiggle room with the cast of characters (Little John, Will Scarlet, Friar Tuck, Much, Allan A Dale, to name a few); as versions pick and choose and reinterpret, I've certainly done the same. Traditionally, the stories see Friar Tuck as a drunken monk, Little John as a brawny woodsman, Much the Miller's son as the quintessential villager, and Will Scarlet as Robin's closest friend.

Will Scarlet is always shown with his knives, usually wearing red, and often portrayed as the moody or more mysterious one of the band. To each of these traditional characters I've made my own adjustments so that I could portray one way that Robin's story might have begun: Tuck is a slightly drunken barkeep, Little John is still brawny but has a heart beneath his flirtatious exterior, Much is (I hope) more complex but still the one who best fits in with the townspeople. Then there's Scarlet—mysterious, moody, and handy with knives, she's obviously connected to the legacy of Will Scarlet and yet wholly different. Other characters, like Allan A Dale, aren't in *Scarlet* because at the time of my story, Rob is still a young man and hasn't met many people beyond the local townspeople and his fellow Crusaders. John and Much, however, are—in modern terminology—his "boys."

I also took liberties with the rest of the history, ballads, and interpretations that have come before mine—especially regarding Marian, and, by proxy, my dear Scarlet. Reading the stories and watching the movies, I always found Marian problematic because, though I had a crush on Robin, I could never see myself as Marian. She was always doe-eyed and waiting to be rescued—not exactly something I identified with, nor what Rob really deserved. Come on, a simpering maiden for the dashing, brave, angsty Robin Hood? To me, true love is about finding someone who not only sees and accepts your demons but also is willing to step up and fight them when you stumble. Marian couldn't do that for Rob, but Scarlet certainly could.

I am intrigued by the idea that history could have been

rewritten to take a girl named Scarlet and, over the centuries, turn her into Will Scarlet—one of Robin Hood's Merry Men. I like to think of history as a very long game of Telephone; it's never going to come out at the end exactly (or even close) to the way it started. So as the legends and ballads got passed along— and because there's a long tradition of writing women out of history and an inability to believe that a mere girl could do all that Scarlet does—people heard the story wrong and passed along their changed versions of it.

Is it possible that Will Scarlet might have been a girl? Absolutely. Like I said, there's virtually no historical fact, and the legends mostly started from ballads that were spoken and changed several times within the course of a day, much less over centuries. Women like Eleanor of Aquitaine prove that medieval women could be tough and smart and incredibly cunning. So why couldn't Scar really exist?

There will always be people who think a woman—especially a young woman—isn't capable of all that Scarlet believes she is. I don't buy it. If history didn't leave a place for a strong (and yes, sometimes unbelievably grumpy) young woman to exist, then it is my pleasure and delight to shake things up and start making some revisions.

A ROBIN HOOD SAMPLER

READ

Lasky, Kathryn. *Hawksmaid: The Untold Story of Robin Hood and Maid Marian.* New York: HarperCollins, 2010.

Lawhead, Stephen R. *Hood.* The King Raven Trilogy, Book 1. Nashville, TN: Thomas Nelson, 2006.*

Lawhead, Stephen R. *Scarlet.* The King Raven Trilogy, Book 2. Nashville, TN: Thomas Nelson, 2007.*

Lawhead, Stephen R. *Tuck.* The King Raven Trilogy, Book 3. Nashville, TN: Thomas Nelson, 2009.*

Lee, Tony, illustrations by Sam Hart and Artur Fujita. *Outlaw: The Legend of Robin Hood.* Cambridge, MA: Candlewick, 2009.

McKinley, Robin. *The Outlaws of Sherwood.* New York: Greenwillow, 1988.

Springer, Nancy. *Rowan Hood: Outlaw Girl of Sherwood Forest.* New York: Puffin, 2002.

*denotes books for adults

WATCH

The Adventures of Robin Hood. Directed by Michael Curtiz and William Keighley. Burbank, CA: Warner Brothers, 1938.

The Real Robin Hood. Directed by M. David Melvin. North Hollywood, CA: Herzog & Company, 2010.

Robin Hood, Seasons 1–3. Directed by Foz Allen and Dominic
 Minghella. London: BBC, 2006–2009.
Robin Hood. Directed by Wolfgang Reitherman. Burbank, CA:
 Walt Disney, 1973.
Robin Hood. Directed by Ridley Scott. Universal City, CA:
 Universal Pictures, 2010.
Robin Hood: Men in Tights. Directed by Mel Brooks. Los Angeles:
 20th Century Fox, 1993.
Robin Hood: Prince of Thieves. Directed by Kevin Reynolds.
 Burbank, CA: Warner Brothers, 1991.

SURF
Robin Hood: The Facts and the Fiction
 www.robinhoodlegend.com
"Who Was Robin Hood?" History.com video, 3:16
 www.history.com/topics/robin-hood/videos#who-
 was-robin-hood

ACKNOWLEDGMENTS

I knew I wanted to be a published author when I was in the first grade; all along the way, I've found naysayers and rejections aplenty, but what has really stuck with me is the true generosity of spirit that so many people have offered me. This list is a shabby microcosm of all the people who truly deserve my thanks.

To my superstar agent, Minju Chang, thank you for being the first one to believe in Scarlet. Your enthusiasm and passion have gotten us this far, and I'm so grateful.

Thank you to my amazing editors, Emily Easton and Mary Kate Castellani, who both loved Scarlet as she was and also saw ways to make her shine that little bit more. You both inspire *Wayne's World*-esque "I am not worthys"!

Thank you to the rest of the team at Walker and Bloomsbury, including Jennifer Healey who, as a copy editor, picks up on things that my mind can't even process (I used that word *how many times?*), the foreign rights team, and the design and marketing teams. I've heard it takes a village, but in reality it just takes one amazing publishing house. Thank you all for being a part of it with me.

To Panera Bread—refillable Diet Coke and/or tea is a godsend. Cheers. To the W Boston hotel, thank you for letting me write in the wee hours of the morning.

To Alex, Iggy, Ashley, Nacie, Leah, and Renee—beta readers, test dummies, cabinets that I throw emotional pasta against, you are unconditional friends who cheer me on, support me, distract me, and occasionally give me vivisection faces when you know I'm wrong. Nothing but love.

To Connie Chapin, Greer Underwood, Meaghan Delahunt, John Burnside, Debbie Harris, the incomparable and very much missed Catherine Doyle, and all the other English teachers who have supported and taught me, I was forever changed by the love you have for your profession. Your students are listening, and you are changing their lives. Thank you.

To Kev and Mike—whoever thought my biggest cheerleaders would be two dudes? Thank you for always standing beside me and laughing at me until I remember to laugh at myself. Best brothers ever.

To my mum, who knew with absolute certainty that this day would come and yet also acknowledges that it's a bit of a miracle that it did; and to my dad, who gave me a great education, love, encouragement, and a total addiction to books (but I still don't want to read *Stranger in a Strange Land*. Sorry, Dad!). You both taught me what joy there is in the written word. Thank you.